CHASING BLISS

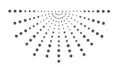

MICHELLE JO QUINN

D1432057

Cover Designer: Alyson Hale, Spellbound Cover Design

Cover image: DepositPhotos

ISBN: 978-0-9951506-5-2

Print ISBN: 978-1-7750256-0-3

To my sister, Shekinah,
and my own personal gentle giant, Cathy,

I'm lucky to have you both in my life.

www.michellejoquinn.com
BLISS SERIES BOOKS
Planning Bliss
Proposing Bliss
Chasing Bliss
Finding Bliss
Santa Bebé - A Christmas Bliss Special

BLISS SERIES SPIN OFFS - COMING SOON!
When He Falls (A New Adult Romance)
When She Smiles (2018)

**DON'T MISS UPDATES ON UPCOMING WORKS,
SALES OR GIVEAWAYS, SIGN UP FOR MICHELLE'S
BI-WEEKLY NEWSLETTER:
BIT.LY/MJQUINNNEWSLETTER**

I bent my knees and scooped up my bestie into a massive hug. Let's get something straight, I was no hugger. I had hugger-radar, and it came in handy whenever I met people who just loved to give hugs. It didn't matter if I felt like a marble statue as soon as they made contact, or that I growled like a feral lioness before they even stepped forward. Huggers were huggers. End of story.

And I'd become one.

Not being able to see Nica as soon as she'd flown in from Paris with her now-fiancé, Levi, was torturous. She'd gone through some crazy events in Paris, and I wasn't there to help her. I'd had family drama before, not that I'd ever share, but being in the middle of some other family's shitstorm wasn't any better. This woman shouldn't have gone through that alone. I'd been powerless to stop her from getting hurt. Thank the ever-loving Universe she survived and came home unscathed. And happy. And engaged!

"Chase...can't breathe," she wheezed against my leather jacket. When I released her, her face was blotchy, and she had a dent on her forehead with the same diameter as the snap of my jacket.

"Sorry...I lost my bearings for a sec." I threw her a crooked, unapologetic grin.

Nica placed a hand, one that was adorned with a huge

sparkler, on her chest. "I almost suffocated between your boobs. Next time, give me a warning."

"Holy smokin', would you look at that!" I grabbed her hand. She preened and let me scrutinize the piece. "Art Deco. Nice. What year?" I'd seen the ring before, when her fiancé asked me to help out with his proposal, but on Nica, it shone even brighter.

She shrugged, a blush heating up her cheeks—the modest bride to be. "1940's. His grandfather gave it to his grandma. Isn't it sweet?"

"Sweet?" I scoffed. "I bet he got laid."

"Chase!" The red on her face intensified as we both laughed. She rolled her eyes and admitted, "Maybe just a little."

"A little? Ha!"

Nica covered her face with her hands, stifling a snort. "Okay, a lot, but not because of the ring."

"Mmm-hmm. Where's the lucky bastard now?"

I leaned my butt against her glass desk, and over my shoulder I watched Nica walk around it to rearrange the magazines and files the way she always wanted them—organized, OCD freak-style. Gotta love her for it. Without her, our little event planning business, Bliss Events, would have burnt down to the ground even before it was set to open, and I would have turned to ashes with it. Nica had saved me. She didn't know it, and I wouldn't know how to tell her other than being loyal to her, but she had.

"He's outside, waiting for his brother to finish smoking," Nica replied as she sat down.

"The shit-disturbers are here?" I glanced over my shoulder to Nica, and scrunched my face up as though bile just filled my mouth. Two Laurents in this small office. Just what I asked for this morning—coffee, donut, and egotistical men. I'd never met the brother but I could only assume his head was as inflated as Levi's.

Nica gave me the "Chase behave yourself" look. I scowled at the window, which faced the lot, and crossed my arms over the front panels of my jacket. "Am I right or what?"

"Give them a chance." She sighed. "You know Levi's staying put. I'm not letting him go anywhere. We're getting married and that's that. And his brother Alex is not so bad once you get to know him."

I snorted, scoffed, and snorted again. "Nica, you think that about everyone." I turned around to face her, bringing my palms down on her desk. "'He's not so bad,'" I imitated, "'He's only a bit of a handful, but he's really sweet. You're going to love him. He's Levi's brother. Enough said.'" Yes, I could be a handful as well, but Nica knew I'd scale Mt Everest for her; all she had to do was ask.

"Glad you missed me too, Chase."

I heard the remark, soaked in sarcasm, behind me. Levi sauntered over to his future wife. I looked up to the flat ceiling and hoped that I wouldn't become a murder suspect today. Nica reached for one of my hands and smiled. Her fiancé (vomit) smirked at me before leaning down to give Nica a kiss (double vomit). A joke about only a mother being able to love him played on the tip of my tongue. But I caught Nica's pleading gaze, and I had to retract my fangs. For now.

Straightening up, I heaved a sigh and extended my hand. All for my best friend. "I heard congratulations are in order." We shook hands. I spread my lips into a flat smile, and muttered between my teeth, "You lucky sonofabitch." Levi dropped my hand, and I wiped mine on my jeans.

"Chase, play nice." Nica tilted her head, exasperated at my antics.

"Fine." With an eye roll, I continued, "I promise not to set your tuxedo on fire on your wedding day."

A snigger came from behind me, and I turned so fast I got whiplash. My eyes felt like they were about to pop out of their sockets. The muscles on my temple twitched.

Trouble sat on Nica's office couch, with dark, mussed, James Dean hair, and decked out in full leather. His booted feet were propped up and crossed over the dainty coffee table, which Nica and I had spent hours sanding and refinishing to perfection. And he smirked like the devil.

"Chase, meet Levi's brother, Alex," Nica piped up behind me.

I always thought life was a bitch. A bitch who loved to inconvenience me. It had been years since I'd met someone like this guy—Alex. He twirled a cigarette around his left index and middle fingers. Fingers that girls would notice. Fingers that women would clamor for a chance to lick. Fingers that undoubtedly symbolized riveting pleasures, and pure, white-hot ecstasy. Fingers of a man who had rendered me speechless.

Say something. Anything!

An almost-word gurgled from my mouth, which brought another snigger out of Trouble incarnate. He locked gazes with me as he stood, all six feet and five inches of hot-damn hotness, and stalked to where I was frozen. Instead of shaking my hand (not that I offered mine), he leaned forward and placed two swift kisses on both my cheeks. Warmth ebbed in me, blossoming from the tips of the miniature hairs on the back of my neck, and down to the little polished nails of my pinkie toes.

I wheezed, about ready to pass out, and willed myself to breathe and get a grip.

Oh, I got a grip all right. My hands, of their own traitorous volition, raised and grasped at the lapels of his leather jacket.

His blue eyes burned into my being, reached past into my retinas and captured my soul (apparently I had one, despite what others believed). His lips, full and red, quirked at one corner into a blasted, knowing smirk.

"Pleasure to meet you too, Chase." If sex was a person and spoke, it would sound like Alex—decadent and smooth with an exotic accent. The beautiful bastard ran his bottom lip between his sparkling teeth, inches from mine. My core tightened. And I knew then that he had me. Unfortunately, he knew it too.

This was so. Freaking. Inconvenient.

Life was a major bitch.

❧

"Drink your scotch and stop pouting." Nica gave me her warning stare. I should tell her it made her look constipated, rather than threatening. The art of the scowl couldn't be taught. It was a skill which one mastered with practice, and which I had perfected to a tee.

I jutted my head forward, away from the back of the leather booth, slouching as I glared at my bestie. She'd invited me to have dinner with her fiancé and the brother. I could be doing better things, like color-coding my underwear drawer or refilling my non-existent spice jars. "Why am I here?" I asked.

Nica unfolded her napkin, refolded it into a freaking swan, and rearranged all her utensils. She'd chosen a fancy-pants restaurant for this lovely gathering (note the big ass hint of sarcasm there).

"To celebrate my engagement, and to talk about my wedding." She beamed at me.

I called BS. We could be talking about the wedding at work, while finishing off a couple of bottles of wine clients had given us, and a bag of chocolate eggs I'd found stashed behind one of her frilly storage boxes. Nica looked everywhere, except at me. She was a horrible liar, which made her a good person in my books.

"I could have asked Jake and Sandrine to be here too, but they're still in Paris." This girl was killing me.

I should count my lucky stars they were out of the country. Jake was Nica's ex, and Levi's best friend, and Sandrine was Jake's new wife and Levi's cousin. How messed up was that situation? And people said the world was such a big place. Puh-lease! It added to reasons why I shouldn't be here. I didn't want to have to face Alex again. Not after that embarrassing moment in Nica's office. I shuddered at the memory of him...Alexandre Laurent—such a pompous name—and the way I'd reacted to that ingratiating smirk of his as I held on to his jacket like it was a freaking life raft.

As soon as I'd realized what I'd done, I let go of him as though I'd suffered third degree burns on my hands. I'd checked them too, back and front. Alex had chuckled, low and hushed, and God help me, oh so freaking sexy. I'd made a poor excuse of having to check on something work-related and dashed out of Nica's office, *my* cheeks burning for once.

And now, we sat, Nica and I, in front of each other, waiting for Levi and Alexandre. After chugging my drink, I winced and said, "We can talk about your wedding plans at work."

She was going to ask me to do something that wouldn't

bode well for me. No wonder she'd ordered me a double scotch before I arrived.

"Spit it out, Nica, or I leave." I leaned forward, crossing my arms over the white linen tablecloth.

Nica straightened in her seat, ducked her chin and peeked under her lashes. "Can you show Alex around San Francisco?"

I was about to throw my napkin down and run out when she grabbed my arm, held on with a death grip, and spoke rapidly. "Please, hear me out. Alex has never visited San Francisco, and he's here for less than a week. I feel like you'll be able to show him things that interest him. You guys are kind of the same, you know."

I sputtered out a response, "Gah... Wha... Nica? Could you insult me more?"

"I wasn't trying to insult you! Chase, please." Cue her doe-eyed look.

I was off my seat, gathering my stuff. "Why can't Levi do it?"

"Levi has to go to Napa. Alex is going there at the end of the week, and Levi has to make sure it's up to par. And before you say it, I can't, because I have a million things to take care of that piled up while I was away." I narrowed my eyes at her, and she had the audacity to pout. "Please, Chase, he's not that bad."

I shook my head, furious at my so-called bestie for putting me in such an awkward position. For once, I couldn't go with Nica's plan. Not when it meant being alone with Trouble. I could still smell his musk comingling with his leathers. It smelled like a big mistake.

Once we were alone in her office, Nica had sat me down and expanded on the situation between Levi and his brother Alex. "Alex was engaged, years ago." She fluttered her eyes and double-checked that the door was shut tightly before continuing. "The girl, Simone, cheated on him and with someone so close. Alex's initial suspicion was Levi, but he claimed innocence, even when Alex beat him to a pulp." She paused, mulling the rest of it in her head. There was more to this story than she'd wanted to share. "The fight caused a riff between the brothers, which lasted over a decade. But they're starting to patch things." I'd speculated as much. Most of the time, only two things came between brothers— money or a woman. Involving myself in this circus could cause a lot more issues than any of us would want. *No, thanks.*

Nica must have seen the determination in my eyes. She took the damned napkin again and this time, folded it into a rabbit before saying, "Okay. I thought I'd ask. Maybe Jewel will do it." She reached into her purse for her phone and typed a message, I assumed to Jewel, our friend and colleague. I hated to disappoint Nica, since she'd never disappointed me. "There. Done." Before she could slip it back in her purse, it vibrated. "That was quick! Jewel's more than happy to do it. You're off the hook."

Alex would be safe in Jewel's company. Safer than with me. I would most likely end up punching him in the gut once or twice. Jewel was a sweet girl, a little excitable at times, but she was nice and smart and pretty in that girl-next-door some guys find attractive. She was a ray of sunshine to my constant thunderstorm. And I was sure she wouldn't kick Alex out of bed if he asked for a tour of that, too. My chest constricted and my breath became ragged. Not only was I imagining one of my friends cavorting with Trouble, I was greener than Shrek because of it.

"Chase. Chase!"

Something thumped against my jacket sleeve. I caught it, looked down at my hand, saw a piece of unbuttered roll, and muttered, "What the hell?"

"What's up with you? I've been yammering here and you weren't even paying attention." Nica tore another chunk off her roll. Her gaze flitted over my right shoulder, her eyes lighting up.

Before he spoke, I felt him. "Well, hello again." *Alex*. I shivered despite the heat that suddenly overtook me. That voice shouldn't have been too familiar, and worse yet, it shouldn't make my knees weak. Alex and Levi stood behind Nica. Levi bent down to plant a slobbery kiss on Nica's lips, and Alex peered at me.

"Yeah, and goodbye," I snapped.

"Aren't you staying for dinner?" Alex asked.

Three pairs of eyes stared at me. Nica's were pleading. Levi seemed entertained. And Alex...well, if he'd stop licking his lips I might be able to focus on his eyes. As I dragged my gaze from his lips to his eyes, I was lost in their blue depths.

"Perfect, *après vous*." Alex waved his hand toward the booth. I imagined those hands running over my legs under the table, up my thighs and...*Stop it, Chase!*

"I have to go," I said, and rushed out of the restaurant.

When I stepped out, I welcomed the coolness of raindrops on my face, positive there would be steam coming off me as cold rain met my heated skin. My body had warmed up under Alex's gaze. Hell, who was I kidding? My temperature spiked when I met him and had stayed that way the whole day because I did nothing but imagine him naked...with me.

"You forgot this."

I turned. There stood Alex under the eaves of the restaurant, with my helmet in his hand. His face conveyed nothing, but the fire alarm in my body screeched. Why couldn't I get hold of myself when I was near him? "Maybe one day, you could take me for a ride?"

Are. You. Kidding. Me?

Oh, I'd ride him all right.

I tried to grab my helmet but the bastard hid it behind him, so I pressed against his chest. *Breathe, Chase, breathe.* Ah hell, that was a bad idea. My heartbeat sped up when I got a good whiff of his cologne. I straightened and stepped back. "Give me my helmet." I had to raise my voice to fight against the sound of the rain.

"You've been drinking. Should you be riding?" Alex asked.

"What do you care? Give me my helmet." I sounded childish, which angered me more.

Alex shook his head, walked away from me, and headed back into the restaurant. And like a petulant child, I stomped my feet but stayed put. Hell no, I wasn't going to follow him. I trudged down the street, cursing Alex under my breath.

When he returned, he grabbed my hand, and asked, "Where is it?"

I stopped short and pulled back, remaining glued to the paved ground. "Where's what?"

"Your motorcycle. I'm taking you home," he bit back.

"No, you're not."

"Stop acting like a child and show me."

"I'm not showing you anything!"

Alexandre might have had enough, for he strong-armed me, his whole body flush against mine. He spoke in a gravelly, dark voice, which made me quiver. "You will do as I say. You'll show me where your motorbike is and tell me where you live, or I will..." His lips were inches from mine. I could almost taste his unique flavor through his breath. Even with the rain pelting us, his scent overpowered my senses.

"You'll what?" I challenged him, tilting my head up

slightly so that I could read his eyes. My stomach flipped at what I saw in them. He was burning me with something I'd forgotten existed, igniting dormant desires. I felt my knees buckle, and at that moment, I was grateful he had wrapped an arm around me, or I would have collapsed to the ground. "It's around the corner." I gave in after swallowing the thick lump in my throat.

Alex let me go, but kept hold of my hand, muttering in French. We trudged through the rain until we got to my baby, my classic Harley. He swung a leg over it, while I stood aside, quirking an eyebrow.

"Do you even know how to operate this?"

"Just get on before the rain turns heavier."

It didn't matter. I was already all sorts of wet. He handed me the black helmet. I didn't bother arguing with him about not having one for himself. The ride would be short. I could've run to my place in less than half an hour, or taken a cab if I wanted, but I didn't want to leave my baby out on the street in the rain. What I wanted was something else, something I didn't understand.

I settled behind Alex, snaking my hands around his waist, and groaned as I discerned taut, muscular abs under his shirt. The Harley rumbled between my legs, and I held on tighter to Alex. I stiffened and kept distance between us. While we rode, I tapped his shoulders instead of telling him which turns to take. Somehow he understood and got us to my apartment in one piece.

Once my motorcycle was parked in the carport, I ran up the steps, jingling my keys in my hand. The problem with him driving me home was that he needed a way back. "Come on in and I'll call you a cab," I offered, avoiding eye contact.

I made a silent promise to myself not to rip his clothes

off. But when I turned around he hadn't followed me up the steps.

"No need. I've got a ride back." He jerked his head to the side just as Levi stopped his car. These bastard brothers were going to hell. Why did I feel like I'd been played? "We better head back to the restaurant. Veronica's waiting all by herself." His subtlety at making me feel guilty wasn't all that subtle.

My keys dug into my palm. My teeth gritted. I didn't risk speaking for fear I'd beg him to stay. Beg him! I did not beg. I unlocked my door and slammed it as soon as I walked in. A deep exhale came out as I sagged against the steel door. What had gotten into me?

Nica's words rang through my head: "He's here for less than a week." If I could avoid Alex and all his sexiness, I could spend the rest of my years in San Francisco unscathed and untouched. I could live with that.

Mamihlapinatapai

I managed to stay clear of Alex the first week he was in San Francisco.

Jewel took him everywhere. The first day they were due to meet, she sought me out and asked for suggestions. At first, I'd shrugged, and told her to consult the great Google. But she said she wanted things to be perfect for Alex, after all, *he* was perfect. And single. So was Jewel.

Once I tamped down that alien feeling of envy, I relented and listed spots to check out in the city. They returned to the office in the afternoon, laughing, having a ball. It turned me sour. Well, more sour than usual. Annoyed as hell, I left the office as soon as I could.

That night, sleep evaded me. While still in bed, I found myself thinking of other places *I'd* take Alex. I'd compiled a list for Jewel every night since, and each morning I'd hand it to her and warn her that the list was for her eyes only. Some of the places I'd written down were my secret, favorite parts of the city.

One in particular was The Wave Organ on the Marina, where I found myself every time I wanted to be alone. In a city as big and as populated as San Francisco, there were still places you could lose yourself. I felt like I was opening myself up to another person, someone who didn't even know I was doing it. And I wasn't talking about Jewel.

Every time Alex and Jewel returned from their outing, you would think I'd make myself scarce, like a sane person would. No, I waited for them to come back and chat about their day. Either I was in my office, with the door slightly ajar so their voices would carry, or I'd make myself leave my office and walk to the small kitchen, where they perched on the stools, looking over photos Alex had taken. Not once could I get myself to ask to check them out.

Whenever I was around Alex, there was a constant prickle on the back of my neck, like someone was burrowing into me with his eyes. Sure enough, when I'd glance over at him, he'd be staring fixedly at me, as though he'd just broken through the wall I'd built through the years, and could see *everything*.

I felt exposed.

There was a secret message written in the air. The current of desire was so thick it nearly choked me.

It was a silent game we played, to see who would surrender first. Secretly, it thrilled me and gave me something to look forward to. But the only time I'd ever make a move was in my dreams. In the light of day, I grasped at all my strength and forced myself to stay rooted in place, letting him think he would never get to me. I thought I'd won, until he left for France.

On the first night, knowing I wouldn't see him the next day, tightness bloomed in my chest. Still, I refused to admit I missed Alex.

"It's just heartburn," I lied to myself.

For the next few months, his visits were infrequent. Oftentimes, I'd hear he'd been in the States when he was already gone. But I would always know when he was around. Every fiber of my being felt him, and those heated glances had seared themselves into my mind.

Without another word or touch, I'd connected with Alex.

It scared the ever-living crap out of me.

❧

I would have been able to ignore it if it weren't for Levi and Nica's wedding, when everything else went to shit. To say I couldn't recall how it all came about would be a complete lie. Everything began with a simple...

"Look...and tell me you don't want that."

"Want what?" I narrowed my eyes at the couple across the way.

"That. Love, marriage. What Levi and Nica have. They're so lucky." I glanced at Jewel, noting the silly, dreamy look on her face. She sighed, wrapped her arms around herself and swayed on the spot.

Jewel, much like Nica, was a hopeless romantic. They believed in crap like true love, love at first sight, and soul mates. Yadda-yadda. It was a load of Grade A turd, if anyone asked me.

And yet, my gaze slid past the newlyweds on the wooden floor, swaying to their first dance as Mister and Missus, and I spotted the Troublemaker. He'd been flush against the photographer from a wedding magazine that wanted to cover Nica's big day. He openly flirted, and they laughed, drank together, ate at the same side of the long table during dinner. Not that I'd paid much attention. I had managed to bag the interest of the only other eligible man in the wedding.

Out of fifty guests, half were women. Ninety-nine percent of the men were married, balding or gay. Since I was the Maid of Honor, I was expected to hook up with someone at the end of this. Those were the unwritten rules. Thankfully, Alex wasn't the only single man here. There was also that guy standing at the bar. If I could only remember his name.

It sounded like Jerry or Barry. Or was it James?

Franklin? Franco? Shoot. No, I recalled noting that he resembled James Franco. Well, the James Franco lookalike had gotten me a drink, and he was back at the bar again, re-filling my glass. I'd drink anything to survive this night. Not that I didn't love Nica; I did. I'd give her my firstborn if she asked, or steal someone else's for her since I had no intentions of ever having a child. And admittedly—not out loud—Levi wasn't bad for her.

What tortured me was witnessing Alex and Miss Big Shot Photographer practically necking in front of all of Nica and Levi's guests. Had they no shame? I scoffed when missy pie threw her head back and laughed at whatever inane thing Alex had whispered in her ear.

James Franco lookalike slid right back in front of me, blocking my view of Alex and his...whatever-she-was, handing me a tumbler containing two shots of scotch.

Jewel gave me a questioning look when I, in the most saccharine voice I could muster said, "Thanks...darling." (I really should try and figure out what his name was). I knocked back the liquid, letting it burn down my gullet, before I grabbed James' arms, and dragged him to stand to my right. I sent a quick side-glance across the dance floor, and as soon as Alex looked our way, I pressed my lips onto James' mouth.

I felt him melting underneath me. Wait, that wasn't right... He was supposed to be getting harder, not... swooning? Was James swooning over my kiss? I inched away from his lips, and stared into his eyes. Sure enough, he had a glazed look on him.

Questions filtered in my mind. Did I even ask his name? What else was I missing? I scrutinized his features. Wait a dog-gone minute...

"How old are you?" I asked the swooning James Franco. There was something amiss.

"Seventeen. I'll be eighteen in three months," he drunkenly answered.

"Ah!" I let go of his arms, and he fell backwards.

The music ended, and the guests applauded the newlyweds. The only people who'd paid attention to seventeen-year old James Franco and me were my friends, Jewel, Mateo and Gerard, who'd helped the little swooning boy up from the ground.

My eyes darted back to where Alex was—checked if he was still flirting and was relieved to see he'd left. However, that relief was short-lived when I spotted him a second later, guiding the photographer toward the main house. Everyone else was outside, waiting to get down to the dance floor. Alex and his twit would be alone in that big house. It didn't take a genius to posit what they'd be doing there, possibly in one of the bedrooms or bathrooms, all by themselves.

"Chase, what's wrong with you?" Jewel lightly slapped my arm.

I growled at her, but my wrath had no effect on Jewel. She knew me too well. "Did you see what you did to the poor boy? I thought he was gonna piss his pants." She nudged her chin toward the young— too-young—James Franco, being consoled by Mateo and Gerard. Were those tears I saw in his eyes?

I should go apologize, but what I said instead was, "He shouldn't be drinking anyway. He's underage."

"You just kissed him." Jewel propped a hand on her hip. "And he wasn't drinking. He's had juice all night."

"I—" *wasn't thinking. I was jealous. I was trying to prove a point to someone who didn't even notice me* "—need another drink." I headed to the bar and ordered a drink, which easily turned into more than one. I downed each one quickly, trying to drown the green-eyed monster in my gut.

Jewel was right to ask what was wrong with me. Ever since Trouble with the capital 'A' walked—no, freaking strutted—into my life, I'd had nothing else to think about but him.

                              ❦

Nica hadn't said a word to me prior to her wedding, even though I knew she knew. Best friend vibes.

Whatever occurred inside the house with the photographer happened fast, embarrassingly fast. I sniggered internally, but only to quell my jealousy. Alex emerged with the photographer, laughing, their arms hooked together. As soon as they hit the dance floor, Alex let her go and danced with Nica, Nica's mom, Lily, and her sister, Maggie. And practically every woman after that. He even pulled one of the hired servers to the floor. I watched it all from the safety of my almost drunken stupor.

"You need to ease on the booze, girl. I can hear your liver screaming for mercy," Gerard, ever the drama queen, told me with the flamboyance of a showgirl.

He and Mateo decided to take a break from dancing and hydrate, joining me by the bar. Mateo peeled the wineglass from my grasp and exchanged it with a bottled water. "Drink this. Did you even eat anything at dinner?"

"Yes, *Mom*, I did." I rolled my eyes at Mateo, but uncapped the bottle and took a sip of the water. Truthfully, I couldn't remember the last time I'd gotten this drunk. I hoped not to turn into one of those blubbery women I'd seen in the weddings I'd been to.

Gerard cleared his throat, taking my mind off my unfinished thoughts. "Drink up, bitch." He pushed the water to my lips, and it trickled down my neck.

"What the hell, G?" I'd just grabbed cocktail napkins off

the bar and dabbed at the cool liquid when I felt it—the prickle. I looked up to Gerard and Mateo, who were staring and smiling at something past my shoulder. I decided to wait and not turn.

"Fancy a dance?"

Breathe, Chase, breathe.

It shouldn't have mattered that his voice could cause my stomach muscles to tighten, or the neurons in my brain to cease all synapses. But it did.

My eyes widened, and I continued to stare at Gerard as he twirled his finger, signaling for me to turn around. *No freaking way!* But I did, because Alex was behind me, and my body—the traitor—did everything it could to get closer to him, without my permission.

The first thing I noticed up close was how he filled out the suit he wore. For a globetrotting photographer, he had a body I could stare at...not that I would. Never... I didn't have to. When it came to Alex, I was hyper aware of everything about him. I knew if I flipped his right arm over and pulled up his sleeve, I'd see a script-like tattoo, which ran from his wrist to his inner elbow. If I took another step, I'd smell leather and mint and not the suffocating scent of cigarettes.

But none of it mattered. He wasn't good for me, no matter what my brain tried to make me believe.

You're no good for him.

"What?" I asked, schooling my face to something neutral—and that was a challenge all on its own.

Alex *freaking* smirked and brushed his dark hair with a hand. "I've danced with just about every woman here..."

"And me," Gerard butted in. I cocked my head to the side and sent him a warning glare.

"Yes, and you. Excellent moves." Alex's teeth sparkled. *Flirt.*

"Thanks. You too." Gerard was outright flirting back. I'd be worried if I didn't know Alex was as straight as, well...Levi. Wait, no! I wasn't worried. Gerard was married, and his husband was snickering away behind me.

Alex returned his focus to me, and continued, "Well, as I was saying, I've partnered up with everyone that counted, except you, Chase."

"No."

Gerard gasped, and I sneered at him when I turned, showing Alex the back of my head. I gulped down the water and reached for my wine.

Alex did not relent. "C'mon. You're the maid of honor. I'm the groom's brother. We have to dance at least once."

Without looking back, I replied, "I said no. I don't dance." *Breathe, sip some wine, swallow it down, and push all the jitters away.*

"Everyone dances," Alex retorted.

Gerard nodded. "Mmm-hmmm. Everyone."

"Shut it, G," I muttered under my breath, and then the little hairs on my arms stood as Alex closed in. I could feel the heat of his skin. I could smell that intoxicating scent.

And felt his hot breath on my ear. "One dance. One song. One hand."

What the snit? "One hand?" Now, I was curious. "What do you mean one hand?"

Alex was so close to me that the vibrations of his voice trembled against my coal-hot skin. "Dance with me and I'll only keep one hand on you at all times."

I scoffed. *No way!*

"This I have to see!" It was Gerard who said it. I sent him another warning glare but he pouted, and mouthed, *you owe me.*

Eff-to-the-uck. He got me there. Gerard and I had been friends for so long and the number of favors I'd asked from him all these years had piled on. He'd never asked for his markers, and this shouldn't even count. But I knew it did. And if I didn't agree to a dance with Alex, Gerard would make me suffer. I begged Mateo silently, but he just smiled and half-shrugged.

I knocked back the wine I had in hand, and agreed, "Fine. One dance, one song, one hand." I pointed a finger, bared my fangs at Alex, and narrowed my eyes at him. "If even a single digit of your other hand twitches my way, it's over."

Alex widened his lips, from ear to ear. He was enjoying this, the jerk. I made a note to step on his feet every chance I got. He offered a hand to me, and with a bit more hesitation, I took it. While we made our way to the dance floor, my hands shook. I caught sight of Nica with Levi talking to some guests. They looked at us with shameless smiles.

I remembered watching the two of them dance at Jake and Sandrine's wedding. They could have set the entire tent on fire, the way they moved together. Of course, it was the night that had changed everything for them, and in a way, for me.

I'd never been a fan of change. I was comfortable with my life.

Once we were on the floor, the big band switched from a fast beat to a slow ballad. Alex turned to face me, but I kept my gaze lowered. In my five-inch heels, we were almost the same height. Alex snaked his right hand around my waist, kept his left hand behind his back, and we swayed. I didn't recognize the song—it was in French—but Alex knew it by heart. And while he moved he sang it to me, his stubbly cheek pressed against mine. With a light grip on my waist, he tugged me closer, placed one of his legs between mine, and led me gliding around the floor.

I closed my eyes as his fingers whispered over my bare back, tickling the nerve endings along my spine. My heart was beating wildly by the time his hand left my lower back and stroked up the side of my ribs and down along the length of my arm. With a flick of his hand, he raised my hand up and ghosted his knuckles along the outside of my arm. Then he clasped my hand and somehow, made me twirl.

This man was like a drug. He'd invaded my senses and woke up dormant feelings. My body hummed and zinged. I felt alive. And I didn't like it one bit.

Somehow I was able to talk, but I kept my eyes closed. "Had a good time with the photographer?" If I could take it back, I would, though only because I sounded jealous.

Alex chuckled in my ear. "So you were watching."

"I wasn't," I lied. "But it was hard not to notice."

His chest rose with a deep inhale, and with an exhale, he said, "I showed her a few of my photographs."

"I guess it didn't impress her, since you guys were there less than five minutes."

He blew a frustrated breath in my ear. "You don't think I can give anyone pleasure in that short of a time?"

I screwed my eyes tighter when he flicked my hand again, and I turned. "I wasn't talking about..."

His hand returned to the small of my back, and he stopped. The song was done. How long it had really taken was unclear to me. My exhale was shaky once I opened my eyes, and saw no one else but him. Everything else around us was a blur.

When Alex had danced with other women, after every song ended, he'd lifted each woman's hand and kissed the back of her fingers. Waiting for him to step back and do the same with me secretly thrilled me. Except he didn't do that.

Instead, Alex's intense gaze burrowed into mine for what seemed like eternity. He leaned in and whispered, "The guesthouse in fifteen minutes, and I'll show you how much pleasure I can give a woman." Then he stepped back and walked away, leaving me trembling in my Louboutins and gasping for more air.

Dysania

The bed hadn't felt like a boulder last night like it did now. All the same, I couldn't get myself to leave the comfort of the blankets.

My muscles whined as I stretched my arms. Every nook and cranny was sore. Even in the sleepy haze, memories of last night flashed my mind. I snapped my eyes open when I realized what I had done, and with whom.

I'd done it. I'd had sex with Alex. So much for staying away and standing my ground. What was it with the man that made me break my own rules? Over and over again?

I winced. I was stronger than that. I was supposed to be immune to his charms.

Groaning against the back of one hand, I massaged the throb in my head with the other. I blamed it all on the alcohol. How much had I consumed? Probably half the vineyard and then some.

This was all Levi's fault.

First, he swooped in and took my best friend away from me. Then he conveniently made up with his brother and brought that beautiful piece of man to San Francisco. And he freaking owned a vineyard! Who owned vineyards? The Laurent brothers, that's who.

I could hear Nica's voice in my head, tut-tutting me. And she was right. This wasn't Levi's fault. I hated to admit it, but I knew he'd take care of my bestie. He'd better or I'd string him up by his balls. Speaking of balls...

I was alone in the bedroom. Had that bastard left? Dined and dashed? Screwed and skedaddled?

It hurt to turn my head or move my body. My head pounded from the booze, my body from... I wasn't entirely sure. My mind was fogged up. The exact events of last night were a blur. All that was clear were the kissing, the sound of clothes ripping, and a whole lot of skin. Pumping and pounding. Laughter and fun.

I couldn't help the smile from spreading on my face. Ugh, thank God I was alone. If I gave myself time, every single moment of the previous night would come knocking on my brain's door.

As I sat up, or rather, slid my heavy ass off the bed, I felt tenderness in places I had forgotten about. I wasn't the reserved kind. I had a reputation, although the rumors weren't always true. Let me rephrase that: the rumors were never true. I did not sleep around. I made out with people in public, and left before anything got too heavy.

Nica knew. I suspected a lot of the people in the office knew as well, even though none of them had said anything out loud. Not that they would dare. Nica had tried to talk to me about correcting what people were saying about me, but at a certain point, it had gotten beyond fixing. So I'd let it ride.

Alex was gone. I would wring his neck next time I bumped into him. However—I rubbed the sleep from my eyes—I shouldn't have been doing anything with him in the first place. He'd only made things more complicated.

I curled my toes over the cool floor when another distinct feeling crept in: guilt.

I hoped that whatever it was that had inspired me to hop in the sack with Alex was now far gone. I couldn't let this happen again. People could get hurt. Me, for one.

As I looked around the room—one of two in the

guesthouse—I was surprised. I expected a mess. Alex had been staying here for the past three days. It was spotless. Even the dress I'd worn last night hung neatly over a chair. I could have sworn Alex had dropped that on the floor by the door after he practically ripped it to shreds. Or was that me tearing his shirt off? There was no sign of that, either.

Did Levi hire a cleaner? Had the cleaner been here while I was asleep?

Unless...could Alex be a neat freak?

I spotted his suit jacket folded over the ottoman at the foot of the bed, a telltale sign that he hadn't left the vineyard. There weren't any other signs of his clothes, though. Or my underwear. I reached for my phone, which lay on the bedside table. Someone had definitely cleaned up after me. *Us.* I had stuffed my phone in the elastic of my stocking during the reception, and I was pretty sure it had clattered on the floor when Alex had peeled off my stockings with his teeth.

According to the time on my phone, if I didn't hurry up, the rest of the people in the main house would find me sneaking back inside. I couldn't risk that. I stood and felt a tingling between my thighs, which I'd received from Alex's trimmed beard. Next time, I'd have to tell him to shave.

No! There wasn't going to be a next time!

I made my way to the attached bathroom to relieve myself, get cleaned up, and find my way back into the house before brunch. When I opened the door, Alex sat up, tilted his head and grinned. "Good morning, *hayati*. Aren't you a sight for sore eyes?" He dangled an arm over the side of the tub, and raked his eyes over my body. My *naked* body.

"What are you doing here?" I grabbed the towel off the rack, and wrapped it around myself.

Alex fluffed the pillow behind him, and rearranged the quilt over his bottom half. "I tried sleeping on the floor after you kicked me out of bed, but apparently, you thought that wasn't far enough. For your information, darling..." Alex regarded me from under his lashes. "I do not snore. You do, though." He waved a hand at me, his eyes gleaming with undisguised humor.

I was ready to scream, or punch him, and I wouldn't even feel bad about messing up his beautiful face. "I do *not* snore!"

He chuckled and pulled a pack of smokes out from under the quilt. "I think everyone across the field heard you." He paused, squinting at the window and scratching his beard. "I swear I heard the coyotes howling in response to your mating calls."

Cursing under my breath, I frantically looked about for something I could throw at him. Where's a piece of rock when you need one? I should carry one around with me at all times, like those old ladies who pack bricks in their handbags.

Alex chuckled again, low and deep. And, my oh my, was it sexy. "Look at you. You're so worked up. I thought after all that we'd done last night, you'd be more relaxed." His eyes, clear blue as the cloudless sky, filled with everything salacious.

I saw the soap dispenser on the counter and went for it. It felt heavier in my hand than I thought it would. This could give him serious damage. I held it up, leveled with my shoulders. Silently shot a warning at Alex.

His eyebrows drew together. "Aw, come on, *hayati*, put that down." He raised his palms in surrender and smiled at me. God, I hate to love that smile. Alex pushed the quilt aside, revealing his own weapon. "There's room for one more in here." Then he waggled his eyebrows.

"You've gotta be kidding me." I placed the soap dispenser back on the counter. "I'm outta here."

"Darling, why the rush? Brunch isn't for another hour."

"Which is why I have to leave." I tightened the towel around me. "There's no way I'm letting anyone find out that I spent the night with you." I'd meant to say that last part under my breath, but from the hurt that crossed Alex's face, I knew he had heard it.

Should I apologize? Maybe, but I had too much pride. And he told me I snored. Telling a woman she snored was like saying she smelled of garlic, or her ass looked fat in her jeans.

I stood before him, waiting for whatever else he wanted to say, but when nothing came, I turned to walk back into the room and get dressed. I heard his lighter flick open and smelled the cigarette. "Could you at least wait until I'm out of the room? That's going to stick on me, you know, and I'm going to end up smelling like you."

"You didn't seem to have problems rubbing all over me last night. You even said that you loved the way I smell." *Smug son of a…*

My hand paused over the doorknob when he said it. I couldn't let him get to me. Everything had been a terrible idea, even this moment. The tic on my neck began from irritation. Slowly, I faced Alex, ignored how sexy he was in that tub with the bedding surrounding him and that stick between his fingers. Those fingers. When my core tugged, the ache and pooling heat between my legs reminded me of how much of a delight those hands had been on me last night. But enough was enough. And I was sticking to my guns. Last night was a mistake.

I glided closer, loosening the towel around me, peering at him with hooded eyes and licking my bottom lip. Alex responded so well. So quick. Baited once again. One corner of his lips tilted up, and he pushed the quilt away. I leaned over the tub, my mouth inches away from his. I crossed an arm over him, and turned on the tap, letting cold water gush into the tub before jumping back.

"*Merde!*" Alex yelped as I ran right out of the bathroom, slammed the door behind me, and let laughter fill the room.

For a single second, my thoughts flitted back to Alex, and it hit me so hard how much I'd come to memorize all his features. His lips after they'd been on mine, his eyes when he climaxed, how the muscles over his stomach tightened as he hovered over me, how his chest rumbled when he laughed, and how his breath tickled my ear when he rasped out my name.

I hurried out of the room, zipping back into my dress, no longer caring where I'd left my underwear. I picked up my phone and my shoes and ran barefoot back toward the main house, blocking out every single moment that had happened the night before. Never again. I didn't often give myself a chance to make mistakes; I couldn't afford another one like Alex.

After a long shower, scrubbing off any hint of what had gone on, and getting dressed for the day in my signature blacks, I stepped into the large solarium where a long table was set up for brunch.

Nica was the first one to greet me. "There you are, sleepyhead!" She raised her arms and welcomed me into a hug. Yes, I allowed her one hug because, well, mainly because I was too exhausted and hungover to fight it. "Your hair smells good."

I pulled away from her and gave her a questioning look. "I didn't change my shampoo." There was something different about her. A higher level of keenness in her eyes.

"Oh...well, it's nice." She smiled sweetly, but nervously, and returned to her conversation with Levi.

I eyed her curiously as I took the seat next to her. The

rest of our group had taken seats, except for Alex. I ignored the hitch in my breath as his name popped in my head. I focused on the spread on the table instead. Pastries and fresh bread, cheese and butter, salads and fruit, and all sorts of preserves occupied the middle of the table.

"Did you sleep well last night, Chase?" Gerard spoke from across the table as I reached for a piece of rye bread. He quirked his brow, and I raised my own.

"I did. Yes. You guys?" I poured myself a glass of water.

"Oh, we slept very well, even with all the noise." Mateo nudged Gerard with an elbow.

"Noise? What noise?" Nica asked Gerard.

"Yes, what noise? I slept in the guesthouse for two nights and I didn't hear any noises at night," Levi added, turning to Mateo and Gerard too.

Wait a second... "You guys slept in the guesthouse?" I asked. A lump lodged in my throat. I thought Alex and I had been alone in the guesthouse. I gripped the water glass harder. I had to tell myself to leave it on the table lest I crush it in my fist.

Gerard cocked his head to the side, addressing Levi with a flourish of his hand. "Oh, it sounded like growling or maybe groaning. Very animal-like. Ow!" Mateo nudged Gerard again, harder this time.

"It was fine, guys," Mateo told Levi and Nica. "It wasn't really that bad. My husband has an overactive imagination." And yet, Mateo couldn't look my way.

Gerard tilted his head at me and grinned. They knew I'd been with Alex. I looked around the room to see if anyone else had noticed Gerard's insinuation. Nobody else seemed to have given it another thought. Levi's grandmother was busy chatting with Lily. Maggie, Nica's sister was telling Jewel how she had managed to snatch the bouquet from Isobel's hand last night. June, Maggie's boyfriend, focused on his cellphone. Jake and Sandrine, new parents, still looked half asleep.

Nope. No one else knew. I'd have to pull Gerard aside later on and beg him not to blab. People didn't have to know. People shouldn't have to know what I did or didn't do behind closed doors. Or who.

"Good morning, everyone." Speak of the devil.

Alex walked in with the sun shining on his back. His hair was still wet, and the white shirt he wore clung to every toned muscle of his torso. He made the rounds, and greeted each person with either kisses on the cheeks or a hearty handshake, and a tight hug from Nica, Gerard and Lily.

When he reached me, I stiffened and dropped my gaze to my lap. He bent down and just said, *"Hayati."* His face didn't touch mine, but I felt the zap of electricity on my cheek, all the way down to my tailbone. Then he pulled back the empty chair beside me. How had it not crossed my mind that once he joined us, he'd most likely take the only unoccupied seat?

None of my actions made sense when it came to Alex.

"Hmmm. Everything looks good today." He clapped his hands and rubbed them together.

"Did you have a good sleep, Alex?" Gerard started again. I sent him a look, which I hoped told him he'd better protect what was most precious to him if he didn't shut his trap, but he ignored me.

"I had a fabulous sleep, and a wonderful bath this morning," Alex replied, reaching over for a slice of bread. The bastard. "How about you?"

"Good bath, huh?" Gerard eyes widened in glee. "We heard animals growling last night." I saw the quirk of a smile on his lips.

Alex spread butter on his bread, not glancing my way or

Gerard's. "Animals, yeah? I think I may have heard those too."

My jaw clicked as I ground my teeth together. Alex reached a hand forward again, this time for the jam. But unlike the last time, I felt his other hand over my thigh. I wasn't ticklish, but he startled me, and I hiccupped.

Everyone at the table turned to me. My hand flew to my mouth. "Sorry about that." Alex's hand trailed up higher. My skin heated underneath my jeans.

"Coffee, anyone?" Anita, one of Levi's employees in the vineyard, entered the room carrying a pot.

"I'll have some." I raised my hand. When I dropped it, I pushed Alex's hand away. I didn't bother looking at him, terrified to know what his gaze would do to me, or what else it would reveal.

Anita came over and poured coffee into my cup. "Alex, coffee?"

"That would be delightful. Please." He raised his cup but Anita waved it away.

"I'll come to you." Anita stepped between us, and I was happy for that break.

I took my chance to stand and pick up my cup. "You know, I think I'll head out and get my stuff ready," I told Nica.

"You're not even going to eat?" she asked, staring pointedly at my untouched bread.

"Not really hungry. I wanna hit the road soon."

"Why don't you stay for another day, Chase?" Levi asked. "Everyone else is. We'll have a good ol' American barbecue and a pool party. I can show you the cellar today."

I shook my head. "No." I let grumpy Chase out. "I've got shit to do at work since you're taking Nica away for two weeks." With that, I headed out the door, not caring who said what or who continued to stare at me as I lifted the coffee cup to my lips with a jittery hand.

※

Half an hour later, I was once again wrapped in a tight hug. Nica is a hugging machine when she's happy. I held onto her wrists and pried her off me. "Okay, you. I'll see you in two weeks."

She stepped back and held hands with Levi. "Yeah. I'll check in every now and then."

"Ugh, please don't. Knowing you, you'd want to share." I sent Levi a quick glance. "There is such a thing as TMI, Nica. You can show me pics from your trip when you get back." I swung my legs over my bike, put my helmet on and started my Harley. "I make zero promises the business will be standing when you return though."

Levi laughed but Nica's eyes turned almost bulbous. She stared up at Levi with worry on her face, and he leaned in and kissed it away. I looked away from them, and far off the distance, I could make out where Alex stood, a cigarette between his lips, watching me.

One last time, I'd let myself think of him. Nothing more. He'd managed to turn my world upside down. I flicked my visor down and saluted the newlyweds before riding back to civilization, and sanity.

*S*olivagant

I loved the open road, but I hadn't been paying attention to how beautiful my surroundings were.

I wasn't in such a rush to head back to the city and to work. It would be completely empty seeing as how everyone who worked for us (and mattered to me) was staying in the vineyard for a couple more days. But I just had to get away from Alex. I didn't know what I would do if I was constantly near him. I couldn't risk it, not for a few wicked lays with a man who magically knew how to push every one of my buttons.

Alcohol had clouded my judgment last night. And I was afraid after being with him, I wouldn't even be able to blame a state of inebriation for having my way with Alex again. All I needed was him. His scent. His touch.

My wrist flexed as I pushed on the throttle. Distance. Distance from him would be good for me. I wasn't sure when he was leaving the States, but it had to be soon. I bent my wrist again. Another half an hour and I'd be home. I'd lock myself indoors until I heard the news that Alex was thousands of feet above the earth.

Then I heard it. A mechanical sputtering. "No, no, no, baby." I tapped my bike. "Shit." I'd been stupid. This was bound to happen. My mechanic, Glen, had taken a look at my Harley two weeks ago and had warned me. I had been too busy thinking about the wedding and Alex that I'd completely ignored Glen.

I guided my bike over to the side, and shook my hair as I took my helmet off. It was a glorious Sunday afternoon. I'd passed a few people along the way, but they were going at a leisurely pace. They'd reach me eventually, but I had zero patience.

I searched my pockets for my phone. Then realized I'd left it there, on the nightstand in the bedroom I hadn't slept in. Not good. I'd have to wait for someone and ask to use their phone. There was no way I was leaving my baby behind. I'd camp out here if I had to.

Several minutes later, the first car came toward me. But whoever it was passed without slowing down. Bastard.

I'd pulled out my emergency kit from the saddlebags and placed mini-pylons behind and in front of my bike. Thankfully, Nica had insisted I bring food with me since I didn't eat breakfast. How could I eat when a hot-as-Hades man was feeling me up under the table? I'd slipped my jacket off and had a sip of the water when I spotted another car coming. No, not a car, a truck. A cherry red Ford Raptor.

It looked familiar. Could it be? I'd seen one of Levi's employees driving a similar one when I'd arrived at the vineyard. Using a hand to block out the sun, I squinted. It was the same truck from the vineyard. Perfect. Maybe they could even help me load my bike in the flatbed. Their trucks were outfitted to carry heavy loads. Maybe luck was starting to favor me.

But as it neared, I realized the man driving wasn't the same one I'd seen driving it the previous day. He stopped in front of me, stuck his head out of the open window, removed his sunglasses and plastered a grin on his face. My knight in a shining Ford was Alexandre Laurent.

"A little trouble, *hayati*?" he asked, maneuvering the truck closer to the side of the road, killing its engine before stepping out. A little trouble I could handle. He was a lot more than a little trouble. But did I have a choice?

"Yeah, I just need to borrow a phone to get it outta here," I told Alex, keeping away from him and my arms crossed tightly over my chest. The killer grin on his face never wavered. I mentally slapped myself to stop the swoon that was about to come.

"I could take a look if you want." He tucked a hand in his pocket and out came my phone. "You left this back there when you were trying to get away from me."

"Wha—? I wasn't..." I shut my mouth and pressed my lips together.

It hurt that he knew me so well. It shouldn't have been possible. We'd barely talked. The most we'd said to each other were the dirty things we had uttered while in the throes of passion. My nipples hardened upon remembering them. Alex had a filthy mouth, but he hadn't only talked the talk, he walked it too.

Shit. I needed to concentrate. I grabbed the phone from him and pressed the button. Nothing but black, like my mood.

"It's dead," I said accusingly, as though he had caused the battery to drain.

"Guess you forgot to charge it." He made his way to my bike, inspecting it under the sun.

"Just give me your phone so I can call someone," I snapped, sending him a death glare.

Alex stooped low, checking on the gears of my baby. "For someone who needs help, you're not very pleasant," he told me without looking up.

I fumed. "Alex, please give me your phone, so you can go on your merry way."

"Try again, *hayati*." He kept his eyes on my bike.

"Shit, Alex, I already said please. I'd like to be on my

way before it gets dark." This time, Alex tilted his head up to the cloudless blue sky. Yeah, I got the point. Darkness wouldn't be coming anytime soon. "And stop touching my bike. What the hell do you know about fixing a motorcycle anyway?"

Alex stood and walked around to the other side, fiddling with parts again. With smugness in his voice, he said, "Two-thousand ten Heritage Softail Classic, whitewalls, chrome-laced wheels. Fifteen eight-four cc motor, and let's see...ninety-two point two pounds of torque at...three thousand rpm. I would have gone with complete Vivid Black, but the Merlot is a nice touch." Okay, he got me. He knew a thing or two about bikes. "I toured with a Triumph for years."

"Well..." *Think, Chase, think.* I tried hard to ignore the pooling of lust in my belly. "I don't want your hands or your clothes to get dirty." *Weak.* What could I do? Alex looked like a supermodel, talked like a mechanic, and screwed like a nymphomaniac on death row.

He chuckled, lower than I'd ever heard before, but not so low that it was easily ignored. My body noticed. I remembered Alex over me, trapped under his luscious gaze, my legs wrapped around his hips, as he pumped into me.

"You're so beautiful," he'd said last night.

I'd exhaled, hard, and replied, "You don't have to throw compliments, your dick's already inside me." He'd chuckled, and the reverberations shot all the way to my core. It had sent him into a fury and his movements had become more frantic.

Alex peeked up at me from behind my bike. "You know I don't mind getting a little dirty, Chase." He winked. Another blow to my failing control. Thankfully, he focused on my bike. "Tank?"

"I never leave it less than half full."

"Tire?"

"Are you shitting me? These are new." I pointed at my tires.

"You can never be too sure, *hayati*."

I rolled my eyes. "What does that word even mean?" I screwed my lips before saying, "It's the gearbox. It's shot. I was supposed to bring it in last week, but I forgot." I squeezed the bridge of my nose in annoyance.

Alex stood, anger present on his face. "And you've been riding it all this time? Do you have a death wish?"

Damn, Alex angry was pretty hot too. "No, not particularly. I've been busy."

Alex swore under his breath, and rubbed his hand over his forehead, leaving a streak of grease on it. "Help me load it then." He ran around the bike toward the truck.

"Or just give me a damn phone," I snapped once more. Why couldn't he just listen?

He spun around so quickly it startled me. "Help me load it, or you stay here and wait for the next person to come. As far as I know, my brother owns half this stretch. A tow could take a lot longer. Your choice, Chase." It was always my choice. Even last night, before we'd entered the guesthouse, between kisses, he'd told me that if I'd wanted to stop or leave, I'd been free to do so. But I hadn't.

"Why are you being so difficult?" I spat.

"Why are you running away?"

Whoa. I did not expect that. This little back and forth had brought him closer to me. Without my heels on, he was almost a head taller. His shirt was thin, and the heat emanating from his skin was hotter than the sun above us. His eyes bored into me as he waited for my reply. He knew there wasn't anything coming. Not today. Probably not ever.

"Help me load her up." He strode back to the truck, massaging the side of his head and muttering in French.

Watching him pull down the ramp from the back of the truck, I breathed a sigh of relief. Even if I tried to hide his effect on me, it was too late. Alex had known all this time. Now that he figured out I was keeping distance from him, would he actually let me?

꩜

I received my answer when we arrived at my doorstep. We'd dropped my Harley off with Glen, and I didn't bother with introductions before I gathered all my stuff. Alex didn't offer me a ride to my place; he just assumed. I hadn't bothered to argue. There would have been no point.

The drive to my place was quiet. When I got out of the truck, he killed the engine and stepped out too.

I reached in for my bags in the back seat. "I can bring my stuff in, no need to..."

Alex was on me in an instant, bracing his hands over the top of the truck. When I turned, I was pinned between him and the passenger door. "You didn't answer my question." His eyes blazed, but I refused to read what they wanted to reveal.

"What question?" I knew which one.

"Why are you running away from me?" Alex trailed his hand over the side of my face, down my neck, and past my shoulder, but he kept his eyes on me. "You can't say you don't want me."

"Alex, please," I breathed out, and shuttered my eyes closed.

"Ask me in, Chase." I had a feeling he wasn't only talking about inviting him inside my house. He wanted more.

I squeezed my eyes tighter, and shook my head. "Alex, I can't."

"Why?" He pressed his whole body on me. All hard, and toned, and wanting. "I know you want me." He took my hand, and I thought he would guide it toward his crotch, but he didn't. He brought it to his chest and let me feel the thundering underneath. "I want you too. Feel this. This is all your doing. There's more to this than something physical."

Shit. This was going at the speed of lightning, and I had no idea where the brake was. "Alex..."

I lost my voice when Alex claimed my mouth. He licked my lips apart and declared himself ruler of everything sane in my life.

I was in dangerous territory from the very beginning. All of my guarded walls tumbled at his touch. It had taken years to put those up, brick by brick of carefully-laid protection to stop anybody from ever getting in. A battle had started within me—the fight to savor everything that was Alex, and the memories of the person I once was. No, more than that...the person I would always be but had never exposed to anyone.

*

We didn't make it to my bedroom the first time.

Alex laid on his back as I rode him, fast and frenzied in the foyer of my apartment, ignoring any protestations from somewhere deep in my mind, and the hard bite of the floor on my knees. I expected some bruising tomorrow.

I begged myself to let me have this—whatever this was —once. Just for today.

The fury continued into my living room, with me bent over my charcoal grey sofa. The fabric scratched my skin, but nothing would scar me more than once this was over. The third time, we'd found ourselves in the kitchen, pretending to rest for food or drinks. We'd feasted on each other instead.

By the time we reached my bed, the sun had gone down. I was spent.

Alex panted beside me, stretched out on his back, while I lay on my stomach. Our faces were inches away from each other. Our breath commingled in the air. His lips spread into a wicked smile before he laughed. And I joined him.

There wasn't anything humorous. It was a bubble of emotion we both understood and couldn't help but give into.

What were the chances of finding someone who just got you, especially when you're not searching?

"Come back to me, Chase." Alex tapped my forehead, and leaned to place a tender kiss on my shoulder. "Where did you go?"

"Nowhere," I answered with a small smile, and wondered if I'd read Alex right. What was he really asking from me?

He reached over and wrapped me in his arms. "Good." A deep breath raised his chest as he took in the scent of my hair. "You smell so delicious."

I hummed. This was too much. A guy inhaling my scent meant something. I made an excuse to be free of him, of that moment. "I have to go to the bathroom."

"Why?" I raised a brow at him. *Possessive much?*

"I have to pee. You want to help me with that too?"

"I'm sorry. That didn't come out right. Go on. I'll be waiting." He folded his hands under his head, looking comfortable and at ease.

Panic wrung my throat when I saw myself in the mirror. Mascara smeared around my eyes. My lips blood-red from his kisses. My cheeks blazed the same tint. It was too easy to be blinded by the possibilities Alex and I could have together whenever I was with him. But as I stood, alone, wracked with guilt and shame, it was obvious we could never be.

I splashed water over my face, cooling my heated skin. Several deep breaths calmed me before I returned to the bedroom. To Alex.

He was propped up with a pillow behind his back, his hair sticking out all different directions from all my earlier tugging and pulling. The taut skin of his toned chest was marred with love bites and scratches, and he held an open book in his hands. "Interesting read." It was a library book, Hawthorne's "The House of Seven Gables". After sending me a knowing smile, he continued reading.

I reached over and grabbed it from him, snapped it closed, and placed it on my dresser on top of other books.

It didn't upset Alex. He quirked his lips into a teasing smile. "I was wondering what was jabbing me on my back." His eyes wandered over my room. Piles of books were everywhere. "Do you always sleep with books?"

Come on, Chase, get rid of him, my subconscious reminded me. "Most nights." I turned away and picked out a shirt and panties from my drawer. If I was going to end this, I couldn't be standing in front of him nude.

"Let's go grab dinner." He sounded so casual, like what we'd done wasn't horrible.

My head snapped back at him. "No." He was studying the lines of fingernail scratches on his left shoulder. Scratches I'd created.

"All right," he said, sounding entertained. "How about we order in? I'd say I would cook for you but we've already discovered you don't keep much food in the house." His voice had a thrill of humor and sweetness in it. He was killing me, my heart swelling until it was ready to burst.

I focused on getting dressed. Alex shuffled behind me, pulling on his boxers, and then wrapped his hands around my waist, pressing against my back. "I'm going to wash up. You decide what you want for dinner. I know what I want for dessert." I kept silent and let him head to the bathroom.

My bed was a testament to my shame. No man had ever been in it. The only people who'd ever set foot in my apartment were my friends. Only Nica had been inside my bedroom when she helped me paint the walls a dark purple. And yes, books were my only bedtime companions.

With the throbbing pulse in my head, I grabbed the sheets and pulled them right off the bed. Alex reappeared as I bundled them in my hands.

With a firm voice, he asked, "What are you doing?"

"What does it look like I'm doing?"

He continued to talk even though I didn't turn to face him. "It looks like you're changing the sheets. Are you that ashamed of what we've done?" He didn't wait for an answer. Alex grabbed my arm and spun me around. Hurt and concern filled his eyes. "What's after this? Are you going to take apart the flooring in your hallway too? Or burn your sofa to the ground? How about your kitchen bench? You're going to get rid of those too?"

"Why do you even care?" I snapped at him.

Alex huffed and shook his head, producing a dry, humorless chuckle, while he picked up his neatly folded clothes from a chair and started dressing.

"Why are you here, Alex? What were you doing driving that truck? Where were you going?" I didn't know I'd wanted to ask those questions until I did.

He calmed a bit, and regarded me with those blue eyes.

"Jewel found your phone, and I made an excuse to see you again. You didn't even say goodbye."

I scoffed. "We had one night, Alex. That was it." His grip on my arm tightened.

"And we had today. What is this?" Alex spread his free hand between us. "One night and one day. Those are all I get? That's it?"

It was more than I should have given in the first place. He would never understand, and I wasn't willing to open up just yet. Not to him, at least. "Yes."

Alex dropped his hands. His shoulders slouched forward. His eyes tried to read mine, but I wasn't entirely sure what he'd see in them.

I steadied myself. I gathered the hem of my shirt in a tight fist. If I touched him, I probably wouldn't let him go. But I needed to. I had to. The more he stared at me, the more I could feel myself falter.

A mixture of confusion and anger flooded in his eyes, and in the end, Alex gave up and walked away. But if I thought that was the end, I was wrong.

Numinous

The marks on my skin from Alex stayed for about three days: a pinkish darkening under my collarbone and the top of one breast, and faint bruising on my knees.

I would have loved nothing more than to stay in my apartment and sulk but I wasn't like that anymore. *Chase* did not pout under the covers. Not for anything, especially not for a man. No matter how sinfully good-looking he was. Plus I did promise Nica I'd take care of the business while she was on her honeymoon.

By Tuesday, everyone was back from Napa Valley and work was in full swing. No one mentioned Alex. I tried my hardest not to think of him, but there were few reminders I couldn't ignore. The muscle soreness wore off the next day, thanks to a stop at my favorite watering hole, Davidson's, followed by a hangover, which gripped my skull.

Once I sobered up and wasn't too busy with meetings, I would remember to eat, head to the gym, then home to shower and sleep. This had been my way of life for a few years.

The quiet nights in my bed were the most difficult to take. I couldn't even crack open a book without remembering him doing the same thing just a few days ago.

On day four, when I stumbled—due to lack of sleep, too much booze, and not enough Nica time (*curse you, Levi*)— into work, I thought I'd hit the end of it. No more suffering. I slapped my head until I was awake enough to go through my day. Without Nica around, I'd have to rely on Jewel to tell me which meetings I had to attend and which events I needed to prioritize.

With a cup of freshly-brewed coffee in my hand, I joined her in her new office, and found her with Gerard *ooh*ing and *ahh*ing over her computer monitor. I walked around and checked out what they were fawning over. They were photos from Nica's wedding.

"Are these the ones for the magazine?" I asked, sipping coffee. They were magnificent. Nica would not be disappointed.

Without taking her eyes off the screen, Jewel answered, "No, Alex just sent them."

Lucky I hadn't taken a sip of my coffee again or it would have ended up all over Jewel's desk. A high-pitched ringing blasted in my ear. And it came with the shooting pain on the right side of my face. I'd dislocated my jaw when I was twelve, and it hadn't been the same since. Every time I'd get stressed, the tension spread on my face. I walked out of there without another word, gripping the coffee mug hard, and at my resolve harder.

What would Nica tell me? Relax? Get over it? No, she would ask me why. Why was I so hung up on not starting or continuing any semblance of a relationship with Alex. And if I didn't want it, why was I being so hard on myself?

I wasn't ready to explore the answers, yet. Most likely, I would never be ready.

My phone buzzed on my desk and it pulled me away from unwelcome memories. Nica's selfie popped up. I snatched it and answered right away, ready to give her a hard time for even calling me during her honeymoon, even though I secretly delighted she did.

"I don't want details, Nica. I don't want to know if Levi

wears boxers or briefs," I said as I accepted her call, bypassing the pleasantries.

Her laughter blasted in my ear. "Right now he hasn't got any."

"Spare me, please." But I couldn't help but laugh with her. The first laughter I'd let out since Alex had left. I rubbed my temples, expelling thoughts of him. "Why are you calling me if your husband's naked?"

"Just want to know how you are." There was a pause. A pause was never good, not with Nica. This wasn't a random call.

"I'm fine, Nica." Although, I wanted to scream and bash my head against the solid wood desk in front of me. If I opened the can of worms I'd hidden for so long, more questions would follow, and there were answers I wasn't willing to bring to the surface. My phone buzzed against my ear twice, signaling I'd received a text message. I ignored it. "Anything else? I have work to do."

She laughed again. Boy, she was one happy camper. When her laughter trickled down, she said in a hushed tone, "Alex is leaving today."

Ah, so now we had the reason why she called.

"So?" I bit my lip to keep from letting any more bitterness out. If she were with me, and we had my emergency kit (aka booze and chocolates), maybe I'd be more forward.

"Nothing. I thought you should know." Right. 'Nothing' was a loaded word to Nica. Nothing meant everything to her.

"Well, thanks for telling me. Everything's fine here." I squeezed my eyes shut and pinched the bridge of my nose. I could feel another headache coming. "You just keep your legs open for your husband and don't worry about us. Bye, Nica."

I hung up. Bad idea. Nica would read something from it. I never ended a call like that with her. I hoped she wouldn't call back. My phone buzzed twice, again, and I decided to read my messages.

Bad idea number two.

They were from Alex. His beautiful face, sleepy eyes and mussed up hair on a pillow smiled at me from my cellphone. I didn't know how he'd got my number or when he programmed his number into my phone. His message was simple but it gripped my chest.

I'm sorry I left.

What could I say to that? Apparently, something genius:

How did you get my number?

He responded immediately. My heart twitched. I pounded on my chest, cursing the damned organ.

I'll tell you when you say you forgive me.

Was he serious? I had nothing to say to him. Nothing I would be willing to admit. I tightened the hold on my phone and dropped my head on my desk. Why was this happening now? Why with someone like him? I'd been free for ten years.

I thought it would be easy. He seemed like a player to me, with his bad-boy swagger and his panty-dropping smile. He could charm pennies off a poor man. I'd met enough men like him, but none had affected me like Alex had. I hadn't let any man affect me in such a way. Not for a long time.

The younger me would have run as fast as possible the moment he had entered the room. But the younger me did not exist anymore. What was left of her were painful memories, which had branded into my brain and chipped away a corner of my heart.

Beyond the physical, I knew what I craved. And

counting the physical, I hungered for it even more. Alex. I thought I could erase my past but it turned out, I'd only put a Band-Aid on it. Stupid me.

Before I could stop myself, I sent Alex a message:

You're forgiven. Now leave me alone.

What he said after threw me off balance.

For now, I will. But when I return, I'd like to take you out to dinner.

After the way I'd acted he still wanted to...date me? Maybe he was as crazy as me. Two peas in a fucking pod. I fought the urge to reply back, and instead, I stared at my phone, trying to read the invisible message.

I managed to survive the weeks after without any repercussions. Nica returned from her honeymoon and announced her pregnancy, which she'd been keeping from me since her wedding. I berated her for not telling me right away, even though I understood her reasoning. It was something she needed to share with Levi for a while before they became overwhelmed with other people's reactions to the news. Perhaps I was too involved in my thoughts because it hadn't registered that Nica hadn't touched a drop of wine on her wedding day. My best-friend radar needed tuning up.

A week after, Alex came back as well. He made good on his promise to ask me out for dinner, but we never did go out. Dinner meant more. Dinner meant serious.

Since then, every time he was in San Francisco, he would send me a text message to meet him somewhere. I was the first person he'd contact, and secretly it thrilled me.

He never came to my apartment, and I never invited him back there again. I was fine seeing him at a hotel, where we'd have explosive, mind-numbing sex for as long as our bodies would allow. Yet, every single time after, guilt would eat at me, and I'd lash out at him. Sometimes he'd argue back; other times he would stay quiet and just let me yell.

It was unhealthy; we both knew it. As sick-sounding as it was, I'd look forward to the arguing as much as I did the sex. But I'd always known I was built with a few missing gears in my brain. In between, we had a great time. He would make me laugh, and he'd make me pensive. He would challenge me in so many ways. Sometimes, he'd make me jealous by showing me photographs of women he'd had "sessions" with, although I'd never admit it.

There were the few times when we would talk about the places he'd been and what had brought him there. And as the skies darkened and the moon appeared in the sky, he'd close his eyes and succumb to sleep. I would leave as soon as I felt the heaviness in my own eyes. Staying over would mean too much. More dangerous than having dinner. I wasn't ready.

Assignation

*L*et me share a secret. Hannah was my second name, my *secret* second name. Hannah meant "favored" or "grace". Grace, meaning effortless beauty or charm of movement.

My second name did not suit me. I had zero grace, and I lacked charm. What I did have was a wicked body. An ass that wouldn't quit (thanks to my fabulous trainer, Diego) and boobs which stayed perky (it also helped to have connections with people in the lingerie business along the western coast). And I wasn't ashamed to use them.

But boy, did it suck at times. More like, all the time. I supposed it was my fault. Nica had warned me time and time again that it would bite me in the ass.

I tried using my brain.

I hungered for knowledge, thirsted for facts. I absorbed clues, hints and wisdom, even from the most bizarre sources. That was me. I was a curious sort. For years, I'd been told that knowledge was power. Well, that was true enough. But I also learned, the hardest of ways, that some men, if not most, disliked smart women. So I had to be wily. And I discovered most men responded better to hot women. It wasn't fair. It was unjust.

Non-secret number three: I was a hypocrite.

Women hated me for how I looked. Men hated me for what was in my head. Put two and two together, and what have you got? Me. A Diva. Queen Bee. I had a reputation. Like anything else I'd worked hard for, I cared for that reputation. Women thought I was a big bitch. Men thought I was an easy lay. Neither of them were right at all.

The only person who truly knew me was Nica. But there were things even Nica didn't know. Some secrets were meant to be buried, hidden in the dark for decades, never to surface into the light. Other things I wanted to keep because they were too much fun.

Case in point—Alexandre Laurent, who just sent me a message.

Room 505. Half hour.

His damned text message was enough to wet my panties.

I stared at my phone for a good minute or two. My mind had often told me not to reply. To stay put. To resist. But the rest of my body rebelled and screamed, "Alex, oh, Alex!"

The vibration of my phone had me jumping. It almost hit the pavement, but thank goodness for quick reflexes, I caught it before that happened. Nica's drunk-ass face from her bachelorette party appeared on my screen. She'd asked me to delete and change the picture, but what kind of best friend would I be if I did that?

"Yeah?" I answered with little flourish.

"Did you get it?" Good ol' Nica. Business as usual.

"You know it." I swung my leg over my bike, ignoring the salacious looks I was receiving from male passersby. Apparently, biker chicks were hotter than hot.

"Oh, thank God. I was worried there for a bit." Nica sucked in a deep breath and released it in a heavy sigh.

"You doubted me? I'm hurt." Even though I knew she couldn't see me, I placed a hand on my chest.

"Pfft. I didn't doubt you *could* get it. I was worried about what you had to do in order to get it."

"Relax. He only asked for a blow job."

"Chase!"

Imagining how red she would be right now, I guffawed into my phone. "I'm kidding," I said, rolling my eyes. "I just made out with him for five minutes."

"Oh gross, I think I'm gonna be sick." Veronica made a heaving noise. What else was new? At a little over six months pregnant, we thought she'd be over the whole morning sickness thing. We guessed wrong. "Tell me you're joking about that too, Chase."

I shrugged. "Do you really want me to answer that?"

"If you have to ask me that, it means yes. Just come back so we can start the morning meeting. And brush your teeth before you come in."

"Got it, boss." I should brush my teeth, because Nica was right. I did make out with Stefano. I didn't enjoy it...much.

From any vantage point, Stefano resembled a Greek god with thick, jet black hair, hazel eyes, and teeth as white as the pearly gates. Not that I'd seen them—the gates, not the teeth. I was more likely to see the underworld's welcoming committee.

As beautiful as Stefano was, he sucked at kissing. If he had been searching for my tonsils, he had completely bypassed them. I'd cringed as an extra gob of spit had made its way into my mouth. And those perfect teeth I'd mentioned? They'd knocked against mine while he'd gone further in for the search of my epiglottis.

But I needed something from Stefano, aka DJ Beatzz (never forget the extra Z, unless I wanted to be banned for life from any event he was spinning at). DJ Beatzz was the hottest deejay in town, and I had to connect with him for a rather important and impromptu event. Thanks to my best friend's six-page spread in a popular wedding magazine, our company, Bliss Events Designers, had evolved into something über-popular. We'd been commissioned to plan a Hollywood's starlet's party, and the twenty-year-old princess wanted DJ Beatzz.

So there I was, choking on someone else's tongue. Stefano was a self-professed playboy, and I was just his type. After a sickeningly long make-out session, and a little boob-grab, I'd gotten Stefano to comply.

He had wanted to do more. If my phone hadn't vibrated —and I hadn't been able to use that as an excuse to escape —he'd probably thought he could get to third base. Not in this lifetime.

My phone buzzed again. Another text message sent. Nope, not just a text message. My throat became parched when I opened the photo Alex sent.

What was it about him that turned me into...this? A wanton woman. I didn't pine for men. I didn't go all gooey-eyed for anyone. But Alex had superpowers, I was convinced. And he freely used those powers on me anytime he damned well wanted. I cursed him as I stuffed the phone in my jacket pocket, put my helmet on, and rode my bike to see him.

꩜

The San Francisco hotel where he'd asked to meet was in full swing, considering we'd been getting fabulous weather. I narrowed my eyes, taking stock of the place to make sure no one I knew was around. I knocked a knuckle on the wooden counter when I approached the front desk.

An energetic girl who could barely look over her station smiled at me. "How may I help you, ma'am?"

I squinted at her and growled. Ma'am? She had to be kidding, right? Leenda—her name tag told me—stepped back and her eyes widened in fear.

"Anything for Chase?"

Leenda gulped before she spoke, "May I have your room number?"

"Five-oh-five. Last name Laurent," I said, remembering his message, and my stomach flipped.

Dear Leenda focused her attention on the screen in front of her, and opened a couple of drawers before handing me an envelope with my name scrawled on top. I snatched it and muttered a quick thanks.

"Have a nice day!" Leenda piped up behind me.

If the girl only knew what kind of day I intended to have. *Ugh, what am I thinking?* I warred with myself. I shouldn't be doing this. How could I let Alex think I was this wanton woman, ready at his beck and call?

Simple. I *was* a wanton woman, ready at his beck and call. He knew it. I knew it. I hated that he knew. I even hated it more that he knew I knew he knew, because he'd found it fascinating. The bastard.

Before heading to the elevators, I turned right and entered the hotel's bar. I nodded at the good-looking bartender without taking a seat. "Double scotch. Neat."

"Got it, beautiful." He returned a couple of seconds later with my drink. I heard a chuckle come from him as I guzzled it down, and slammed the glass on the bar top. "Want another one?"

The liquid burned my insides, but it served two purposes: get rid of Stefano's flavor in my mouth, and get the butterflies in my stomach drunk enough to settle. I shook my head and handed him a twenty. Then I dashed to the elevators, stepped into the first doors that opened and listened to the thrumming of my heart.

I pulled the envelope out of my back pocket as I stood in front of room 505's door. The key slid in, the red light turned green, and I turned the handle. In three seconds flat, I was pulled in and my back was instantly pressed against the wall beside the door.

His hands were all over me. So were those luscious lips. Alex muttered accented words as he nipped at and licked my ear, my chin and my throat. I couldn't understand what he was saying. My eyes had shuttered as soon as he attacked me. But I knew, I knew, he was naked, hard and ready.

Fiery lips claimed mine. And Alex was the king of kisses. If I could ask to do one thing for the rest of my life, it would be to kiss Alex for eternity. He was that good.

"What took you so long?" he rasped against my swollen lips. He didn't seem to want an answer, but another question came, "Have you been drinking?" He kissed me again, and tasted me. Really tasted me. "Scotch. That's my girl."

That sobered me up...a bit. "Wait, wait, wait." I raised my helmet, wedged it between us. I opened my eyes and looked at him. Yup, he was in all his naked glory. The man had no shame. Not that he had anything to be ashamed of. Nothing. At. All.

"What's wrong? Too rough?" he asked, with that sly grin of his. He shrugged. "I thought you'd like it."

I inhaled deeply and let the air slowly whoosh out of my mouth. "You can't keep doing this. I can't keep doing this." I waved a hand between us, still using my helmet as a shield, pushing him further away.

Alex chuckled and shook his head. "Doing me?"

I threw my helmet at him, but he caught it, and chuckled again. "Shut up!" I rolled my eyes at my weak words. "You can't just text me whenever you're in town and..." I searched my addled mind for the right word. "Horny!" *Wow, A-plus, Chase!*

He dropped the helmet on the bed behind him, and

stepped closer to me, with his arms up into a surrender. "I've been in the Serengeti for weeks, Chase." He dropped one hand and held his hard length. "I can't let this go to waste now, can I?" Then he started stroking.

I closed my eyes and uttered an expletive. Alex was all over me again, trapping me between the wall and all his hardness...

His hand continued to stroke, as the other snaked up my neck and threaded through my hair. Alex gave it a gentle tug, making me tilt my head to him, and opening my mouth to receive his tongue.

A four-letter word garbled inside his mouth as my hands moved and covered his. He let me do the work, using both of his hands to run all over my body, cupping my ass, squeezing my boobs, exploring, exploring, exploring.

My phone buzzed inside my jacket pocket. I knew it was Nica. "I have to go back to work," I whispered.

"Unh..." Alex said. Whatever that meant.

"Alex, I have to go to work," I tried again, while he alternated between kissing my lips, my neck, and my ears. I could see stars behind my closed lids. I was dizzy with his freshly-showered scent.

"I'll be fast."

"Yeah, right."

He sniggered. Alex loved to take his time. He was meticulous in all things. With a flick of one hand he undid the button on my jeans, and I heard the zip go down.

Then his fingers...oh those lovely fingers...dipped past the delicate lace I had on.

"I. Have. To. Go. To. Work," I panted.

He grunted again. "Wall or bed?"

Did it even matter? Even if he had me against the wall

57

now, we'd eventually make it to the bed. Possibly back to the wall again after that. "Bed."

I could feel him smile against my fired-up skin. He knew he'd won. He knew he got me. I shouldn't be doing this, for reasons anyone couldn't possibly understand. For secrets lurking in the dark. We walked toward the bed, careful not to disconnect from each other. His hands were on me, and mine were on him.

I felt the vibration in my pocket again, as Alex's back hit the bed, pulling me down with him. I wanted to somehow communicate to Nica that I was trying to go back to work, but failing. Failing miserably. The buzzing wouldn't stop. It meant one thing. There was something important going on somewhere.

Two people, not counting Alex, had my number—Nica and Jewel. Jewel would often send me emails, and Nica loved to either call or text, but mostly call. It was a Monday morning, and it meant we had a weekly meeting. Nica had made it mandatory for staff to attend it. It would be bad form if one of the business partners did not attend because her secret lover was in town and doing things people only read in erotic novels.

On the edge of the bed lay a robe. I figured Alex had it on before he opened the door. An idea shot through my head. I reached over for the sash of the robe with one hand.

"What are you doing?" Alex paused his kissing attacks, staring at the soft cotton belt.

"Something fun." I shrugged.

Alex grinned. We pushed ourselves up higher toward the head of the bed. It didn't have a padded headboard nailed against the wall, like most hotels had. It had two large wooden finials, one on each end.

"Arms up." My legs were astride his, and I sat back, feeling him getting even harder under me. I rolled my hips and he groaned. "Up." I folded the belt in half as he followed my direction.

I'd read enough erotica through the years, the dirtier the better. They were great resources for times like these. Taking the terry cloth sash, I squirmed up along his torso, and leaned forward to wrap the sash around Alex's wrists and around one finial. Tight enough to keep his hands there, but looser to make sure his circulation did not get cut off. While I did, Alex lifted his head and bit through my jeans. White hot lust shot through me when he pressed his mouth right where my thighs met. He was going to make me pay for this later.

I gave the belt—now his restraint—a tug.

"Good?" he asked.

"Yeah." I looked down at him and smiled.

Then I pushed off the bed, zipped up my jeans, and grabbed my helmet.

Alex wriggled on the bed. His smile, half wicked, half sexy, was an invitation. But his smile wilted when he saw me straightening myself up. "What are you doing?"

"Sorry, I gotta go to work." I really was sorry, more than he could ever know.

"*Non, non, non.* Chase, you can't leave now." Alex pushed his hips off the bed and wiggled them, his manhood swinging like a freaking flagpole. "What about this?"

I bit my bottom lip. Our office better be on fire. "I'm sorry." Walking back to him, I leaned down to kiss his lips, then stepped toward the door, listening to him calling my name in an urgent, pleading tone.

Pulling the door handle closed, I breathed out a sigh. That probably was the hardest thing for me to do. I pushed my hair aside as I faced a couple in their late fifties walking in the hallway. I gave them a curt nod.

Before I could turn at a corner, Alex called my name again. As I looked over my shoulder, I couldn't help but snicker.

Alex had gotten the robe's belt loose—it was still wrapped around one of his wrists and the finial hanging off the other end. Did he destroy the bed? He stood in front of his opened door, in the same state I'd left him in. His hand waving at me to return.

I shook my head, turned around and walked backwards. "Maybe next time!" I yelled, and stifled a laugh as I caught sight of the elderly couple stopping in front of Alex.

Alex faced them, cupped his erection with both his hands, and greeted the couple, "*Bonjour*. Good morning." The woman looked down at what his hands were trying to hide, her mouth agape.

I could only guess what she was thinking. But all my thoughts stuck to how I was going to *miss* him.

As I made my way to the lobby of the hotel, I pulled out my cellphone and checked my messages. There weren't any from Nica. I'd missed four calls from a blocked number. Should I head back upstairs and finish what Alex and I had started? Just as I was making the decision, my phone vibrated on my palm. This time, it was Nica reminding me the staff meeting would start as soon as I arrived. I guessed she decided for me, after all.

When I reached my bike, my phone buzzed once more. It had never been this busy. My provider would have a heart attack at how much traffic my phone was getting today. The message was from Alex:

Have dinner with me tonight. I promise I will NOT behave.

Why? Why would those words even affect me the way they did? My pulse rate increased with the thought of his promise of misbehavior. I chose not to answer. Let him stew for a bit. If I showed up for dinner, he was going to make me pay for what I'd done.

Here's hoping.

&

I shook out my hair, and my dirty thoughts, as I removed my helmet when I reached work. The constant buzzing of my phone was unnerving.

"All right, Nica, I'm already at the parking lot," I mumbled and ran right upstairs to our new digs.

They were waiting for me in the conference room. Nica sighed as soon as I walked in. I puckered my lips and threw her an air kiss.

"Good, we can start," she said, getting off her feet while rubbing her swollen belly. Nica was always nauseous and barfing. What upset her more was that she had gained weight even if she could barely keep anything down. Oh, the perks of being pregnant with a Laurent seed. That was one venue I wouldn't dare explore. I popped birth control pills like they were Pez candies.

I took the seat between Gerard and Jewel. Mateo was across from me, and so were a few of our new staff members, Nica's assistant, Jewel's assistant, and my own new assistant whose name I hadn't committed to memory yet. None of my assistants lasted. Nica told me it was due to the stress I'd put them through. Hey, as I always said, if you can't take the heat, work in the Arctic. I was sure Santa had comparable pay and benefits.

I tried to pay attention. I really did. But Alex kept sending me photo messages, all bordering on pornographic. When my phone wasn't buzzing because of him, the call from an unknown number would cause it to.

Those I readily ignored. I had voicemail. If it was important enough, they could leave a message.

Too often, I would stifle a snicker at the tags Alex added with his suggestive pictures. I'd hide behind my hand and fake a cough. Concerned looks came my way. If I didn't discipline myself, the jig would be up.

One of our interns brought in lunch as soon as our meeting was over. I brought mine to my office, mostly so I could ogle Alex's photos without arousing any more suspicions.

When he stopped texting me, I'd finally focused on a bit of work. Right in the middle of typing up an event contract, my assistant knocked on my door. I scowled at her when she stepped in. She forcibly tried to make herself look smaller, which was difficult for her since she was as tall as me. But she was younger, and I was her boss.

"Nica would like me to remind you that she'd like you to be present at the meeting with new clients this afternoon," she said, keeping her hand on the doorknob, ready to bolt anytime.

Two, three seconds more, I let her squirm. Nica would tell me off later. I knew why she'd sent the girl in. She wanted to test her to see how long she'd last with me. I'd give her two more days before she quit.

"What time are the clients coming?" I asked, propping my feet over my desk. I pulled out my makeup kit to re-apply my eye-liner and lipstick.

"Ahm..." She looked down at the tablet in her hand. Big mistake, she should know this by now.

I got up, taking my phone with me, and slamming my makeup back on the desk. She jumped. "Forget it. I'll head there now. Clean this up for me, will you?"

She stammered. Across the way, I could see Nica watching through the glass walls of her office, hands propped on her hips and shaking her head at me. I shrugged as I headed to her.

"Why do you give Stephanie a hard time?" She wagged a finger at me as soon as I stepped through the door. She'd make a good mother. The Laurent kid she was carrying would cause her headaches for sure, like the little bugger's uncle had given me.

"Stephanie? That's her name? I thought it was Joanne." I headed over to her desk, examining her half-eaten sandwich.

Nica sighed as she waddled to her chair. She looked like she'd swallowed a large watermelon. "Joanne was your assistant two months ago. Stephanie is sweet. In fact, they all are."

"Even the one who set fire to my chair?" I challenged her.

She cringed. "Okay, maybe not all of them are, but you do tend to bring the demon out of people."

I popped a piece of bread in my mouth, ignoring her comment. "So who are these new clients?"

She tapped on her keyboard, and paid attention to her screen. "Not sure. They're from out of town. The woman said she saw my wedding spread and had to meet with us. They should be here in a few minutes."

"Good. So I have time to finish your lunch?" I propped my butt over her desk, as she sent me a glare. It lasted about two seconds, then she waved her hand away. "What event?" I asked before taking a large bite of her sandwich. I was famished for one reason: I needed the energy to face Alex again.

"Wedding." Nica continued to type on her computer. Every now and then, she'd give her belly a rub.

As I chugged the rest of my, er...Nica's juice, she stood

and waved. "Oh, I think they're here. Get off my desk, Chase."

"Fine." I bumped off the desk, not paying attention to whoever had come in.

I wiped a thumb over the corner of my lips when I heard it: a voice I hadn't heard in ten years, calling out a name I thought I'd never ever hear again. "Chastity!"

The blood drained from my face and my eyes widened as I turned away from Nica, and faced Georgia-Anne Buford. "Mom?" I croaked around the lump forming in my throat.

"Mom?" Nica gasped behind me, but my attention was focused on the woman who had given birth to me. Her arms were wide open as she sashayed in her rose pink bouclé suit, pearl necklace and earrings. Her blonde curls bounced over her shoulders.

Suddenly, I was enveloped in Nina Ricci perfume.

"It is you!" My mother wrapped me in the tightest hug, which I could swear she'd done to make my eyes pop out of their sockets. When she let go, she looked me over with a slight grimace on her face. "Oh, look at what you did to your hair." She tutted, pushing my black hair off my cheeks and tucking it behind my ears. "And why are you in all black? Were you at a funeral, dear?" Georgia-Anne pursed her lips and patted both my cheeks.

There was a clearing of a throat, and the shock of seeing my mother was replaced by the disheartening sight of my father standing behind her. "Daddy," I mouthed, choking on the word. A prickling of tears threatened behind my eyes. Not now. *I am not going to cry!*

When he shifted on one foot, my knees buckled. I had to grab the desk behind me for support. The lunch I'd demolished earlier swirled in my stomach, gurgling up to a threat of projectile vomit. The pressure in my head made it feel like it was in between clamps.

Rigidly standing in the doorway, with his hands fisted on his sides, was no other than Daniel Thompson.

He strutted toward me in a way that was confident and predatory. Ten years had done a lot to him. From where I stood, it looked like they were all good. He'd always been tall, but his wiry frame had been replaced with a toned body. His hair was darker and cut stylishly.

As he got closer, I noticed the fine lines running through his forehead, and the slight darkening around his eyes. But there was no doubt in my mind that it was him, Danny. My Danny.

In those hazel eyes, I saw the same look I had seen ten years ago, when I'd left him on the day of our wedding.

Eleutheromania

*M*y body shook with fear, anxiety or excitement—I wasn't sure which. My pulse raced, and the ringing in my ears made its presence known.

The parents I hadn't seen in a decade were now standing before me. Not only that, they'd dragged Danny with them. I stared at him with bewildered eyes. I was wary of where his hands were, rising slowly. He could choke me, slap me, and I wouldn't blame him. I wouldn't even stop him.

Yet, as my chest gurgled with sharp breaths, I swayed in tune to the beating of his heart, and the hint of musk from his cologne. This was Danny, my Danny. My body knew him. My heart remembered him.

His hands made their way around my neck, stopping at the nape, before he, ever so gently, angled his head and covered my lips with his. I was lost in that sensation, in the memories the touch of his lips conveyed. Danny's kiss whisked me back the person I once was.

I had been young, naïve, and utterly in love.

"Ahm...Chase?" Nica's voice brought me back to the present. Still wrapped in Danny's strong, almost possessive arms, I heard her shuffle around. "I'm Veronica, her business partner."

Danny chose that moment to release me. I stood dumbfounded, still unwilling to let go of the desk while my mother blinked invisible tears from her eyes. Where did I even begin?

I faced Nica, but avoided her gaze. "These are my parents, Walter and Georgia-Anne Buford. And this is..." How did I describe Danny?

Danny saved me and introduced himself, stretching out a hand to Nica, "Daniel Thompson."

"Thompson?" Nica's eyes flitted to me—letting me know I was in a lot of trouble with her—as she shook hands with Danny. The fact that I'd been using his last name for the past ten years piqued her interest. Then she turned to my parents. "Mr. and Mrs. Buford, welcome to San Francisco. You mentioned you're from out of town, where from exactly?" Nica displayed no hint of anger or malice. She was calm—unlike me, who was quaking in my boots.

My mother covered her chest where her heart would be with clasped hands, and smiled. "Vermont, my dear, Stowe."

"Stowe, Vermont?" Nica repeated, nodding her head. I was positive Nica was making a list for my comeuppance.

I glanced at my father, who had stayed quiet the entire time. He caught my gaze, and it was enough for me to choke down a sob. He looked older, tired, and beat. I could only imagine the amount of stress I'd put upon him, disappearing for ten years.

"Would you excuse us for a moment? There's something quick I'd like to discuss with Cha—Chastity." Nica, hands clasped, smiled brightly at my parents. "My assistant will take you to another room. Becky!" she called out and within seconds, Becky appeared. "Could you show them to the conference room please, and offer them some refreshments?"

"Sure thing. Hi," Becky greeted my parents. "This way please."

My mother patted me on the cheek, while my father

nodded once before leaving. Danny leaned over and kissed me chastely on the lips. Nica closed the door behind them, and touched the glass, turning it from clear to frosted (perk of having a wealthy husband—cool office doors).

"What the hell is going on? Chase? Chastity? Daniel? Vermont?" Nica waved her hands frantically.

Head hanging, I rubbed my temples as I took a seat on her sofa. "I know. I know. I can explain."

She joined me on the sofa, sitting precariously on the edge. "Please do. I thought your parents were dead?"

Yup, I might have said that, and followed it with 'I don't really want to talk about it.' And Nica never pushed the topic.

"You're from Vermont? Not Texas?"

I nodded, "My daddy's from Texas. I was born and grew up in Vermont." Then I covered my face with my hands.

Nica sighed. "I thought it was weird that you didn't really have a drawl...And Daniel Thompson? Thompson? Chase, are you...married?" She whispered the last word.

"No," I mumbled in my hands, then looked at her, pleading with my eyes for her to understand. "We were...are...engaged." My brows drew together.

"Were? Are? Which one is it?"

"I'm not really sure. We were going to get married, but I left."

Nica's eyes widened when she straightened and gasped. "You didn't leave him at the altar, did you?"

I leaned back, my head lolling on the sofa cushions. "No. I left the morning before the ceremony."

"What? But you're...you would have been sixteen at the time. Was that even legal in Vermont?"

Sixteen. Another of my lies. I wondered if Nica was keeping count. "I wasn't sixteen. I'm not twenty-six, Nica.

I'm twenty-nine." I trained my eyes on her, wracked in fear of losing my best friend.

"Oh my God." She stared at me, trying to read my face. "Is your birthday even June sixteenth, or have we been celebrating someone else's birthday too?"

"No, that's my birthday." I turned my head, and silently begged her for forgiveness.

Nica stood, squared off her shoulders, and held out her hand. "Hi, I'm Veronica Laurent, née Soto-Stewart. My father died when I was five, and my mother lives in Fresno, where my sister and I were born and raised."

"Nica, please." I felt so ashamed. I covered my face with my hands again. "I can explain everything, but not now." I looked up to her. "Let me deal with my parents and Danny first. Then I promise you, everything will make sense."

Nica retracted her hand and crossed her arms over her chest. She pouted. A line creased between her brows. "Fine. But after this, everything on the table."

"Yes, I promise." I stood and spread out my arms, hoping she wasn't too mad to give me a hug. I could really use one. Thankfully, she hugged me, and patted my back too.

"Is your name really Chastity?" she asked against my chest.

"'Fraid so. Chastity Hannah Buford."

"Oh my God."

"I know." We let go of each other and headed out the door.

Even though she waddled more than walked, Nica was still fast-paced. I let her get ahead of me, staring straight ahead into to the conference room. In there, my mother was too busy chatting the ears off of Becky, while my reserved father lifted a glass of water to his mouth. Danny had his hands stuffed in his pockets, watching everything going on outside of the room. I paused mid-step as our eyes locked.

An overwhelming panic churned in my gut.

Danny saw the fear in my eyes, and shook his head as he mouthed, 'No'. But it was too late. With my cold hands on my sides, I backed away and ran toward the exit, once again leaving him behind with unanswered questions.

*

Where else would I go? In a city like San Francisco, it was easy to get lost. But I'd become a creature of habit.

I hadn't seen my parents for a decade, and I never practiced how I'd deal with them once I faced them again. So, I ran. That was what I did.

I would've kicked myself if my legs weren't clenched tight around my bike, speeding away from the source of my duress. I made it to the Marina, to the Wave Organ. I parked my bike and sat looking out to the magnificent water, listening to the waves lapping at the shore, crashing through the pipes and producing ethereal sounds I hoped would clear my mind.

Danny and that kiss, his kiss. His effect on me. The swirling, overwhelming emotions in my stomach. The fluttering of my restless heart. How was it that even though I hadn't felt his lips on mine for a decade, I was still familiar with his taste? That the simplest touch from him would wreak havoc on my senses?

I guessed it was true when people say you'd never forget your first. Danny was my first everything. Was this emotion swimming my gut only a surge of nostalgia?

I couldn't say how long I'd been sitting here, contemplating, but once the place was filled with families, and screaming tots climbing the stones, I headed out and ended up in my next favorite safe place, Davidson's.

My phone wouldn't stop the intermittent vibrations, so I turned it off. *Not now, Nica.*

Benoit the bartender saw me right away, and since he had a sixth sense for when one of his patrons was in dire distress, he slammed a highball in front of me, poured two fingers of scotch in it, and left me alone with the bottle. Ladies and gentlemen, this was how sorrows were drowned. Literally. No matter how many times I'd ended up at this place, the only person I'd ever talked to was Benoit. Sure, men ogled me and propositioned me, but I was protected under the guise that Benoit and I were dear friends. Truthfully, though, all I knew was he was happily married, with three munchkins.

He didn't bother me that evening, but I could feel him watching over me, even from the other side of the bar. More than halfway through the bottle, and when my eyes started to cross, I stood (or fell off the stool, then stood) and saluted him before heading out. I had a running tab at Davidson's but he would never charge me for anything. Not when the bar's silent partner was my best bitch's husband, Levi.

I propped my helmet over my head. Safety first, right? And hugged my beautiful bike between my legs. Before I could start her up, Benoit appeared, looking like he was gearing for a fight.

"I called you a cab. You're not driving anywhere." He stood, feet hip-width apart, arms crossed over his massive chest, angry shitface on his well...face.

"I'm fine." I jabbed a key into my ignition. It wouldn't fit in.

Benoit snatched the keys out of my hand and unhooked

the one for my Harley out of the ring. Two were left: my house key and a storage key. "Cab will be here any second."

"I can't leaf...leave her here!" I slurred.

"I'll bring her in later. She'll be safe inside the bar. You can collect her tomorrow." Benoit cocked his head up. "Cab's here. You need help getting there?" He stretched an arm out to guide me and I slapped it away.

Before I could shut the cab door, I glanced over at Benoit, waiting for me to zoom away, to gain distance from him as fast as possible. I rolled the window down, and yelled out a warning, "She falls apart under your care and I'll make sure you won't get baby number four!" He laughed, loud enough for it to register through my scotched-soaked brain, and then he received a high-flying, one-finger salute from me. I leaned back in my seat and dreaded facing the night.

"Address?" the driver looked over his shoulder, waiting for me to answer.

Where would I go? My apartment wouldn't be my first choice. Not where Nica, or someone from my past would come around. No. I scrubbed my hands over my face and patted my pockets, thinking I would find a solution. Surprisingly, I did.

I gave the hotel address to the driver. It didn't take long to arrive at my destination. It was rather unfortunate since my heart hadn't stopped pounding through my rib cage, and I could have used extra time to corral it back in.

This could be a major mistake. How would Alex react? Was he still staying at this hotel? I slipped in the key card, and was only too relieved when the light turned green.

A lamp was on in one corner of the room. Some of Alex's clothes were piled neatly on the bed. There was no sign of him. Where could he have gone?

I made my way to the bathroom, and flicked the lights

on. The sudden brightness burned my eyes. I caught my reflection in the mirror, and gripped the edge of the marble vanity. A lump caught in my throat. Extending my hand to the glass, I traced the outline of the woman facing me. Who I was and who I'd become were two complete opposites. Tears stung my eyes. I turned away before the first fat tear rolled down my cheek.

My gut reaction was to wash it away. The square, tiled shower called to me. I reached forward and let the water blast. My hands shook, my lips quivered, and my heart squeezed. All I had energy for was to strip my jacket, boots and pants off. All else was fair game. I walked into the rush of hot water, pressed my hands flat on the cold tiles, and let the fountain works start, trying to remember when was the last time I'd cried.

I collapsed down to the shower floor, letting the high-temperature water drown my sorrows. I heaved. I choked on my sobs. I let the memories filter in. The distant, long-ignored thoughts of my past.

And that was how Alex found me.

Caluné

*W*hen I met Alex, I never expected him to be anything other than a wrench in my gut. But he surprised me in so many ways. He showed me tenderness, warmth, and, dare I say, affection.

In this dark hour, I ran to him. Weakened and confused by the state of my life and mind, I sought out the person I didn't think was capable of caring for me. Maybe, just maybe, right alongside the long-forgotten emotions, the thought of being in his arms burrowed deep. I knew I'd be safe with him, cuddled close to his heart. And he let me.

Whatever our relationship was—in the moment of my need—he became my solid foundation. And it hurt to know there was a possibility this time tomorrow...he would hate me.

His voice didn't register until after he scooped me out of the stall. Alex called out to me, "*Hayati.*" Only he knew what it meant. He repeated the word like it was my cradle, a cocoon, which would protect me. "Were you trying to drown yourself? You're more likely to get a second-degree burn." From his low, gruff tone, I could tell he was put off by my actions, but his voice softened when he added, "Talk to me."

I looked at him, my eyes level with his, as he sat me atop the vanity. He held my gaze even as he covered my head with a bath towel and squeezed the water from my hair, quietly, until it was nearly dry. My mascara wasn't waterproof, and I knew I had raccoon eyes, but he regarded me like I was the most beautiful woman in the world. The thought stabbed another hole into my heart. Alex was punishing me, and he wasn't even aware of it. How much more of it could I take?

When he was done with my hair, tucking thick strands behind my eyes, he quietly ordered me to lift my arms so he could remove my shirt, which stuck to my reddened skin. Then he unclasped my bra, and skimmed his fingers over my shoulders, under the straps to remove it. There was nothing lascivious about his actions. He glanced away only to reach for a robe to cover me with, but as soon as he turned to me again, he searched my eyes, questioning me silently.

With the pads of his thumbs, he etched lines under my lids. The deep grooves on his forehead expressed his worry and concerns, that he was trying to understand how to deal with me, what to do next. Alex reached for a small towel, wet it, and proceeded to dab under my eyes.

He raked his bottom lip between his teeth before he spoke. "I wish you wouldn't drink so much."

Not exactly what I thought he'd say, yet fitting all the same.

"We all have our vices." I bit my tongue before I could say he was my vice. I parried with, "I wish you'd stop smoking."

He quit rubbing my makeup off. The towel in his hand had splotches of gray and black on it.

"I did."

"You did what?"

"Stopped smoking." My mouth dropped. Alex loved smoking as much as he loved sex, as far as I was aware.

"When did you do that?" I asked once I found my voice.

He shrugged, and I thought the noncommittal action

was all the answer I would get, but he replied, "Six weeks ago."

"You were here six weeks ago." *With me.*

Alex nodded. There was a flicker in his irises. "Yes. That's when you said I didn't need a cigarette to look badass sexy." His features smoothed into an expression of pure bliss, which added more sparkle in his eyes.

I had said that, but I didn't think he would listen. My gut twisted tighter as I wondered what it meant, if it meant anything at all. Why had he quit when I had asked him? I couldn't formulate the proper words.

He drew invisible lines along the sides of my face. If I hadn't known better, I'd have thought he was committing me to memory. Had someone told him? Had Nica found out he was in the city and had informed him of the situation? No, it was impossible. Nica would be the first one to tell people to mind their own business. Whether she had a clue about what was happening between Alex and me or not, she would keep my secret safe. Although Nica would also try to convince me to explain everything to Alex.

I'm as stubborn as I am cowardly.

There was no possible way I could open up to Alex now. If his own painful past had taught me anything was that he did not tolerate betrayal. There was still the niggling question whether Daniel's appearance was a form of betrayal to Alex.

Alex sighed heavily, bringing my focus back to him and away from the problem which I intended to handle...tomorrow. He rubbed the bottom of my chin. "Have you eaten anything tonight?"

I looked down at my wrinkled fingers. "I had pretzels at the bar," I lied.

"You have to eat something more substantial than that, Chase."

I shook my head. "I'm not hungry. To tell you the truth, I'm exhausted. I just want to sleep."

Alex straightened. Those last words seemed to surprise him. "You're staying with me tonight?"

My eyes drifted back to meet his. I wished so hard I could match the joy I saw in them. "Yes," I answered, because it could most likely be the last time I'd have with him. "If that's okay with you."

"Of course," he said with a smile, flashing his bright white teeth at me. Then he zipped open a small black bag and produced a disposable toothbrush.

I couldn't help but laugh. "You always carry a spare toothbrush?"

"Yes. Chase, I smoked for years, drink coffee, tea, and wine. These bad boys don't clean themselves you know." He pointed at the row of teeth between his stretched lips. He handed me toothpaste and left me to my own devices.

When he came back, he removed my robe and had me wear one of his shirts. It was made of soft cotton and smelled of him. It nearly killed me.

To keep myself from going insane, I probed him, "If you weren't out for a smoke, where were you?"

"Went out for a run." Only when he said it did I notice his running gear. Before I could ask him about it, he continued, "I had to replace smoking with something else. I figured running's as good as anything." I simply nodded, trying to evade the vision of Alex and his already toned runner's body.

A minute later, I didn't have to imagine. I watched him change into his sleeping clothes and brush his teeth. How easy it would be to do this routine with him every single day? I bit back anger at my own thoughts. *Not now. Not ever.* That would be his decision.

Alex held my hand and led me to the bed. Before I could get between the inviting sheets, I removed my underwear, damp from both the shower and the man before me. Alex was sexy. Alex was a forbidden fruit, which any woman could not get enough of, and would eternally lust after.

He let me slip into the bed first, before turning onto his side. He was the big spoon, and I felt safe wrapped in his warm embrace. Our limbs tangled together, making it seem like I was glued to him. I shimmied my buttocks against his front, and felt him grow and harden. But I didn't want sex tonight. I just wanted to be held. I wanted a moment, one that could last a lifetime. One of his hands reached up and brushed through my hair. Every third of fourth time, he would press his lips on the delicate skin behind my ear.

Every single moment of the night, every movement he made caused tension inside my chest. My heart galloped within the boundaries of my ribcage.

For years, I had taught myself not to feel. Tonight, everything was fair game. I cried. I laughed. I feared. And if I wasn't careful, I would let myself fall.

I traced the thick, curved tattoo on his arm. "What does this mean, Alex?"

His breath tickled my ear, and goose bumps burst all over my body as he spoke. "It's Tibetan script for 'Everything happens for a reason'."

Actually, shit happens for a reason. It had led me to live a secret life. It had caused me an enormous amount of pain and sorrow. And it seemed it wasn't over yet.

I was a glutton for punishment, so I pulled Alex closer and let my eyes drift closed.

I woke him up by running my fingers through his hair. I'd slipped back into my pants and bra, and stuffed my underwear into my pocket. I kept his shirt on under my leather jacket.

"Good morning, gorgeous." Alex tuned on his back, propping his head up higher against the headboard. "Leaving already?"

"Yes. It's going to be a long day." It wasn't a lie. I'd been up since the crack of dawn. My mind was filled with the choices I would have to make, and the people I'd have to face.

Alex stretched his arms and winced. He reached for a small container on the nightstand and applied a little amount of strongly-scented ointment on his wrists.

I wriggled my nose as I sat on the edge of the bed. "Is that liniment? You smell like an old man."

"A sexy old man?" He waggled his brows. How could I not laugh?

Moments like this with Alex would be the most painful to remember. Not just the unbelievable sex, and the unexplainable connection we had. He made me smile. He made me laugh. He made me feel good about myself. I would take these memories, dig deep into my heart, and bury them there for all eternity.

I leaned forward and kissed him. With passion. With sorrow. With affection. With everything I had.

"I can't convince you to have breakfast with me?" Alex asked, pushing my hair off my face.

With my lips pressed into a flat line, I shook my head and ran my hand over his cheek. He tilted his head, closed his eyes, inhaled and kissed my palm.

"Bye, Alex."

When he opened his eyes, I met with the impossible. It was beyond lust, beyond physical desire. It was something he had been convincing me we had since we met. A flash lit inside my head. How many times could I let myself lose the people I loved?

"I'll see you later, *hayati*," Alex promised as I stood and headed to the door. It took all my strength to walk away.

Geborgenheit

After claiming my motorcycle from Benoit, I drove to my apartment. When I parked my baby inside the carport, I could sense someone watching me. I faced the street, with my helmet in my hand and my heart in my throat. Shading my eyes from the rays of the early sun, I saw the person who had been watching me.

When he stepped out of his car, I couldn't help but run to him, and cry on his chest.

Walter Buford was a man of few words. What he didn't say, he conveyed in many different, albeit subtle ways.

At that moment, all he did was pat my hair and let me weep, soaking his wrinkled shirt. Belatedly, I wondered how long he's been waiting for me. My father was my strength. He was the only person who had seen me fall apart...until last night with Alex.

"I'm sorry, Daddy." I snorted and sobbed. It wasn't a pretty sight, but without a doubt, he would tell me I was beautiful no matter what.

His large hands cradled my cheeks, forcing me to look at him. His face was hard, lined with unspoken sorrow, grief and pain. Daddy wasn't just built like a linebacker, he used to be one, but around his chin were signs of weight loss. Maybe it was from sadness, or age, or both.

"Why don't we talk inside, Nugget? I could use some coffee." Daddy smiled, a simple, enigmatic, ear-to-ear sort. Then he handed me a folded-up tissue.

"You weren't out here all night, were you, Daddy?" I

wiped the tears and snot off my face, and off my father's shirt.

With an arm over my shoulder, we walked to my door. "Not the whole night, no. Your mother agreed to let me back into the hotel around one in the morning, and Danny took over." My body tensed when *his* name was mentioned. Daddy felt it and squeezed my shoulder. "I came back around six and sent him back to get some rest."

A number of things rolled through my mind as I unlocked my door. I understood why my parents came. I was their daughter after all. But Danny? What was he expecting? I still couldn't figure out why he'd kissed me like that. It was a lover's kiss. The biggest question, perhaps, was why I'd quivered under his touch. Did heart muscle memory exist?

"I'll make you some coffee. You still take it with cream, no sugar?" I threw my keys in the bowl by the door and hung my jacket.

Daddy nodded. His eyes travelled all over my apartment. "This is some place, Nugget." He stuffed his hands in his pockets and rocked back on his heels. "I would never think to paint the walls black."

I led him past the living room and all the way to the kitchen, where it was sunnier and less oppressive.

He stopped at the threshold. "Nugget, I could use the little boys' room."

"Oh, yeah. Down the hallway, first door on the left." He hesitated before he turned. I wanted to assure him I wouldn't be running away from my own apartment, but he was gone before I could formulate a good enough sentence.

I let the coffee percolate, and went to my bedroom to change. It was disheartening to see myself in the mirror with Alex's shirt. I slipped it off and pressed it to my nose. It didn't smell like me. It was all Alex. I wasn't one to keep mementos, but it would be a hell of a battle if he asked for the shirt back.

This morning, as the sun filtered through the white chiffon curtains, I had woken up with him wrapped around me. He was like a serpent coiled around its prey. I had fallen into his trap...or had he fallen into mine?

I hurriedly dressed and tied my hair up when I heard my father open the hallway bathroom door. We had a lot to talk about. I doubted he'd leave here without some of his questions answered.

The smell of coffee filled the kitchen. Daddy stood in front of the large picture window that faced my tiny backyard.

"You want something to eat? I think I have bread. I don't keep a lot of food here. I tend to eat out." My nerves were a jumble. The bell-like clanging of the pot against the lips of our coffee mugs made me twitch.

"Coffee's good for now. Knowing your mother, she expects me to eat breakfast with her as soon as I report back." My father sat on one of the barstools at my kitchen island, and I settled on the other, passing a cup to him. He sniffed the steaming liquid and sighed. "Nothing like a freshly brewed coffee to start the morning, eh, Nugget?"

I couldn't help it. I burst into tears again, covering my face with my hands. I'd missed precious moments like this since leaving home. With my eyes closed, I could almost imagine being back in Vermont, sitting in our sun-filled chef's kitchen, having maple syrup-soaked pancakes and crispy bacon with Daddy. We would snicker and mutter secrets to each other before my mother came down the stairs and forced us to start our day.

"I'm sorry I left, Daddy." I shook my head, and my father pulled me back into his arms, kissing the top of my head.

"Now, now, Nugget. We understand why you left. The whole situation was too much to handle for someone as young as you. But I do wish you'd come to me, at least, before you ran off."

Yeah, like it would have made me feel better. But he had a point. I went to him for everything. Some girls prefer talking to their mothers, but not me. My father was one of my best friends.

I straightened, and in a most unladylike manner, wiped my snotty nose on my shirt sleeve. If my mother had been with us, she would've had a heart attack. I'd warned her no amount of finishing school would turn me into a proper lady, but it hadn't stopped her from trying. "I'm pretty sure Mom blames me for ruining everything."

"Has anyone said you ruined anything at all?"

My bottom lip quivered as I pouted. "Not out loud, but I know what Mom's probably thinking. She had everything laid out for me, and I left." It was true. My mother had wanted to show me a promising future. She'd even picked names for the children—two boys, one girl—I would supposedly have. I'd gone along with it all. For one, she would've made my life even more miserable if I hadn't. Two, she would've turned my father's life upside down, since she'd always been convinced he and I conspired against her. And three, once upon a time, I'd been truly in love with a boy named Danny.

Just thinking about him caused a sharp, acute pain in my heart. "And Danny?" It was all I could ask, while I rubbed the part of my chest where my thumping heart lay.

His eyes flitted to the cup. He licked his lips before lifting it and taking a sip. I knew he understood my question. His forehead furrowed into the deep grooves of a man who'd spent hours upon hours under the hot sun. "That boy is special, I tell yah." He took another sip.

Maybe he was buying time. Maybe he was contemplating on his next few words. But once he turned to me, and I heard his answer, I almost fell off my chair. "Danny still loves you, Nugget. That's why he's here."

To think, after a decade, after leaving him cold and not a note in sight, Danny still loved me. Was that even possible? Insane came to mind. But it was classic Danny. If there ever was a person who'd forgive and forget, and had the ability to love continuously, it was Danny.

"It's been years, Daddy," I muttered to myself more than to my father, looking down at the dark liquid in my cup. From the corner of my eye, I saw Daddy nod. What did this mean? Would Danny expect me to return to him, with him, to Vermont? What would happen to the life I'd built in this city? How would I cope without my friends? Without Nica? And what about Alex?

What Alex and I'd had the night before was something cerebral. Not to mention our hard-to-ignore physical attraction. He hadn't directly asked me to have a relationship with him, not in so many words, and not for a while. We'd been having a blast with our secret rendezvous. He'd been consistent with asking me out for dinner, and I had either declined or brushed his invitations aside. But what had he really been asking me? Was it just dinner? Or something more? Dinner could be more intimate than sex. It meant talks and laughter and sharing. And being in public together.

My thoughts were interrupted by a loud ringing in the small space. I'd left my phone in my bedroom, and hadn't turned it on since yesterday, so it couldn't be mine. My father searched his pockets and produced a sleek, most likely rarely used, smartphone. He leaned his head back slightly, and squinted at his screen. After ignoring the call, he left it sitting on the counter.

"A cellphone?" I asked, and lifted an eyebrow. Daddy was anti-technology. He subscribed to the idea that it had harmful effects on our bodies.

"Your mother insisted I carry one at all times. That was her calling. She checks on me every hour, on the hour." He calmly sipped his coffee.

"Do you think it's a good idea to ignore her call?" As I pressed the cup to my lips, I let a little smile spread on my face.

"She'll be fine. If I picked up I'd have to let her know that you've come home. If I don't answer, she'll think I've fallen asleep again." Daddy nudged me on the side, which reminded me even more of our mornings together when I was younger. "I will have to go back soon, though. Will you come with me, Nugget?"

I wasn't ready. "I'm not sure."

"Would you at least talk to Danny?"

Now, there was a question I was afraid to answer. "I'm not sure," I repeated. "What would I even say? What would he say?"

"You're both adults. You'll figure it out."

"What if he asks me about that day?"

"Then tell him the truth." My father emptied his cup before standing. He nudged a knuckle under my chin and kissed my forehead. "I think it's time you stop running, Nugget."

His words exploded in my head. I felt numb as I remembered Alex asking me to stop running months ago. "I have a lot to think about."

"Yes, you do. I'd better get back before your mother worries and calls the Army." He placed a card on the counter beside my cup and picked up his cellphone. "That's where we're all staying, and my cellphone number is on the front. Walk me to the door, will yah?"

"Yes, Sir." I hooked my hand in the crook of his elbow, and leaned my head on his upper arm. "How did you find me?"

"Your mother saw a magazine article when she was getting her hair done at Savannah's Salon." I giggled, imagining my mother as a 1920's Hollywood actress, resting the back of her hand over her forehead and falling gracefully onto a fainting couch.

"Mom came in for our services. Was it even real? Is there a party?" Daddy shook his head, lowering his eyes to the floor. It was all a ruse.

"You want to know a secret?" my father asked, lifting his back to me.

"Always."

As we reached my door, he faced me, his mouth pressed into a hard line. With every breath, his shoulders rose and fell. "I've known where you've been all this time. I followed you that day, and I saw you didn't get on the plane. If I had been smarter, I would have talked to you and taken you back home. I didn't think you would disappear."

My mouth dropped. "All this time? How did you know?"

"When I realized you weren't coming back, I talked to Frank. You remember him? He was a retired detective. I asked him to follow your movements. He's been reporting to me since."

What was I supposed to say to that? My father had let me go. He'd let me live the life I'd been living all this time and not made a peep? I nodded, because in the deep, dark recesses of my mind, I understood. Without saying it out loud, I comprehended why he did that. I decided not to ask him if he would have done the same exact thing if he had known I'd be away this long. I hugged him instead.

He'd trusted me. He loved me so much he'd let me go.

Before he stepped out of the house, he asked a question I had been trying to figure out on my own. "Why didn't you get on the plane?"

When I opened my mouth to tell him I didn't know, another answer came out, "She wouldn't have wanted me to. She would have wanted me to follow my own path."

Trepidation

y knuckle hovered over the door, waiting for my brain to give it the green light. *Knock, son of a bitch, knock!* I brought my hand back down and took some cleansing breaths as I straightened the wrap-dress over the curves of my hips. I should have said yes to Nica when she offered to accompany me.

After Daddy left, I'd called her and we agreed to meet at our favorite bistro for lunch. I couldn't bring myself to say much, but I was able to tell her a few things. Later, much later, she'd want the entire story. And she deserved it.

"When you're ready, Chase," she had said to me, squeezing my hand over the table and offering me understanding I didn't deserve. But that, among other things, was why she was my best friend.

At my mother's insistent invitation, I agreed to meet my parents and Danny for an early dinner. God forbid my mother eat later than six p.m. Since I'd been aware of the world around me, she'd been proud of her figure and cared for it as much as she'd cared for her designer handbags and shoes. Eating after six made her bloated, or so she claimed. Years ago, I used to wonder if she'd have had kids if she'd known how much work it would take to keep herself looking slim and fit.

What was I saying? I was like my mother! I worked out too much at the gym and wore nothing but designer clothes. Case in point, the dress I had on tonight was off the runway, fresh off a supermodel's back. I had been saving it for a special occasion. Which one—I'd had no clue.

At that moment, Alex's face popped in my head.

No, I wasn't saving this dress for him or the date that would never happen.

"Not at all," I tried to convince myself, but even I wasn't buying it. I was full of crap. I'd bought this dress because I'd thought the blue-grey silk jersey fabric matched his eyes. I'd paired it with nude heels because Alex had once told me how sexy my legs were when I wore heels (and yes, I'd kept them on while he'd had me flat on my back that night).

Thinking of Alex right now wasn't going to help me deal with this situation, *aka* Mom.

I fanned my face. I didn't know why I was sweating. Sweat and silk did not go together. My fingers darted to the statement necklace sitting low on my neck. Fiddling wasn't allowed around my mother.

Okay, get it done, Chase.

I lifted my knuckles again, and this time, I didn't hesitate to knock. It took one second for my mother to open the door, which meant she'd been standing behind it this entire time, probably watching me through the peephole. That alone made me narrow my eyes at her. Then, it took her three seconds to "fix" my hair. I gritted my teeth and formed an un-psycho smile.

"Hi, Mom," I said through clenched teeth.

She air-kissed me and proceeded to sit languidly on the sofa. *Uh-oh.* When my mother posed like an old Hollywood glam actress, it meant trouble was brewing. Mom loved dramatics.

The door shut behind me, but I didn't step forward, keeping that faux smile on my face. "Where's Daddy?" I took in the pricey hotel suite with a wicked view of dusk over the bay as I stayed by the door.

"I'm here, Nugget." He ambled in from the bedroom, patting his forehead with a small cloth. He sat on the gold and cream chair and waved me over to give him a hug.

I had to decide, and fast.

If I got any closer to the middle of the room, I might as well say goodbye to any form of escape at any signs of awkwardness. But I didn't want to hurt Daddy's feelings, and after finding out what he had been keeping from my mother all these years, I couldn't bring myself to disappoint him, again.

"Oh, Chastity, dear, could you bring me an Evian from the Frigidaire?"

I rolled my eyes. "Mom, it's the twenty-first century. We call it a fridge these days." I shouldn't have argued with her, because that meant she'd won. I walked to the wet bar, grabbed a bottled water from the fridge, and brought it to her with a low glass tumbler. Daddy smirked at me as I passed him. I wanted to ask what the hell was going on, but not within my mother's earshot.

As I tried to think of an excuse to skip our night out, I took my time twisting open the bottle, pouring the overpriced water into the glass, and handing it to Mom. "Are you not well?"

She made me wait, taking little sips of the water before speaking. "Oh, it must be the heat." She rubbed a hand over her dry neck. Nuh-uh. I wasn't buying it. She was up to something.

"If you're not feeling up to it, we can cancel dinner." I could go home and avoid having to see Danny.

"Oh no, dear." She paused for a sip. "Maybe your Daddy and I can stay here, and you can head on out with Daniel?" Mother's eyes flitted to the right.

I propped a hand over a hip and shook my head. "No. No way. I'm not going to dinner alone with him. You said we'd go out *together*. All four of us." I glanced at my father, silently pleading for his support. His head was down, and he looked pale. I hated that he was in the middle of this. It was unfair to him. "I'm not doing this." I threw my hands up in exasperation, and walked toward the door.

But a knock stopped me midway. Mother jumped off the sofa—so much for feeling ill. "Oh that must be Daniel."

My shoulders sagged. I'd never win with my mother. As she opened the door for Danny, I again pleaded for Daddy's help. But he was avoiding my gaze. Perhaps he hadn't been able to catch up on the sleep he had missed last night while he'd staked out my place. I pressed a hand over my stomach and inhaled, trying, but failing, to quell my brewing anxiety.

"Hello, Daniel!" my faking-illness mother greeted him as soon as he stepped in. "My, oh my, don't you look handsome. Doesn't he, Chastity?"

My eyes travelled slowly to where he stood. Damn, he did look handsome in a custom-tailored, dark blue suit. My heart thundered, making me all too aware of the effect he still had on me. I couldn't trust myself to speak. I stood stiffly and tried not to squirm under his intense gaze.

Danny and Mom made their way to me. She held my hand in one of hers and grasped Danny's with the other. My mother fluttered—*fluttered!*—her lashes at Danny and then at me as she squeezed our hands together. "Look at you two. Perfect, just perfect."

I rolled my eyes. I might as well go along with this obviously cooked-up scene, dreading to think what the consequences could be if I refused. The lesser of two evils was having dinner with Danny. My mother released our hands and let Danny hold mine on his own.

"I guess it's just you and me tonight." I smiled, and let it spread all the way to my eyes. Danny had done nothing wrong. But something continued to boggle my mind. What the hell he was doing here in San Francisco with my parents? Tonight, I could find out why.

"Seems like it," he said through a barely-hidden smile as Mom resumed her act back on the couch.

He nodded at my father, who'd kept his mouth shut the entire time. I squinted when he shrugged. And here I thought he had my back.

Danny tugged my hand over the crook of his elbow as he bade my parents adieu. I massaged my temple with my free hand. If there was a migraine blooming, I would welcome it wholeheartedly. At least it would serve as an excuse. But my own body betrayed me when all I got was a sore thumb from kneading the side of my head.

&

The elevator ride down to the lobby of the posh hotel atop Nob Hill was spent in silence. Twenty-three floors. People stepped in from other floors, forcing Danny and me to the corner of the mirrored car. He placed a protective, yet not intrusive hand around my waist. If spontaneous combustion was a real phenomenon, I could have had one from the heat coming off his hand alone. His body was pressed close to me but not on me. Classic Danny. Always the gentleman. He'd never been one to take advantage of a situation. Or me—not ever.

A flash of memory flickered. One of him and me on lush grass. We'd had a picnic near a lake. I'd chosen to wear a flirty summer dress, and done my then-blonde hair into a neat braid. I'd straddled his lap and blushed at the feeling of his heat. Danny—younger, happier—

reached up to weave a daisy through my hair. With a push of his arms, he lifted himself to meet my lips with his.

Our first kiss. *My* first kiss.

The elevator signaled that we'd reached the lobby. My breath hitched as I stepped out of the elevator, released from the confines of my own memories. By instinct, my eyes found the exits right away. Just a few strides and I'd be free of him for the night. But I trampled the idea down, and held onto the little courage I had left. I would see this night through.

"It's just dinner, Hannah, between friends," Danny said, catching my hand in his, and giving it a reassuring squeeze. I'd forgotten that, once upon a time, I'd been called by my second name. Only my mother called me by my first name. My father had insisted I was his "nugget", but Danny and everyone else back in Vermont had called me Hannah.

I nodded, not trusting myself to say anything coherent. We made our way out of the hotel, where a silver BMW convertible awaited. I raised a brow at Danny, while he held the door open for me.

"It's a rental," he told me, a smile played on the corners of his lips.

I waited until he sat on the driver's side before I teased. "And what do you drive at home?"

He threw his head back and laughed as he changed gears. "1967 Camaro RS."

I laughed with him, imagining the sleek, sexy car as we drove away from the hotel. "You've always wanted that car. I remember you finding a picture of it in a magazine and showing me. You said, 'See this, Hannah, this is my future car. It will attract all the babes.'"

I caught his gaze and the quick bite on his bottom lip out of the corner of my eye.

"You remember?" From the tone of his voice, I knew he could recall the exact moment he had said it to me.

I had to change topics fast. "Do you know where you're going? I thought we were going to the hotel restaurant."

"I made a different reservation. I was getting tired of staying in the hotel...and Georgia-Anne called me earlier to say it was just gonna be the two of us."

Grinding my teeth, I focused on the road. My mother had planned this entire setup. And Danny? What was he up to? I swallowed whatever had dislodged itself in my throat—fear, loathing, anxiety—and reminded myself that Danny wasn't one to trick people. He didn't play those games. He laid it all out on the table. What you saw was what you would always get.

"Ahm, Danny? Are you sure you know where we're going?" I asked again as I read the street names, and noted the condition of the surrounding buildings. We ended up in the Tenderloin neighborhood. Not exactly the poshest area, although I was well aware of some good establishments which had sprouted in recent years. But I was a local. I knew my way around. I didn't know if he did.

"Yes, it should be around the corner." He confidently maneuvered the car, and stopped in front of a speakeasy. He hopped out and made his way to my side before giving the valet the key to his rental. I secretly hoped he'd purchased extra insurance for that car.

"How do you know this place?"

"This isn't my first time in San Francisco, Hannah. I've been here twice before." He patted my hand over his arm. "For work." I hadn't thought otherwise.

Danny gave his name to the hostess, who undressed him with her eyes. She welcomed us, although more Danny than me, and asked us to follow her to our reserved table. I had to be careful with my decisions and actions. In normal circumstances, I would have ripped her fake lashes off along with her real ones after the way she ogled Danny. But I couldn't lead him on, or let him think I'd made my mind up. So I swayed my hips and lifted my chin as I walked beside him.

When Daniel Thompson entered a room, he commanded attention. His regal posturing, and natural intelligence made people notice. And yes, it didn't hurt that he looked good enough to lick.

I knew how people perceived me. I wasn't a shrinking violet. I was the belle of the ball with sharp claws, curves in all the right places and legs up to my chin. Together, we epitomized a power couple.

As we made our way to the table, right in the middle of the busy restaurant, I sensed all eyes were on us. But I knew one pair in particular was more focused on me than on Danny. It was almost palpable. I harnessed my inner James Bond, and surreptitiously cased the joint.

At a far corner, in a booth, surrounded with shelves of vintage records and funky mood lighting, I spotted Dr. Jake Benjamin, Levi's best friend. I sucked in a sharp breath. What was he doing here? Did he really see me? I wanted to look again and see if I could recognize the other men sitting with him. Could I spend the entire dinner with Danny while Jake sat a few steps away, possibly spying and later reporting back to Levi?

Danny must have felt my hesitation, or read the sudden stiffness of my body as disapproval. "Can we have something more private?" Danny asked the hostess. He handed her a few bills, which he did smoothly, and she complied, taking us further back into the restaurant and away from Jake's prying eyes.

While Danny pulled my chair out, panic began to pour in. Was Levi in the booth with Jake? I was sure I would have noticed. However, if Levi was there, could Alex be there too?

I dug through my memories to recall if Alex ever let Levi know he was in the city. I hadn't spoken to him, or responded to any of his text messages—I hadn't even read them—so I didn't know if he'd mentioned it.

"Hannah?" Danny's voice snapped me out of my thoughts. "Drink?" He gestured to a girl, a server, who stood beside our table. When did she get here?

"Three fingers Lagavulin, neat," I told her without hesitation.

"Wonderful," the girl said, then turned to Danny, "And for you, sir?"

"Just sparkling water for me. Thank you."

"I'll be back with your drinks."

As soon as she walked away, Danny reached for my hands across the table. "Who is he?"

"What—I mean, pardon me?" Was he asking me who Alex was? How did he know I was thinking of him?

"The guy you saw seated in the booth. Who is he?"

I'd forgotten what an astute observer Danny was. But still, he was no mind-reader, and I was thankful for that.

I shook my head and nonchalantly waved a hand. "Friend of a friend. I just didn't expect to see him here, because he's got a little one at home and his wife is pregnant again." It wasn't a complete lie.

Thankfully, Danny bought it and didn't pursue the topic. Our drinks came, and our server—Chantal, according to her name tag—took our orders. I hadn't even seen the menu. Danny asked if I was fine with the tasting menu and my mind was too busy to process anything, so I nodded curtly.

I nursed my drink. Truth be told, I would've liked to ask for the entire bottle and downed it in one go. Danny was in front of me, but my thoughts had wandered to Alex. What would he do, what would he say if he found out I was on a sorta-date with my ex-fiancé?

"Hannah, are you fine with this?" Danny squeezed my hand again.

He was such a sweet man. He'd always been considerate, caring, thoughtful, and incredibly romantic. I couldn't forget how he'd asked me to prom. He'd gotten the entire football team, cheer team and the school band to do a performance after a home game, which, thanks to Danny—the star quarterback—our school had won. All that jazz to get me to say yes.

"I'm fine, Danny." I searched deep within the crevices of my mind for the sweetness I once had, and offered him a saccharine smile. "I'm sorry you have to put up with me and my mood tonight. I didn't think Mom would fake some kind of disease to get out of dinner."

Under the soft, ambient lights, Danny frowned. "Your Mom?"

"Yeah. It's her usual act. You know her and her antics." I picked my drink up with my free hand to take a quick sip, hoping it would calm my nerves.

Danny's grip on my hand tightened. "Hannah, that wasn't the reason. Your Dad...she said your Dad isn't feeling well. And she's right; he had to stay in. This whole trip has been hard on him."

"What do you mean?" Whatever his answer would be, my heart instinctively knew I wouldn't like it as it crashed in a quick tempo against my ribs.

"Your Dad has cancer, Hannah. It's terminal."

My vision blurred as he said the words.

"No. Why would you say that?" I yelled, not caring who heard me.

He held onto me tighter, as I loosened my grip on reality. "It's the truth. Didn't they tell you?"

No, it couldn't be. Not Daddy. He was tough and healthy and...I'd been away from him all these years. What did I know?

I scrambled to get up, the restaurant spinning around me. Danny's voice became inaudible, a mumble. The noise in the restaurant turned into one piercing ringing in my ears. All I could hear was the screaming in my head. Not my father. He wasn't dying. I had to go back to him so he could tell me Danny was a fool. Danny was wrong.

Calm

"*H*annah, stop, wait." Danny's arms circled my waist, forcing my body against his.

He led me back to our table, as I muttered, "Not Daddy. He's good. He said he's going to live forever." My voice trembled. I didn't sound like me. I sounded like the little girl who had once lost a pet cat.

"I'm sorry. I shouldn't have said anything. I thought he'd given you a clue when he saw you this morning." Danny handed me his water and I welcomed the cool crispness down my parched throat. I was choking on sorrow and disbelief. "I'm sorry, Hannah."

"I have to go. I want to see him. I want to know why he didn't tell me." I looked to Danny for answers, which I knew he didn't have. "Why didn't he tell me, Danny?"

What else could he do? He waved to our server and dealt with the payment. "I'll take you back to the hotel."

I found myself back in front of the restaurant, while we waited for the car. The chill on my skin and the heaviness in my chest shook me. Danny, who had been keeping me close to him, took his jacket off and hung it over my shoulders. "Thank you," I said under my breath, keeping my eyes on the ground, formulating the questions I'd ask my parents as soon as we returned.

Danny helped me into the passenger seat, even buckling my seatbelt for me. I smelled his minty toothpaste when he got close. I couldn't even feel bad that he hadn't been able to eat dinner.

Driving back was quieter than the ride there. People, buildings and streets blurred as my eyes welled with tears. But I forced myself not to let go of them. Not in front of Danny.

The silence in elevator ride up was deafening. My jaw clicked and popped, as I worked the muscles around it. Daddy bought the horse I'd fallen from when I'd gotten the jaw injury. I'd cried, pouted, and wailed the entire autumn for that horse. I'd wanted him for Christmas the year before, but hadn't received him until my twelfth birthday. Daddy had bought him for me. Only now did I wonder what had happened to Willy. He had been a good horse, picked just for me. Daddy thought he had a good temperament. But Willy had never grown to like me. It had been clear the first day I'd ridden him—he'd bucked and thrown me off his back.

Daddy had given me the world, and my mother had given him a lot of flak for it.

And he could be dying.

I rushed out of the elevator and back to my parents' room. Before I could reach the door, Danny pulled me back with one hand.

"Hannah, wait. Relax for a bit. There's no sense in going in there with guns blazing. He's tired. He's sick. Your mother has been helping him out, and I'm sure she's tired, too."

He was right, of course, but the stubborn Buford in me wouldn't back down. I slipped my wrist out of Danny's grasp, and turned on my heel to face him. "You had no right to tell me, Danny. No right!"

"Hannah, I understand how—"

I wasn't done. With the heel of my hand on his chest, I gave him a hard shove. "No. You wouldn't understand. You can't possibly understand how I feel right now."

"As a matter of fact I do, Hannah." He held onto my hand again, bringing it back on his chest, letting me feel the hammering of his heart. "Have you forgotten what my life was like before you left?"

I searched his eyes, and found hurt and grief. How could I have not remembered? "Your mom?" Danny nodded. "When?"

"Five years ago. The effects of the last clinical trials she went through eventually wore off. Her condition worsened a few months after you disappeared. She fell down the stairs one night, went into a coma and never woke up." His eyes lowered, and he swept his hair off his forehead.

For as long as I'd known Danny, his mother had been sick. She was a lovely woman, even with her different moods, and there had been times when I wished I had her as a mother instead. Yes, as a teenager, I'd even told my own mother that, just to be spiteful. Abigail Thompson would have been my mother-in-law. Knowing how progressive Huntington's could be, Danny and I had gotten engaged during her better year, while she'd undergone a promising clinical trial, and despite the protestations from my father, we'd proceeded with the wedding plans. Abigail had left this world before she could witness her son getting married. I loved her. I had betrayed her too.

With my temper toned down, I admitted again in a hushed tone, "I just can't believe he didn't tell me." I leaned my back against the gold and cream wallpaper.

Danny joined me, and his shoulders sagged as he stuffed his hands in his pockets. "Maybe he would have but couldn't. Sometimes, it's hard to find the courage to say what you need to say." Somehow, I knew he meant those words more for me than my father.

With a heavy sigh, I straightened. Later, Danny and I would have to talk about our past. Later.

"I'd better do this now before...it gets too late." What I really wanted to say was before I lost courage, but I didn't want to admit it.

My mother was a lot slower opening the door this time. For a brief moment, shock appeared on her face, then she molded it into excitement.

"Back already? Was the food horrible?" I wasn't buying it. Her voice had a tinny sound. She was nervous, anxious.

I bypassed the pleasantries and walked right into the bedroom, "Daddy? Dad?" The bed was empty. I didn't know if I should be thankful or worried not to see him lying on it, weakened by his condition.

Through the opened balcony doors, he called out to me, "Nugget?"

A soft wind blew past me as I stepped onto the balcony. The view was breathtaking. The darkness and light fog were punctuated with lights from the tower and the cathedral. Daddy sat on a lounger, facing the city beyond. Before he could get up, I stopped him with raised hand, and signaled to him to make room for me. I snuggled with him, placing my head and a hand over his chest. My heart prepared to burst.

He sighed before kissing my hair. "Daniel told you?"

I nodded. "I wish you had told me this morning." I angrily swiped away tears.

"And ruin our reunion?" Daddy let out a dry chuckle. He wrapped an arm around me, rubbing one of my shoulders with his large hand.

Wiping away more tears, I looked up to him. "Are you in a lot of pain?"

"Not right now. I'm on heavy medication. Once we return to Vermont, I have another round of chemo to go through." I expected his voice to shake, or hear a tinge of fear in his voice. But my father was a brave man. He had faced many trials in his life. I had no doubt in his mind, he could beat this thing, or at least fight like a hard Texan until the end. "I had to postpone it so we can come and see you."

If there ever was a perfect time to blame myself and the decisions I'd made a decade ago, it was now. He could have been going through his treatments, possibly prolonging his life. Instead, he was here in the city with me, far away from home.

We stayed silent for a while. It was comfortable, unrestrained. It reminded me of the many times he had taken me fishing with him. Just the two of us, waiting for a catch, enjoying each other's company. When the wind picked up and the night air cooled, I led him to the bed and asked him to rest.

"I'll see you in the morning," I promised before leaving the bedroom and joining my mother and Danny out in the living room of the hotel suite.

I couldn't look at my mother when I asked about my father's illness. "What stage?"

"Four. The oncologist has hopes with the newest treatment." The words were like a sword that speared through my heart.

I faltered and reached for the nearest chair. Danny helped me onto it, asking if I needed a drink. I could only nod. "When was he diagnosed?"

"About three and a half years ago. We were told then that prostate cancer had a high rate of survival since we'd caught it early. But it came back this year, with a vengeance. It's spreading." My mother's voice was clear, but it lacked emotion. It was like listening to a recording. It wasn't unlike her. In a huge crowd, she could be overly dramatic, but in a more intimate gathering, she was like a stone. I didn't know which was worse.

The glass of water Danny offered me sweated on the coffee table. I could spend the night staring at it. But I'd been alone for far too long. I'd gotten used to trouble-shooting my own dilemmas, although not a lot of them came my way. It was one of the perks of keeping people at bay. Whenever Nica ran into some sort of trouble, she'd come to me, and I would do anything possible to help her out. There was no doubt in my mind she would offer help and encouragement right now. But what I craved at this moment was time alone with my thoughts.

I stood, shaky on my own feet. "I'm going home. I'll come for breakfast in the morning. We'll talk more then."

My mother glanced at me and offered a flat smile. "That's fine. We have breakfast at seven sharp." Then she looked back down on her skirt, smoothing it out with her hand.

"I can give you a ride home," Danny offered.

"No, thank you. I'm fine on my own," I declined politely.

"I'll walk you down then?"

While we waited for the elevator doors to open for us, I turned to him. "Thank you, Danny, for coming here with them. I'm sure it couldn't have been easy for you."

Danny and my father got along well now. Years ago, Daddy had been angry at him and almost refused to give his blessings when Danny had asked for my hand in marriage. Whatever had gone on after I left had seemingly fixed their relationship. Danny's own father had been absent for most of his life—when his mother was diagnosed with Huntington's, his father didn't hesitate to pack his bags and leave his sickly wife and son.

"I'm here for you, Hannah." He took my hand and kissed the back of it as the elevator doors swooshed open.

Before I got into the cab, he gave me his phone and room number. "Call anytime," he said.

After two hours of tossing and turning on my bed, I gave up on sleep. There really was only one answer to my questions. But before I could fully commit to my decision, there were other matters which required closure.

I dressed quickly in a sleeved shirt, jeans and boots. With my keys in my hand, I shrugged into my leather jacket and made my way to the carport. The night was cool and the smell of incoming rain permeated the air. I had to make it to my destination before the heavens poured.

It took ten minutes to get there. Without hesitation, I rapped on the white door.

"Hi," I greeted, biting my lip, and looking up through my lashes.

"Hey," Danny said as he opened the door wider for me. "Come on in."

The room was lit by a lamp on the desk near the windows. His laptop was on and there were papers stacked beside it. At least I was right to assume he'd still be awake. Whether he'd be open to a discussion was another matter.

As I zipped open my jacket, it didn't escape me that just the night before, and around the same time, I'd been in a different hotel room, seeking solace from another man. I swallowed the emotion that clogged my throat at the thought of Alex, and faced the man who sat on the sofa with me.

He held my hands and pulled me to him. It was time we talked.

Danny talked about moving on once he'd admitted to himself I wasn't returning any time soon. I was right; his relationship with my father had changed when I left. They'd supported each other. Neither blamed the other for my disappearance.

"When he was diagnosed, Walt told me he knew where you've been all this time. I couldn't be angry at him when he explained why he just let you be," Danny informed me.

Then he'd spoken about graduating from Harvard Law, and moving back to Stowe to start his own firm. My father had helped him with his education, paying for all the fees his scholarship didn't cover, in addition to any healthcare expenses his mother had required. My father had felt he'd owed it to Danny for not telling him where I'd been. In return, Danny became my family's attorney, and with a minor in business, he'd managed to turn my father's wealth into something akin to an empire.

Ever since we'd started dating, I knew Danny was as smart as they came. He had big plans, and I would have gone along with him the entire time, if things had worked out differently.

"I'm sorry I didn't say goodbye," I started, wringing my fingers together. "But I'm not sorry I left. I had to."

Danny leaned an elbow on his thigh, propped his chin on his upturned hand and brushed the other through his hair. "I know. I was mad at you for a very long time." He looked at me, studying my passive features. "But I would've understood. We could have postponed the wedding."

Before I could make a reply, he sat erect and raised a hand in front of his chest. I waited for whatever else he wanted to say.

"I'm not mad now. I haven't been mad at you for a long

time, Hannah. Nothing I say now would change the past. All we could do now is to keep moving on. And I'm not gonna convince you to decide one way or another...but Walt needs you. He needs his daughter."

*N*ica's jaw practically unhinged as she stared at me, a weird noise coming out of her mouth. I'd dropped a bomb on her, but if I had waited for the right time to say it, I wouldn't have been able to at all. There was no right time.

With an index finger, I pushed her jaw up, closing her mouth. She placed her Chinese food container on the table, and plastered her game face on.

"What do you mean you're leaving?" Her voice went an octave higher.

I squeezed a piece of breaded chicken between my chopsticks, avoiding her stare. "I'm going back to Vermont with my parents." I tried to keep my tone casual, like there wasn't an eruption in volcanic proportions inside my head and my heart.

San Francisco had been home to me for a number of years. I might have had a different name here, but it was where I built my own roots. My friends had become my family, since I abandoned my own. I'd grown fond of the people, the places, and every single nuance of this lively city. But my duty as a daughter called.

"But...but...but..."

I waved my chopsticks around as I spoke. "All my current projects are done...well, as done as they can be. Jewel can take over most of them, and the rest will work themselves out." I'd spent the whole day making phone calls and sending emails to vendors, contractors, and clients, while Nica had taken the day off to see her obstetrician.

"But you live here. What about your apartment?" she asked.

"It should be good for a few months, then I'll sublet it. I'll ask Gerard or Mateo to look after it while I'm gone."

"So you'll be back? This is just temporary, right?" Nica asked, her voice shaking. Any second now, she'd be crying. As if to prove my point, she sniffled.

I shrugged, and placed my food beside hers. "It will depend on a lot of things." I sat with my legs up on the sofa in her living room. With carefully chosen words, I told her about my father's illness, and the necessary steps he'd have to go through in the coming months.

She stopped pretending she wasn't going to cry and let it all out. Every now and then, she would rub her belly, or reach for my hand. She'd wipe the tears off her face, and constantly blamed it on her hormones.

"I'll be back for your baby shower, though. And I'll visit when that little she-devil is born." I poked her burgeoning stomach, and felt a nudge back. "What the hell? Did she just kick me back?"

Nica blew out an exasperated breath. "Yeah. She's been relentless. As soon as I get any rest, she starts moving around."

I was suddenly squeamish. "I can't believe you have a human being growing in there. Freaking weird."

She slapped my upper arm. "Get over it." Then she sighed. "So you're really leaving me, huh?"

I propped my head on the sofa and watched Nica's bottom lip quiver. "I'm not leaving you. I'm just leaving for now. I'll figure it all out when I get there."

"What if you never figure it out? What if all of a sudden

you choose not to come back? I mean...Daniel...he's back in your life now too. That's a big deal, right?"

Danny. Was he back in my life? I thought after our talk last night, I'd know for certain where we stood.

The sun had risen by the time I'd left his room, and only had enough time to head back to my apartment to prepare for breakfast with my parents. It had been an awkward meal. In the daytime, my father's condition had been clearer for me to see. Since I was aware of what to look for, I spotted every manifestation of his illness. He was gaunt, easily tired, and weak. Before breakfast was over, I'd told my parents I'd be going back with them, but I'd made no promises of staying. I couldn't, yet.

Even with no sleep, and a heavy burden on my shoulders, I'd made it into work and buried myself in it. It helped me forget my sorrows momentarily. My assistant had been shocked to see me there the entire day, and the rest of the gang had stopped into my office to ask if I was okay. I shrugged them all off and scoffed at their concerns. Not one of them had any idea what had happened in the past couple of days. If I were to tell anyone about my impending departure, it was Nica who had to know first, which was why I visited her at home, bearing gifts in Chinese containers.

She propped herself up with pillows against the back of the sofa, returning to her meal. I was going to miss times like this with my best friend. "What are you going to do in Stowe?"

I chuckled at her question, as I'd been asking myself the same thing. "Other than look after Daddy and try not to get pissed off at my Mom? Not much. Be a princess?"

Nica snorted. "A princess?"

Right. There was something else she didn't know.

"Well...have you ever wondered how I survived all these years without my parents?"

"I used to, but after finding out how resourceful you are, I stopped."

I laughed at her remark, digging into my food. "That's true. But a huge part of it was my trust fund."

"Your what now?"

I enunciated the words. "T-rust Fun-d."

"You have a trust fund." It wasn't a question.

"Yes. Before I left home, I withdrew whatever I could from it. My paternal grandmother was a rich old lady, and when she passed, she gave a chunk of her money and properties to me and my...ahm...Daddy. Although I didn't touch it much because we owned a maple farm."

Nica's eyebrow raised. "Say that again? Maple farm?"

"Yes, Nica. Maple farm. We're the biggest producers of maple syrup in the country. Daddy had a knack for business and grew this huge production. Anyway, that's where I grew up."

Nica narrowed her eyes at me. "Who are you?"

"Stop it, Nica." I slapped her hand lightly. "I'm telling you now. I know I've been a shitty friend for keeping secrets from you. Don't think I haven't been kicking myself for that."

Just then, we heard the ding of the elevator, announcing someone had arrived in their penthouse. I continued eating my dinner out of the box.

"Your husband's home," I muttered.

"Hmmm, yeah. With Alex," she added nonchalantly.

I had just popped a piece of carrot into my mouth when she said his name. My heart leapt into my throat. I chewed the carrot quickly and gulped it down with a sip of water. "Alex is here?" I kept my voice low.

Nica nodded, looking toward the hallway where voices

of two men came from, both speaking in their native language. "He called us yesterday saying he's in the city for a bit. It was a bit of a surprise. I thought he'd be back in France. Martina was expecting him."

It was unusual for Alex to come here when his grandmother needed him.

Well, hell. How was I going to escape the awkwardness which was about to rain down on me? I hadn't talked to Alex since yesterday morning. God, was it just yesterday morning? It felt like a lifetime ago. With everything that had happened, hours seemed like months. Their voices stopped as soon as they reached the living room. I straightened and trained my eyes on the fog outside the massive windows.

"Hi, baby!" Nica pushed herself up and leaned over the back of the sofa to greet her husband with a kiss. "How was dinner?"

"Great. I missed you," Levi said. I couldn't look in their direction without wanting to choke myself. "Hey, Chase. Good of you to come and keep my wife company."

I raised a hand but didn't move my head. "Yup." I felt a dull ache on the back of my head. My ear buzzed. I adjusted my vision on the windows and saw the reflection of the man standing behind me. Even in the blurry glass, I could see he wasn't happy. And I felt it like a vice grip in my chest.

"Something to drink, Chase? I've got a couple of great vintages to go with your meal," Levi offered.

"Please." I wanted to tell him to bring both bottles.

Levi gave his wife another kiss before leaving. I listened to him speak to Alex in French, but didn't hear his brother's reply. Not that I would understand the words.

Nica chose that moment to stretch up. "I'm going for a

pee. Be right back." I watched her waddle to the hallway. The pulsating in my ear was like a ticking bomb.

Being alone in the massive space with Alex did not help quell my shaking nerves. When I finally made myself turn to him, all I saw was indifference. We stared at each other for a bit before he shook his head and made his way out to the balcony. Without another thought, I followed him out and was shocked when I saw what he held in his hand.

"I thought you stopped smoking."

He was facing the night sky, and slightly angled his head in my direction, but didn't look at me. "I thought you were single."

Damn.

I sucked in a breath. There was no time for explanations. Not that I was ready for them. "I made no promises," I countered.

I received a humorless laugh. Then Alex turned, inhaling from his cigarette and pushing smoke into the air. I waved my hand, fanning the smoke away from me.

"No, you didn't. You only came to me when you were distressed, and, what is it you American girls say? Led me on?" He was mocking me. "I'd wondered why you kept pushing me away." His free hand gripped the metal rails. "Now, I know." Alex stepped closer to me and with the two fingers pinching his cigarette, he pointed. "Just to let you know, Chase, I don't make it a habit to fuck unavailable women."

Pushing his hand away, I squared my shoulders. I understood why Alex was bitter. Not brave enough to argue his point, I blurted instead, "I want the photos." It was one of the reasons why I followed him out here.

"What photos?" he asked with a menacing tone.

"You know what photos. I want them. All of them. I never signed any release forms so you can't use them for anything, but just in case, I'd feel better if they're in my possession." Lessons for life: never sleep with a photographer. Never let them take photos of you in states of undress. And never ever let them take photos of you while having sex. "You can bring them to my office tomorrow." Before he could say anything else, I turned away and walked back to the living room.

"Chase? You okay?" Nica plopped back onto the sofa.

I grabbed my jacket and helmet, which I had placed over a chair, and avoided eye contact with Nica. "Yeah, I forgot I told my parents I'll go and see them. Tell Levi I'll take that drink some other time."

"Right..." Nica wanted to say more, I could sense it, but she was always good at giving me space. "I'll see you at work tomorrow."

"Yeah, bye."

I didn't know how much of an effect the moment with Alex had on me until my hands trembled. Tears fell down my cheeks as soon as I got in the elevator. I squeezed my hands over my stomach, trying to get a breath in. By the time I arrived home, I was a heaving pile of mess.

❦

"Vermont? Like the mountains?" Becky, Nica's assistant, responded to my announcement that I would be shipping out of the sunny state.

Nica and I had decided it would be best to get the troops together and announce my nearing departure. The best reaction so far came from Gerard, with his mouth popping open and closed, his brain trying to formulate a comprehensive reply. He wasn't normally this quiet, especially with an announcement this big.

"I can't believe your last name is Buford. I always

thought it would be something magical. Like...like..." Jewel rolled her wrists in the air. "I don't know."

"What's wrong with Buford?" I challenged from my perch in front of the large conference table.

"Nothing!" Her voice rose an octave, then she blinked at least five times. Liar. A horrible liar, at that.

Gerard woke up from his semi-stupor, standing on his feet, palms on the glass top. "I can't believe you used to live on a farm!"

Nica sighed and rolled her eyes. This wasn't exactly how she'd pictured it, surely.

"It's a maple farm," I countered.

"Did you have horses, and goats and cows?"

I threw my hands up in the air. "Yeah, but it wasn't that kind of farm. We used to have those for the kids' petting zoo."

"Right."

Mateo finally tugged him back into his seat. "What Gerard means is that we are going to miss you, Chase."

Big Boss Nica added to the sentiment, "That goes without saying. Chase and I have gone through her events, and we'll be allocating them amongst all of you. The biggest one is the twenty-first birthday party. Chase was able to secure Stefano as DJ, and she's contacted all the vendors..." I could feel the tension in the room. This was a huge assignment. Anyone in the room would jump onto the bandwagon to oversee the event with a huge star-studded guest list. "Since it falls on one of your wedding days, Jewel, Gerard gets this one."

With a triumphant fist pump, Gerard shouted, "Yes!" And proceeded to do his victory dance, aka cabbage patch with a side of sprinkler. "Does this mean I get to have her office too?"

Everyone else in the room shook their heads. And it hit

me. I was going to sorely miss these people, my coworkers, friends, and even the assistant whose name still eluded me.

"No. You don't get my office. My move's not permanent."

"Fine." Gerard sulked, though two seconds later, he brightened up. "You know what this means?"

"What?" Jewel perked up with interest.

"We get to throw her a Bon Voyage party!" Another fist pump and victory dance.

The murmur grew in the room, with all of them agreeing to the idea. There was no way of escaping this, so I might as well face it now.

"Fine. Party at my place tomorrow. We'll do it after work, or whenever. Don't bring friends or partners."

꒰ꕤ꒱

"It's so good to meet all of Chastity's friends." My mother grinned, touching the side of her face, eyeing the two good-looking men in front of her. Of course, she wouldn't pick up on the fact they were married to each other.

Gerard choked on the drink he'd just sipped. "I'm sorry." His eyes watered. "Did you say Chastity?"

Here we go.

"Oh yes, Chastity," my mother proudly said, "I named her myself."

I gave Gerard a look that said I'd take the ice from his glass, shape it into a shiv and jab it in his eyeball if he didn't stop snickering. But he ignored it, grabbing my mother's hand, and placing it over his large arm. "Tell me more, mother dear, tell me more." Naturally, my mother swooned.

Mateo shrugged, a silent apology, and followed my mother and Gerard. I emptied my glass and walked over to the makeshift bar. As I dropped in a couple of ice cubes and a good three fingers of scotch, I watched the interactions happening in the room. My past had collided with my present. It felt surreal.

On the sofa, Levi and Nica chatted with Danny. A few words filtered toward me from their conversations, such as 'investment properties', 'profit margins', 'brand identity', so needless to say they were talking business. My father was delightedly surrounded by Jewel and the assistants around the kitchen island. His hands flew everywhere as he described the mischievous little girl I had been.

As I sipped my drink, I wondered if my life wouldn't have been as bad as I thought it would if I'd been honest from the beginning. Now my past was revealed, and my friends and coworkers were very accepting. Okay, my friends were accepting; the assistants were afraid of me but they would gladly listen to any tidbit they could use later on to blackmail me. I would have done the same.

My past and present didn't collide. They smoothly fitted into each other. Yet, I couldn't ignore the deep ache in my heart. And I knew why.

Alex.

I missed him.

Even if I could figure out a way for him to fit into my life, I wasn't sure he would want to, not by the way he had reacted the other night. I stupidly retrieved and read all of Alex's texts last night, and it crushed me. I tried not to read between the lines, but the words, which I had initially ignored, were flashing like Vegas lights. Alex had wanted to be with me. He had been trying to get me involved in more than just a sexual relationship all this time. Now, my moment with him was up. End of the line for me. He wasn't someone who gave second chances.

And I still had to figure out Danny.

I refilled my glass and chugged the contents. The ice clinked against the crystal tumbler as my hands shook. My chest constricted. I forced out a ragged breath and tried to take in a soothing breath of air. It wasn't happening. I had to get out or I would faint.

The steps I took toward the front door weren't rushed. I tried to appear calm to whoever was paying attention, which was probably nobody, as they were all too busy getting acquainted with each other.

As soon as the cool night air hit my face, my eyes welled up. I cursed myself for being such a pansy. I hadn't cried this much since leaving Vermont, and I'd had more valid reasons to cry back then. What was going on with me? Did Alex mean more to me than I'd like to admit? And now that we couldn't be together, I was acting all broken-hearted?

I sucked in a shaky breath and swiped at the tears rolling down my cheeks. There was no running away from this. My father was terminally ill. I wouldn't find any way to forgive myself if I didn't go back to Vermont with him, and be by his side while he went through harrowing procedures. I patted my eyes dry and prepared to walk back in when someone on a motorcycle stopped in front of my house. I knew it was Alex before he even took off the dark helmet.

Grateful I had just ceased freaking out over the loss of what we could have had, I calmly climbed down the steps to see what brought him.

Thoughts of hope and reconciliation burst within me.

I almost tripped over my own feet before I reached him. He looked damned sexy on that bike. *Curse him!* My libido screamed at me. But his impassive expression gave nothing away.

We stared at each other. I stuffed my hands in my back pocket. Touching him would be the death of me.

"I brought you this."

"What brought you here?"

We spoke at the same time, which made a hint of a smile lift the corner of his lips.

Hope. There was hope yet.

I took the small Manila envelope he had taken out from inside his jacket pocket. I turned it over in my hand, wondering what was in it.

"The pictures you asked for," he explained, with a steady voice. "I've made prints but they're all there, I believe."

"I—" Should I look at the photos now? Should I check if they were all there? I had no idea how many he'd taken of me, of us, and I had no clue if I would be able to survive whatever emotions could come crashing down on me once I did. I dropped my hand and raised my head. "Thank you," was all I could say. Anything else would betray my emotions.

Alex offered a smile, which did not glimmer in his eyes. But it was something. "Chase, what I said the other night..." He didn't say more. His head cocked up as something caught his eyes behind me. I was afraid to find out what caught his attention. What if Danny had seen me leave and now decided to check on me? I gritted my teeth and prayed I was wrong.

"Nugget?" My father's curious voice boomed from behind me.

I released a sigh of relief before turning. "Daddy? Is everything okay?" The other difficult part was to keep my dad away from Alex. I didn't know how to explain him or his presence to my father. I jogged to meet my dad at the steps but he waved me away and continued walking to where Alex got off his bike and stood beside it.

"Good evening, sir," Alex politely greeted, extending a hand over to my father. "Alex Laurent. Pleasure to meet you."

"Walter Buford. You can call me Walt. Are you Levi's brother?" Alex nodded. "Why don't you come in and join us?"

I stiffened as Alex glanced at my direction, head tilted to one side, daring me to answer for him. But he turned back to my father and shook his head. "I have to go. I've got a long drive tonight." Alex patted the leather seat on his Triumph.

"That's a nice-looking motorcycle yah got there, son," Daddy said. I about fainted when he called Alex 'son', even though I knew it meant nothing. "Where're you headed?"

Alex looked over his shoulder, out to the slanted road, to the view of sparkling stars and shimmering city lights. "Not entirely sure." Then he stared at me, with a gaze that bored into my whole being. "Wherever my heart leads me." My chest tightened.

"Hmmm. You'd best be careful then. Our hearts can be wild."

Shivers ran through me as I heard Daddy say the words he'd often said to me ever since my interest in boys had begun.

Alex licked his lips before swinging his leg over the cushioned seat. "Wise words. I'll keep it in mind." He propped his helmet back on his head and, before sliding down the visor, he bid me and my father goodbye. I wanted to hug him. Hold him. Kiss him. Taste him...one last time.

Daddy gripped my hand and squeezed while we watched Alex zip away. My heart hurt. "You're going to be all right, Nugget. You are going to be fine."

Metanoia

My dearest Hannah,
Take a risk, while you're young and don't be afraid
*   to make mistakes.*
Pack your bags and see the beauty out there. Out in
*   the open. Past the borders. Past the paved*
*   streets...*

I could recite the words from memory, from the letter I'd kept hidden. How many times had I read it through the years? However, I'd never taken even the first step to freedom and adventure the letter had promised. Instead, I'd hidden from all that. I'd run away, yes, but I'd built a wall to protect myself and keep others out. Where was the freedom in that?

Now, I was faced with a challenge. Back to square one, to my starting point. Would it be different this time around?

Except for me, everyone else had settled in their seats on the plane Levi had happily provided for us, which I'd been grateful for. Every bit of comfort it offered was helpful to my Dad. I grasped the leather-covered seat backs as I walked along the aisle to the first empty spot I could access and plopped my ass on it.

"Hannah, are you okay? You've gone pale." Danny, of course, noticed everything.

I cleared my throat and sank deeper into the cushion. "Never better."

He unbuckled his seatbelt, moved to the space beside me, and unglued my hand from the soft fabric I had a vice grip on. Danny leaned closer, muttering into my ear, "Fear of flying?"

"I'm sure it will pass," I lied.

Danny wrinkled his forehead. "You've flown before, haven't you? Years ago, the first time you left...or is this because of what happened?"

"No. I've never been on a plane." It was all I could offer as a reply. I refused to open old wounds. I doubted it would help the situation.

"Hello, my name is Sophie, I will be your attendant for the duration of the flight." A statuesque woman, with a French accent, stopped in front of us. Her pristine hair and perfectly pressed dress added to my anxiety. How could she be so perky? This was her job. She chose to get on a plane and walk around in six-inch heels while tens of thousands of feet up in the air. "Would you like some champagne?"

"I think I need something stronger. Horse tranquilizer maybe?" I said, and Sophie giggled. My own emotions did not change, and thankfully, Sophie saw it.

She straightened and smiled. "Levi made sure there was Scotch available for this flight. Neat?"

"Yes please. Bring the bottle." I massaged my temples, while clicking my jaw. This was a nightmare. I was grateful to Levi for lending us his private plane for the trip back to Vermont. The luxurious and roomy jet was much easier for Daddy to travel in. His condition had worsened overnight, and it was important we get home so he could start his treatment right away.

Danny released my hand and helped me with my seatbelt. "I can talk you through the whole thing if you want. I've taken flying lessons for small planes, but I don't think there's much of a difference."

"No. That's not going to help." I looked straight ahead where my parents were seated. I shouldn't worry about my own fears when my father was quietly suffering.

My mother caught the look on my face. "Oh, Chastity. Are you not well? I've got something for you."

"No, Mom, it's fine." Sophie came back, handing me a glass half-full of amber liquid. I knocked it back, winced, and stretched out my arm for another. She didn't hesitate to refill it. Sophie was trained well. I liked her more now.

"We will be taking off shortly, and I can help your father move into the bedroom and rest while we're in the air," she informed.

The thought of being 'in the air' twisted my gut again.

"Here, sweetie, take these." My mother handed Sophie something, and the attendant passed it to me.

There was a loud mechanical noise outside, and I didn't think to check the pills my mother gave me. I swallowed them and drank the rest of my scotch. My breathing increased. There was a slick cover of sweat on my skin. If I were a skunk, I would be spraying stink all over the place.

Danny stayed quiet beside me, but he kept his hand and arm available for me to hold onto anytime something made me jump. When he asked if I thought it was a good idea to keep drinking, I growled at him and dug my fingers into his skin.

My blood pressure hit the roof. My stomach grumbled. My head continued to pound like a jackhammer. Moments later, blackness consumed me.

❦

I'm falling. The mechanical noise continued as I fell and my entire body thudded on the floor. *What the hell?*

I opened my eyes and wanted to scream. This was

worse than flying. Where the hell was I? And what was that buzzing noise?

Shit. My phone! I held myself up, pulling at the side of the bed to get back on it and grab the vibrating phone from a side table.

"Nica!" I yelled into the smartphone, while rubbing my sore bum.

"Chase? I've been calling for hours. Are you okay?"

I let my eyes wander. "I think I died and went to chintz hell."

"What? Did you say 'chintz'?"

I took in the decor, if one could call it that, and described it to my best friend. "It's pink. It's floral. It's everywhere." The garden flower-printed pink fabric covered the sides of all six dormer windows, and swayed above me on the canopy of the four-poster bed, matching the pillowcases and coverlet, and to top it all off, the fabric was also used as upholstery for the wing-back chair in one corner of the room. The walls were bubble gum pink. Thankfully the trims and ceiling were painted white.

"What are you talking about? Where are you?"

"I think I'm in my old room, except it's not my room. It's never been this pink and girly, even when I was younger." I rubbed my behind as I tried to find comfort on the bed.

"I'm sure it's not that bad."

"Hold on." I raised my phone, took a few pictures, and sent them to Nica.

"Oh my gosh."

"Yeah. I gather my mother got carried away while I was gone. I'm afraid to find out what the rest of the house looks like."

"Well...how was the flight?"

I shook my head and instantly regretted it, squeezing

my eyes shut. "I honestly don't remember. Mom gave me some pills to take and I think it knocked me out cold. I don't even know how I got home."

As I tried to recall any bit of the flight, there was a soft knock on the pink door. Danny's head poked in when the door opened. "Oh good, you're awake." His smile widened as he walked in. It was eerie having him standing in my childhood bedroom again. Good thing I was still fully clothed.

"Nica, I'll call you later. Danny's here."

"Yeah, no problem. I just wanted to say I miss you already. We all do."

"I know. I miss you guys too. Talk soon."

When I ended the call, I looked back at Danny. "Sorry, I didn't realize you were on the phone," he apologized.

"Don't worry about it," I said, replacing my phone back onto the table. "Nica was just checking up on me. My head's killing me. How did I get here?"

Danny crossed the room and poured water into a glass from a pitcher on a sideboard, then sat on the edge of the bed and offered the drink to me.

"I guess the Valium and scotch cocktail hit you hard. You were out even before we took off."

I almost sputtered the water. "Valium?" He nodded. "The pills my Mom gave me? What the hell is she doing with Valium?"

Danny shrugged. "You'll have to ask her." He gave me a look of concern. "How do you feel? Hungry?"

"Not really. Just... I feel like I've gone through the ringer. Did you help me up here?"

"Yeah. Don't worry, I bench more than what you weigh." Wow, so not what I wanted to hear. "That didn't come out right. I mean..." He rubbed the back of his head.

"Relax, Danny. Thanks for your help. And for your information, I bench more than what you weigh too."

He smiled, wide but softer at the corners, and it lit up his eyes. A tug in my belly caused me to pull at the fabric of my shirt, like it would release the pressure I felt in my abdomen.

Danny dropped his focus to the floor. "Your parents are resting now. Your Dad's doctor just left, and he left his card for you." He handed me a thick, cream business card. "You can call him if you have any questions. But you should eat, then rest for the night."

"Are you staying here?" When he tilted his head up, our eyes met. "I mean, here at my parents' house. Not in this room."

"No. I have to go to my office before I head home." Danny stood and pressed a kiss on my forehead. "It's good to have you back, Hannah. You have my number if you ever want to talk. I'll come by tomorrow morning."

"Yeah, thanks, Danny."

"Welcome home, Hannah."

When he walked out of the room, I fell back onto my pillows and contemplated the whole scenario. I was back in Stowe, living with my parents, sleeping in this pink froufrou bedroom. My father wasn't well. My mother carried Valium in her purse. My ex-fiancé had access to my bedroom, and seemingly, everything else in my life here.

How could I move forward? Would I? What would happen to the life I left behind?

I groggily got up and zipped open one of the bags I brought from San Francisco. I'd refused to pack all of my things. This was temporary. My father would go through his chemo and defy the odds. My mother would find something else to redecorate. And Danny...I wasn't too sure about Danny, yet.

My heart dropped when a package spilled its contents by my feet. I sat on my haunches and gathered the photos from the floor. I didn't think Alex had taken this many pictures of me, or any of us. But the evidence was there.

There were photos of me asleep, awake, reading, contemplating. And of Alex and me kissing, laughing into the camera or just being goofballs. I didn't even recall any of these being taken. We looked so happy. We *were* happy. Then I wondered, *where were the nude photos?* I shook the envelope and a USB fell out. I suspected the rest were on it. I didn't have the guts to look at them. As uncertain as I was with Danny, I refused to think of where Alex and I stood. If there was even something for us to stand on.

Komorebi

*T*he distinction between what my life was like in San Francisco and what my life would be like in Stowe became evident on the third day. Courtesy of women who lunch (and gossip, and criticize).

Night number one was hazy from the accidental combination of anti-anxiety meds and scotch, heightened by the squeezing pain in my heart when I went through Alex's photos. When I woke the next day, I was a pile of mush. I donned my largest pair of sunglasses to keep my mother from asking why I appeared to have grapes inside my puffy eye bags.

To think that my real first day back would have been easy was major BS. I'd skipped breakfast after a long shower, and moseyed on to accompany Daddy to his appointment with his oncologist, his general practitioner, his mechanic, his barber, his new farm manager, the vet and the recently pregnant cow, and Daddy's lawyer, Danny. By the time we met with him, I had a migraine and couldn't stomach the thought of sitting through another meeting.

Didn't these people know my father was sick?

I'd asked my father that exact question. As a reply, and to shut me up, he'd patted my arm and said, "I ain't dead yet, Nugget. The business ain't gonna run itself." He'd added that being back at home had given him enough energy, or in his words, superhuman powers.

It had resulted in me pulling my hair out. Not all of it,

of course, but a good wad, enough to cut into short strips and sell to the next toupé maker I'd come across. Not that I knew one, but the day was young yet.

By sunset, I was in bed, not bothering to change into pajamas, and passed out from all the day's activities.

When the bright sun spilled into my still-pink bedroom on the third day, there was an uncanny texture in my mouth. Upon close inspection, and after a quick checkup with my pediatric dentist, who resembled the crypt keeper in his ancient years, I discovered I'd gnashed my teeth overnight, causing one of my fillings to pop out and turn into a fine, sand-like product in my mouth. Stress was getting to me. Stowe was getting to me.

After the dentist, I returned home, where my mother and her posse awaited to scrutinize each and every inch of my being. Women who lunch. They insisted they should be called ladies, but their definition of a lady was a far cry from mine. They played the "Point out what's wrong with Chastity Hannah game".

One said, my hair was too dark for my complexion.

Another argued, my complexion was too light for my hair.

"She could use a haircut."

"She needs a facial and less whorish makeup."

"She needs an entirely new wardrobe. Only women who hide secrets wear black."

Well, damn woman, you got me there.

Meanwhile, the Novocain from the dental visit had worn off. My eyes twitched when I overheard one of the women saying I could stand to lose a few pounds. I had trouble determining who was who since they all dressed alike (pearls and twinset, pressed pants or a floral skirt, or a fugly floral dress), they all sounded the same (high pitched with a tinge of annoying), and they were either called Georgia, Georgia-Anne or Georgiana. One was called Wendy, but she was clearly the black sheep of the group, having worn jeans and a sweater with rhinestones, and stating that my leather-trimmed leggings did not make me look like I was a part of the local motorcycle gang.

From head to toe, through and through, each one had a comment about my appearance, but not one brought up my disappearance ten years ago. I refused to argue or point out the obvious, because Mother Dear was their head honcho, and I still didn't know how long I'd be living under her roof.

As soon as I was released from their scrutiny, I ran straight to the backdoor, past the outdoor pool, and through the woods until I hit a small, familiar lake. I dropped on the grass and breathed in the fresh air. The flickering sunshine weaved itself between the lush dancing leaves of mature trees. I'd forgotten about this place. As a little girl, I'd often trudged through the forest in the middle of the day, sat on this very spot, and dreamt of jetting off to a faraway land and having my own (mis)adventures.

In that moment, surprising even myself, I thought of Charity, and asked the whistling wind what would have happened if she'd never left.

Nature had no answer for me.

સ

The best way to sneak back into the house without detection from my mother, who had always claimed she was allergic to cooking, was through the kitchen where Chef Paul passed me a helping of lasagna. I devoured it within minutes. When I stood up to check on Daddy,

Dishwasher Paul told me my parents had gone to an afternoon tea with the Mayor and his wife.

I went straight to my bedroom and searched for my phone. I stared at it before I could figure out what to do. Should I call Nica? Gerard or Jewel? No matter how much I'd love to chat with any one of them, there was only one person whose voice I would pay millions to hear right now. Unfortunately, due to a hasty and drunken decision, I'd erased Alex's number, texts and voicemail messages. If anyone researched my life through my phone, that person wouldn't find any trace that I'd ever been involved with the motorcycle-riding, globe-trotting, sex-on-legs photographer.

Like a magnet, my eyes drifted to my closed closet door. Hidden inside was an envelope full of memories.

I couldn't go there again. Not now. Not yet.

Instead, I had a soothing bath. But even that turned into a disaster, when a flash of memory of Alex cursing in a bathtub after I'd switched on the cold water invaded my thoughts.

I'd panicked the last night I'd seen him outside my apartment. Why didn't I kiss him? Why didn't I hold him tight and ask him to stay with me, or fly with me back here? Why didn't I tell him how I truly felt?

Sitting up in the tub, I splashed water on my face and rubbed my eyes while I admitted once again how much I missed and ached for him. If I had been honest, would he have understood?

No, he wouldn't have, not according to his past behavior. Alex would have turned his back on me and left the way he did, searching for what would make his heart happy, complete, and to start beating once again. I saved myself from a huge heartbreak. The challenge now would be to convince myself of the unavoidable truth. Alex and I weren't meant to be together.

Since I didn't know when my parents would come back, I decided to explore the rest of the house. But I couldn't stomach the visual abuse my mother had applied throughout the eleven-thousand square foot home, and the house was as dry as the clubs and bars during the prohibition. I ran to the garage and borrowed one of my father's cars.

Stowe was a gorgeous town, attracting tourists from everywhere with activities and seasonal events throughout the year. My drive along Main Street brought fond memories of my childhood—standing wide-eyed on the sidelines as a four-year old during parades, holding my Daddy's hand and spreading melted ice cream on my face as much as on my Sunday's best, my annual volunteer work in the Maple Festival.

I parked in front of a quaint shop filled with trinkets Nica would appreciate. Every single piece I'd picked up would have suited Nica's old apartment. Now that she was living with Levi, I wondered if kitschy doodads would suit their contemporary decor. I did pick up a few colorful onesies for little girl Laurent. My favorite? Had "Shits and Giggles" printed in pink, sparkly curlicue script.

Late July weather was in full swing, and instead of the cooler night air I'd gotten used to in San Francisco, Stowe's summer nights were perfect for a nightly stroll. No one bothered me. Tourists avoided me— a scowling woman in a black shirt and jeans— and the locals ogled and whispered amongst themselves. With a population of just over four thousand, and me the prodigal daughter of the richest man in town, the news of my return had travelled fast. Whenever I saw a curious person, I veered away from them, which resulted in me getting lost.

My feet needed rest. I'd stupidly left my cell phone in my bedroom, and I didn't have anyone's phone number memorized yet. Even worse, I couldn't figure out where I'd parked the damned car. Annoyed at myself, I plopped on a sidewalk bench. When I read the sign over the black and white awnings, I huffed a sigh of relief. I crossed the street and stepped into Daniel Thompson, LLP's office.

"Hi there!" a perky—too perky for this time of the day —voice greeted.

It came from a petite woman perched behind an uncluttered desk. Her smile was infectious, and my mood lifted, but instead of returning her smile, I narrowed my eyes. Why was she so cheery? It was nearly nine o'clock, and she was still at work. Something did not compute.

"I'm Tiana," she said, walking with an outstretched hand to where I planted my feet by the door. "How may I help you?"

I lifted a brow at Tiana. She was a lot shorter than first glance suggested, but she had major curves. Her peach skirt and cream blouse reminded me all too much of how Nica dressed. She wasn't my best friend's doppelgänger, but Tiana could pass as Nica's cousin twice removed. This alone should've melted my iciness, but it only did a little. I shook her tiny, manicured hand.

"Chas—Hannah. I'm Hannah. Is Danny still around?"

A quick look of surprise passed over her face when I said my name, but as a professional, and I assumed, Danny's secretary, Tiana was quick to smooth her features. She nodded. "He is. Would you like to have a seat? He should be done with his phone call in a bit." Tiana leaned in and whispered, "Bad divorce, cheating husband, but you didn't hear it from me."

Oh dear, we've got a live one. A gossiper. She was nothing like Nica.

"I thought Danny practiced business law?"

Tiana pressed her lips into a thin line, and nodded again. "Mmm-hmm. Yup. But it's a favor for a friend of a friend."

The interior office door opened, Danny walked out, and my throat clenched. Men on the cover of GQ had nothing on the way Danny looked, strutting out of his office, wearing a three-piece suit. Smarts and good looks, a lethal combination. Not to mention, Danny had been incredibly sweet with me.

"Hannah? Hi!" When he reached me, his lips tickled my cheek. "Is everything okay?" He looked from me to Tiana, who said something about a report she had to file.

"Everything's good."

Danny cocked his head to one side and scratched his ear.

"Okay, I got lost. I went for a drive and now I can't figure out where I left the car."

Danny chuckled heartily. "Where did you park it?"

"Near the city hall on Main?"

"You are on Main. Let me grab my keys and I'll walk you to your car."

"Okay." Why did I all of a sudden feel I was in my teens again? Was it because of Danny?

While he went back into his office, I contemplated what I could say to Danny so I wouldn't have to be alone with him. My mind blanked, and it was too late when I heard Danny bid Tiana a good night, and ask her if she would be fine locking up. She shushed him away and waved at me with a cheery "good night".

As soon as we were outside his office door, Danny took off his suit jacket, undid his tie, and rolled up his shirt sleeves. I had expected to see a tattoo on his arm, and I had to mentally bitchslap myself when I realized I had just compared Danny to Alex. Danny spoke quietly as he led me down the street, greeting some of the locals. I kept my head low. By tomorrow morning, the local paper would be filled with assumptions about Danny and Hannah.

"How's your dad today?"

"He's doing well. He starts his treatments next week," I said, stuffing my hands in my jeans pocket.

"After the party, then."

"Party?" I stopped in my tracks, and grabbed Danny's arm to force him to face me. "What party?"

Danny looked away, clearly uncomfortable. "Your mom didn't tell you?"

"No. What party?" I waited to hear the horrible possibilities.

He took in a deep breath and released it slowly. "It's your welcome back party, Hannah. Why do you think the Gee-gees were at your house today?"

I lolled my head back. It was bad, but it was exactly what I had expected to hear. "Is there a way to stop this?"

"I'm afraid not."

"I cannot let this happen. You know how she gets. She's going to make this entire thing about her, Danny." My hands shook. Danny held onto them, and pulled me to him. His hand rubbed over the tension built over my shoulders and neck.

"It will be fine, Hannah. I'll be there with you the entire time..." He lifted my face up so I could stare into his hazel eyes. "Can I be your date?"

I bit my lip and agreed, "Yeah, that would be good."

Danny quirked one corner of his lips. "I still have a tux

hanging in my closet." I wondered if it was the same one he was supposed to wear on our wedding, which was the same one he'd worn to prom.

"I'm sure it only needs a few minor adjustments." He laughed, and I playfully slapped his chest. He held me tighter and kissed my forehead again. "Come on, let's get you to your car."

We continued walking, and at some point, his hand touched the side of mine, then he intertwined our fingers. I wasn't going to admit it out loud, but I also didn't want to lie, Danny made me feel safe. He made me feel wanted. He made me feel.

*H*eading back to my parents', I saw how empty the roads were, and I couldn't resist speeding. I was driving a Porsche Carrera after all, circa 1990. If I'd had my Harley with me, I would be doing the same thing. Ten years ago, I would have been the person who'd tsked at such reckless behavior. It would be easy to say that living in San Francisco had given me need for unruliness, but San Francisco wasn't my first destination after leaving home. For at least a couple of years, I moved around to different states until I settled by the bay.

The reckless behavior came from me, from within.

Those few months after leaving Vermont, I was careful. Once I stopped checking to see if someone was following me, I let anger get to my head. Everything pissed me off. There was nothing stopping me. I was either going to live with wild abandon or die young. Either way, I didn't care. It wasn't until I met Nica that my wild ways pared down. Like a dirty mutt found by the side of the road, Nica had cared for me and forced me to see the proverbial silver lining.

When Daddy had told me about hiring his old buddy Frank, a private investigator, I was appalled, and then curious as to what the PI had reported to my father. Some of the shit I'd gotten into wasn't for the faint of heart.

As soon as I saw the figure standing in front of the massive house, I screeched to a stop, the tires of the Carrera throwing dust and gravel in the courtyard. Daddy looked pissed off, and boy did his stance—feet hip-width apart, large arms crossed over his massive chest, head raised—bring back memories. His anger had never been toward me, of course, I had always been his good girl. But I'd witnessed his ire at Charity time and time again. I killed the engine and stretched out of the car, the gravel crunching underneath my boots.

"She runs well," I said, throwing the keys at him.

He caught it in the air. Good to see he still had his quick reflexes. I'd have felt horrible if they'd smacked him on the head. Daddy nodded once, relaxed his entire body, and smiled. I released a sigh, not even realizing I'd been nervous enough to hold my breath.

"How was your trip to town?" my father asked.

I shrugged before I hugged and kissed him on the cheek. "It was fine. Glad to see the gossip mill isn't dead around here."

Daddy chuckled as we walked up the steps to the wrap-around porch. He sat on the swing, patting the cushioned seat beside him. I sat with my head on his shoulder. How many times had we sat on this very porch during nights like this? He'd always been open to me. He'd treated me like his equal, even when I was younger and too naive for the world. My last night in Stowe had ended the same way.

It was the night before my wedding. The night before a letter had somehow found its way to me and changed the course of the last ten years. It was the last letter from Charity.

"Do you miss her?" I asked because I had to know.

Daddy wrapped his arm around me and held me closer to him. "You know I do."

"Mom doesn't. There's no sign around the house she even existed." A silent wind blew, and the cicadas began their serenade to the night.

"Your mother has been in denial for years."

The heaviness of what we were talking about pressed down on my father. His sighs became deeper and the muscles of his arms tightened. "What happened after I left?"

He shook his head, and for a moment, I thought he wouldn't answer. "Your mother went ballistic. She blamed me for losing both her daughters. She said I was the wild one and you girls inherited the genetic anomaly from me."

"Genetic anomaly?" I raised my head to look into his eyes. There was hurt in them, in the deeper blues than mine.

"Those were her exact words. I didn't deny it. If I hadn't taken risks myself I never would have met her. You wouldn't have existed. But she didn't see it that way, not for a while."

I leaned on his shoulder again. "I bet she would never admit she was the reason Char left in the first place."

"Of course she does, Nugget. That's exactly why there are no photos of your sister around the house. Your mother thinks it's a constant reminder of how she has failed as a mother." I let this truth sink in, and wondered if all of my mother's gaiety wasn't a ruse to cover up what she really felt. "Tell me though, Nugget, what did you think you were going to accomplish when you left? Did you think you were going to find her?"

It had been my plan, and I hated to admit it now. I'd known it was futile even before it began. Charity had been missing for five years when I left Vermont. Several years before that, she'd run away. Char was eighteen when she'd told our parents she'd wanted to travel and see the world, to experience life in faraway places, to not be bounded by borders and rules, to figure out who she really was. Who she could be. When I turned six that year, she'd sent me a *wayang golek*, an Indonesian puppet doll used for theatre. The presents had continued until I was thirteen, when my sister was never heard of again.

I had intended to use a piece of the doll's fabric in my bouquet. In the morning of my wedding, while going through boxes in my closet to look for the puppet doll, I'd come upon Charity's unopened letter, buried under photos and mementos. It was addressed to me. I'd ripped it open and read it.

Take a risk while you're young, Char had said in her letter.

What could she have meant? *Was it somewhat similar to the risk I was taking marrying so young?* I'd wondered. But there had been no danger in being Danny's wife. I'd been completely enamored with him. I'd thought I wasn't taking a risk.

"What risk, Char?" I'd asked myself and the humid summer air around me.

And without hesitation, I'd left to find her and ask her myself.

Did I think I was going to find her? Maybe I did, once upon a time.

"I hoped I would," I answered my father. "When I got to the airport, somehow I knew she wouldn't have wanted me to. She'd wanted me to live my own life and find my own happiness."

Daddy kissed the top of my head, and breathed in. "Not a day passes that I don't wish your sister would one day reappear, that we would find a photograph of her in a magazine, much like how your mother found you. I'd never stopped having you looked after while you were gone. And trust, Nugget, when I say I have yet to stop searching for her."

❧

After reading Char's letter for the umpteenth time, I laid my head on the soft pillows, listening to the symphony of nature around me, and the soothing noises of a house settling for the night. Charity, even in her wildest days, had been creative and organized, and my mother had relied heavily upon her talents and skills. Years before, while my father was healthy and admired by all, Mom had pushed him to run for governor. My mother had hopes and dreams. She'd made use of Charity for fundraising events, for Daddy's campaigns, and whatever she and the Gee-gees, the name Danny came up with for her posse, would come up with. But the pressure on Char had been too much. She hadn't wanted to be a part of any of it, but day in and day out, she'd done what she was asked.

Nica reminded me of Char, with her innate ability to turn the most boring event into a flamboyant affair. And that was why I'd attached myself to Veronica and never let go.

I dialed her number.

She picked up right away, sounding groggy, "Hey, Chase."

"Are you in bed already? That little creature tiring you out?"

"It's not that. We arrived early this morning and I'm just catching up on my sleep." Nica grunted and the ruffling of the sheets told me she was trying to sit up in bed.

"Arrived where?"

"Oh right." She paused for a yawn. "We're in New York City."

"What are you doing there?"

Nica spoke through another yawn. "Alex called and asked us to come." His name through my phone made my heart beat in allegro. "He rode his bike all the way here. Anyway, he asked us to come and meet someone."

"Who?" I sucked in a hiss, hoping Nica couldn't tell the trepidation in my voice.

"A girl. Levi said she must be someone special for Alex to get us packing in a rush..."

My throat closed up.

Steadying my breathing, I returned to the conversation. Nica was telling me about the party Gerard took over for me, how successful it had been.

"Hey, Nica, I have an idea."

Nica stammered, "Y—Yeah?"

I gripped my phone tighter and ground my teeth together, trying to keep myself from falling apart. "Why don't you come and visit me here, since you're so close?" I cleared my throat so my words came out crystal clear. "Bring Levi...and Alex and his girl." I might have swallowed that last word. "Mom is having a party for me this weekend."

"A party? I don't know if we can make the party, but I would love to see you. I'll talk to Levi when he gets back. He's at a fashion show with Alex, playing model."

"What? You know, I don't even want to know what that means, but okay. Just call me and let me know when you're all coming." And I could make Alex see I was just as happy with Danny as he was with his special someone.

ALEX

*T*he light had been hitting her features just right.
If I'd angled the camera another degree to the
right, I would have completely missed the little smile
playing on the corner of her lips. She had no idea I'd taken
the photo, and for a second, it had seemed perverse to do
it, but I had to capture the moment she said my name in
her sleep.

I'd waited for her to say more. But she'd only followed
it with that smile. It was rather brilliant. Beautiful. One
that poured out of her soul and melted the iciest of hearts.
It was special...unique. She wasn't the kind of woman
who'd offer anything so pure to just anyone. *I* mattered to
her. She smiled because she thought of me.

Did she also dream of me?

"*Hayati*?" I'd gently swept a finger over her hair. She
didn't stir.

Though I would remember it forever, keep it carved in
my heart, the photographer in me had to catch it on film. It
was the moment I'd known I wanted to be with her and
only her.

"Are you ready?" A tinny voice distracted me.

I cleared my throat, and moved the cursor up the screen
to close the window on my MacBook, trembling as though
I'd just been caught watching pornography with my

trousers down. I couldn't even remember how long I'd been staring at the photograph. At *her*.

Cara, with all her youthful exuberance, skipped to me and arranged herself on the sofa, her legs folded under her. "What's the matter, Alex?" She drew her brows in and cupped my chin to face her. "Are you kicking yourself for saying no to Levi and Veronica?" She pouted.

Pulling away from her, I grabbed a handful of my hair and tugged. "Not at all," I lied. "There's nothing there for me." I fiddled with my watch, and refused to look at her, fearing she'd see the truth in my eyes.

"I heard it's nice there all year 'round." She slid all the way to the other end of the sofa and leaned her head on the armrest, while she swung her legs over my lap. "I wouldn't mind seeing Vermont. I've never been there."

"You've never been anywhere, Cara," I reminded her, and evaded the topic altogether. "But I'm taking you to France to see Martina before your mother changes her mind...again." I pushed her legs off my lap, but she instantly brought them back up again. Whoever said sisters were sweet had brothers. "Get off, Cara, I have to shower and get ready for tonight."

Cara propped herself up, quickly leaned in to sniff me, and lay back down. "Yeah, you need it." Her laughter filled the lounge.

I pushed her legs off again with more force this time, without hurting her. Cara was as fragile as a girl her age can be, even though she tried to deny it. "Did you make reservations?"

"Duh." She rolled her eyes.

"It's a yes or no. I don't know what 'duh' means." I reached forward to close the lid on my Mac and headed to the bathroom.

"Yes, I did. I had to use my celebrity status to get it too. You owe me one," she proudly said.

I turned back to face her. "How about I pay for dinner? Is that good enough?" She shrugged and flipped her hair over her shoulder. I took it as an affirmation.

In the glass-enclosed shower, while I tried not to think of the woman who had been haunting me in my sleep, a jarring thought came to mind. Slipping out of the stall, I grabbed a towel and haphazardly wrapped it around my hips, letting soapy water drip all over the rug as I dashed back to the lounge. I found my Mac off, and Cara had returned to her room, where I could hear her singing some obscure pop song. Leaving her alone with access to my laptop had bad written all over it. In a matter of minutes, she would have blogged the goings-on of my life to millions of her social media followers.

The first time I'd experienced the wrath of Cara's blog entries was the time I'd introduced myself as her half-brother. She'd stood dumbfounded, but little did I know, behind the quiet reception, she was formulating words to her next blog entry. For days afterwards, I'd received emails from random strangers about the heartfelt story of an older half-brother who sought out his younger sister, estranged by the fault of our father. I'd thought it was bizarre.

Then I began receiving attachments of naked, supposedly "single" women of all ages. It turned out, Cara's second entry had been about my single status, and she'd even included a photo. I'd forced her to take down the posts and got a new email address. Since then, I'd been careful about leaving too much valuable information around her. If Cara found out about Chase, I could only imagine what she would feel compelled to do.

Earlier in the week, Levi and Veronica's visit had made its way to her blog, even before their plane touched down in New York City. Levi wasn't too thrilled about it, but his loving wife thought it sweet.

Before returning to the shower, I vowed to delete all of Chase's photographs. There was no sense of holding onto them, not when she had clearly moved on. *Tonight*, I told myself, *tonight I'll rid myself of those memories*. I would let go of her, once and for all.

By the time I went to bed, after an exhausting dinner with the talkative Cara and her friends, whom she had completely forgotten to inform me were joining us, thoughts of Chase haunted me once again. Her voice filtered into my lulled mind. And if I closed my eyes and forced myself to remember, I could smell the scent of her skin, feel the way the ends of her lush, dark hair tickled my chest while she laid her head on it, and see the complete rapture on her face when she climaxed.

Not since my late ex-fiancée, Simone, had I felt anything like this.

Sleep wouldn't come tonight, and hadn't since the day she left. Giving up on it, I walked over to the desk and fired up my Mac, bringing up the photos as soon as I could.

Let me soak her in for one more night, recall the laughter we'd shared together, the feel of her warmth around me, the beat of her heart, the ragged, sweet breaths she released in ecstasy, just for tonight. And tomorrow...tomorrow I would stop chasing the woman who refused to have me in her life.

L'appel du vide

CHASE

*D*eft fingers traced lines over my naked back, followed by hovering lips. My skin raised, serotonin pumped furiously out of my brain. I loved this feeling. I loved the way he could turn my insides into mush. He was my serenity.

"Don't be afraid to take a leap of faith." I was reawakened by a burning desire for a man who had asked me to take a chance with him.

He whispered my name the moment he filled me, and recklessly I fell into the throes of passion. "Open your eyes, *hayati*."

I did.

Oh, how cruel the world could be. When I blinked my eyes open to a pink, floral chintz room, and found myself alone in bed, the weight of loneliness crushed my heart against my chest. I shouldn't be dreaming of *him*, but I did because my mind hadn't been filled with anyone else but *him*. Whatever happened to "out of sight, out of mind"? Clearly, it had worked for him. Why couldn't it be the same with me?

I needed a distraction, something to keep myself busy enough I wouldn't be thinking of *that man*, who, henceforth would remain nameless.

My phone rang. I snatched it from the bedside.

"Yeah?" I was disgruntled.

"Good morning!"

Before I grunted my answer once again, I coughed to clear my throat. "Good morning, Danny."

"Still not a morning person, I see," he joked.

I tried to release a chuckle but it sounded like I was choking on spit instead. "Mornings and I have an understanding." At least I'd thought so until I moved back here. The summer sun in Stowe loved to get up early. In San Francisco, there were days when the sun didn't show up until past noon, hiding behind the heavy clouds until it was ready. My kind of sun. I also had had lined blinds to shut out the world. My kind of window dressing.

Danny's chuckle was different though. It was rough around the edges but sexy and smooth through and through. "I was just talking to your Dad, and he said he's hoping to take you to the farm today."

"Oh, is he?" It was nice of people to plan my days for me around here.

"He said you've been bored out of your head. So I was wondering..." Danny's voice lowered. "...if I can take the afternoon off, can I meet you at the farm and take you for a little picnic?"

I pinched the bridge of my nose and cracked my jaw. Danny was sweeter than cotton candy. When was the last time I went for a picnic? When was the last time I'd gone on a date?

"You know what, Danny, I'd like to go for a picnic with you."

"Are you sure? It sounds like you're not fully convinced."

He might be right. But what had I told Nica when she came home from Paris after realizing she was in love with the wrong man? (Who turned out to be the right one after all, but that was beside the point). I told her to "buck up, sistah from another mistah." It was time I sloughed the whine off me.

"I would love to go on a picnic, Danny," I said again, and this time, with a smile.

"Perfect. Dress for the heat today. It's bound to be a scorcher."

After getting off the phone, I had a long shower and rummaged through my luggage for something to wear. I hadn't unpacked. That would make all of this too real. I pulled out a black tank and ripped jeans. Since I hadn't worn shorts in San Francisco, mostly for safety reasons when I rode my Harley, I would have to make a pair. I cut the jeans shorter and frayed the edges. Over a black lace bra, I donned a tank top, which read, I'm cute as hell, which incidentally, is where I came from. With a pair of Converse, I was ready for a high-heat, high-humidity day.

When I reached the sunroom where my parents always had their breakfast, my Mom's glare was enough to melt me on the spot.

"If you think you're leaving the house with that shirt on, you've got another think coming, Chastity!"

I rolled my eyes and begged my father silently to get her off my back. He kept his eyes down, focusing on the local newspaper, but there was a telltale shake of his shoulders from a silent laugh.

"I'm almost thirty years old, Mom. I can—"

"Then dress like one."

I grunted and groaned and colorful swear words danced on the tip of my tongue. Daddy glanced up from his paper and gave me a pleading look. Fine. He'd better know I was doing this for him. I ran back to my room and picked out a different shirt. A grey tank, which asked people reading the block letter print if my sass was too much for them.

No way was I facing off with my Mom again. She could make me feel like a pouty teenager. And besides, I was still angry at her for not telling me about the party. I went to the kitchen and had a better time eating breakfast while listening to Paul-squared bicker. They reminded me a little of Mateo and Gerard, but I wasn't going to ask if either of the Pauls were gay.

God, I missed my friends.

Our farm was a twenty-minute drive out of Stowe. Well, the edge of it was. When the boundaries kept going, I asked Daddy how much land he had taken over. He responded with 'lots'. I made a mental note to ask Danny later.

We brought with us, in an attached trailer smelling of animal dung, the new cow. It was an adorable Holstein. As she made her way out of the trailer, I patted her bum, feeling sorry for the black and white, which would be used for dairy and freshening.

Several people my father greeted seemed to recognize me. Daddy would, seconds later, inform me who the people were. They were a polite bunch, clearly hard-working, much like Daddy. Since he was expected not to work at all, I kept a wary eye on him. If he even lifted a strand of hay, I'd scold him.

Soon after, Danny arrived, and he was as well-known to the workers as my father was. He strutted in jeans and a plain white T-shirt, confidence oozing from his pores. Okay, maybe it was sweat, but even that made him look appealing. I found my throat suddenly as dry as a stack of hay.

As Danny neared, his eyes wandered down to my chest and I caught him grinning at the words on my tank top.

"Your Mom let you wear that out?" he said before he kissed the cheek I offered.

"I evaded. She saw my first choice and got me to change, though."

Danny let out a small laugh. He led me out of the barn after we said goodbye to my father. Daddy's right-hand man said he would to report to me if he lifted a finger and promised to get him back home safely.

"Have fun, Nugget," Daddy said.

Even when we were younger, Danny had always been a gentleman. He opened the door for me, and helped me get settled in his massive Ford truck. I spied the picnic basket sitting on the backseat, and let myself relax.

"Where are we going?" I asked as he settled in the driver's seat.

Leaning a hand on the back of my seat, he reversed the truck, and answered, "Down toward the lake, then we'll go for a canoe ride."

"A canoe ride? You can't be serious."

Danny paused and smiled at me, "I don't ever joke about canoes, Hannah, you know that." I gave him a playful push on the chest. He captured my hand and kissed my knuckles. And he kept it held in his as we drove north toward a lake Danny and I had frequented when we were younger.

Sure enough, when we got to the edge of the trail, a canoe was waiting for us.

We paddled for a bit. The water was dark green and calm. We pulled the oars in and settled for a picnic on a canoe.

He was reliving our first date. Although some of the details were more elegant and adult this time around—wine, cheese and crusty bread, a bowl of sliced fruits, jam and honey. And unlike the last time we did this, Danny had remembered to bring me sunscreen. Years ago, I'd returned home red as a Maine lobster after being in the sun for too long. And blissfully in love.

Reminiscing was too easy, especially when we were ignoring the obvious. He was on a date with his runaway bride. Despite having talked about it back in his hotel in San Francisco, before I decided to move back, I still wasn't too sure if he had completely forgiven me. Would I have if he had done the same thing? No, I would have tracked him down and castrated him.

After lunch, we paddled again and ended up at the other end of the lake. We tied the canoe around a tree. Danny dragged me to another part and pointed at a rope hanging off a large branch.

"Remember that?"

"Yeah. What happened to the tire swing?" At the end of the rope, instead of an old tire, which had been there last time I was here, was a long, thick handle, a branch.

"I replaced it," Danny said while he pulled off his shirt and his jeans, leaving his boxers, thankfully.

I stood with my mouth to the ground. Damn, what a body! How he stayed single all these years was bewildering. "What are you doing?"

His grin went from one ear to the next. "Going for a swim." And without hesitation, he ran, screaming, reached for the handle, swung his body up and released as he rose high above the lake. Moments later, his head bobbed up and he waved at me, urging me to do the same. "Come on in, Hannah! The water's great."

I bit my lip before stripping down to my undies, kicking

off my shoes, and taking off to join Danny in the water. I gasped when the rope pulled me up into the air, and screamed when I let go. The water was a great coolant after being under the hot sun. We were like two teenagers splashing at each other and chasing one another into and out of the lake, taking turns on the rope swing.

As the skies clouded over, we laughed and treaded water. And in another second, we were holding onto each other. My breathing slowed as Danny held me in his strong arms. His hazel eyes turned brooding, his lips puckered.

Caution bells rang in my ears.

"We better go." He raised his eyes to the clouds. "It looks like it might rain after all."

I followed him out of the water and put on my clothes, which instantly got soaked the moment they hit my body.

"We don't have far to go," Danny said, and I just nodded.

I helped him pull the canoe in and carried the picnic basket while he carried the oars. He seemed to know the lay of the land. I followed him quietly.

Just that morning, I had dreamt about another man.

As I wasn't paying attention to where I was going, my foot caught a root poking out of the ground and down I went.

"Hannah! Shit!" Danny dropped the oars and ran back to me, and my wounded pride.

"I'm fine." I sat on the ground, bending my knees to assess the damage. Blood seeped out of the broken skin on my shin up to my right knee, and my right palm and arm.

"Yeesh, you're bleeding."

"It's just a flesh wound, Danny."

But he ignored me. He scooped me up in his arms.

"Please let me down. I can walk," I protested, although my hands made their way around his neck.

"Your ankle might be strained. I have a first aid kit in the house." He ignored my protestations and kept moving.

"What house?" As I asked the question, a log cabin appeared on our line of sight. "You live there?"

Danny nodded. "Don't worry, it looks better inside."

I didn't know why he had said that because even from the outside, it was quite a place. It had a shingled roof, a porch and a balcony jutting out on the other side, facing the water. The greenery, shrubs and flowers around it were well cared for. When we reached the door, Danny asked me to open it.

"You always leave your house unlocked?"

"No one comes around here much. It's just me and you." Was it just me, or was that heavy with innuendo?

He wasn't wrong, though—it did look better inside. Actually, it matched. The house was professionally decorated. Danny couldn't have done this on his own. Maybe he had even lived with a woman before. Maybe he brought one-night stands here.

Danny propped me on a light blue couch, and asked me to stay put while he went to grab the kit. I barely had time to snoop before he came back with a large first aid bag. "I'm a volunteer firefighter." Why wouldn't he be?

After he'd cleaned up the mess I'd made on my leg and arm, he brought me a change of clothes, a Harvard shirt and boxers, and carried me to the bathroom.

"Just throw your wet clothes in the hamper and I'll put them in the dryer. Then I'll make us dinner."

"Dinner?"

"Yeah, is that okay? Or...do you want to go home now?"

Did I? What did I want? Return to my parents' house where I'd continue to ignore the pain and sorrow surrounding me? Or stay with Danny and let him take care of me, much like he had years before?

"Hannah, what do you say?" His hazel caught the light, even though they were surrounded with thick dark lashes. He looked hopeful as he bit his lower lip.

I touched his chin and made him release his lip. "Yeah, I think I'll stay."

*I*f I had to name the emotion pouring out of my heart the moment I opened my eyes and saw Danny beside me, it would have been nostalgia. It was immediately followed by soul-sucking, punch-to-the-nose guilt. I didn't want to admit to myself that I was conscious of the reason why. I wasn't going there. I refused to think of *him*.

But I couldn't help but question myself. What was wrong with me? I lay beside one man and thought of another as I did. This was becoming somewhat of a habit. When did I become this person? This woman? What was I doing with Danny when I constantly thought of Alex…er…*him*?

Danny was unaware of any of this, of course. Despite the amount of talking we'd done the night before out on his deck, I hadn't told him about Alex. He was *my* secret. I choked up at the thought. Alex wasn't mine. And he would never be mine.

Here, I had Danny. Relaxed, charming, caring, not to mention extremely good-looking. He was perfect in every way. Perfect on paper. Perfect in the flesh. Yet, my heart still cried out for Alex.

I sat up, cradling my head in my hands and rubbing my eyes. Without even a thought yesterday, I didn't put make up on. Why? Was I reverting back to the old me? To Hannah? If that was the case, what would happen to Chase?

Danny moved beside me, curling his arms around my waist. "Why are you up so early—" He peered at me through one opened eye. "—on a Saturday?"

I pushed his messy hair off his forehead. We'd fallen asleep in our clothes. Well, I was still in his clothes, borrowed while mine dried. Déjà vu was all over this moment. By the time we'd been engaged, half the clothes I'd wear to bed had been Danny's. Back then, I'd been an early riser, accustomed to my father's routines, even on weekends.

"I have to get back home before the parental units start to worry."

Danny pulled me back down to the bed and kissed one of my shoulders. "I'll drive you home. Give me a minute to wake up."

That was easy. I thought he would at least try something this morning considering he didn't try anything last night. Who would believe me if I told them nothing happened? Sadly, I knew a bunch of people who would ask.

Danny didn't even try to kiss me, even though there were plenty of perfect times to do so.

Danny released me and pushed the blanket aside. "There's a spare toothbrush in the bathroom," he said as he sat on the edge of his bed. The mattress sagged under his weight.

And that was that. The walk to memory lane ended.

❧

Having left his truck on the other side of the lake the previous day, Danny had the chance to let me ride with him in the Camaro. It was a sexy car, as sexy as the driver. But my God, he was a careful driver. No matter how much I urged him to speed a little, Danny refused. I rolled my eyes when he said he had a reputation to keep up.

When I reached home, it was difficult to sneak through the kitchen. A few trucks were parked along the road to the house. Caterers, party suppliers, florists and all their staff worked on the Buford grounds. All for a party I didn't ask for. I nodded a greeting at Paul-squared, and ignored their delighted looks when Danny followed after. The caterers brought their own employees in, taking over one-half of the large kitchen. Chef Paul didn't seem to mind, which was odd. I'd known other people in his line of work who'd get bent out of shape when others used their space.

"Hey, guys," Danny greeted the kitchen staff—ours and the caterer's. "Can I get a plate, Paul? Bring it over to the sunroom." He grabbed a cup from a cupboard and proceeded to pour coffee into it.

This made me raise my eyebrows up to my forehead, thinking, "Make yourself at home, Danny." Then I checked myself. I was the stranger around here. He might even have hired the two Pauls. Last night, he'd explained in detail what his role was in my father's business. Basically, without Danny, our business would have sunk years ago. As a gesture of gratitude from my father, he had given Danny a large piece of the farm, where his cottage now stood. Although with Daddy's big heart, he'd probably given him more, and I wasn't talking about land.

"Hannah? Hannah?"

I shook my head when Danny snapped his fingers in front of me. Who does that? I narrowed my eyes at him. "Yeah?"

"Are you having breakfast with us?" he asked, raising a cup to his lips.

I shook my head again. No way. "I'm going to shower and change."

"Okay. Won't you at least say good morning to your parents?" he practically ordered. Ordered, not suggested! Chase would have reacted, but Hannah...Hannah always complied.

"Yeah, I should."

I followed him to the sunroom, where my parents sat finishing their meal. My mother had a smile on her face the size of the iceberg that sank the Titanic. Daddy was a little amused and paid more attention to his cup than to us. Mom preened when Danny chose the seat beside her.

"Oh, Chastity, your dress for tonight's party is in your boudoir."

Boudoir? My dress? "You got me a dress?" I was half-crazed. I imagined finding a pink frilly dress made with yards of tulle and bedazzled with rhinestones. "Mom, I have a dress picked," I lied. "And speaking of which, thank you very much for telling me about this party." I let the sarcasm hang in the air.

Mom didn't pick up on it, or she chose to ignore it. Her earlier grin reappeared. "You're welcome, dear," she said in a sing-song voice.

My mouth hung open, but before I could throw a retort, I caught my father's pleading look. My jaw clenched. Danny seemed oblivious to all this. I left the sun-filled room without another word.

❧

I fumed in the shower, murmuring within the glass and tiled walls. I pushed aside the garment bag when I opened the closet to access my luggage, pulling out a black jersey dress.

A knock interrupted my hair-drying. I groaned, tempted to shout "go away" to whoever was on the other side.

"Nugget," my father called.

I dropped the towel on the vanity and walked to the door, leaning back against the wood. "What is it, Daddy?"

"Little chat? I brought coffee and pancakes. Paul said you like them."

I twisted the doorknob and grabbed the tray from Daddy.

We sat on my bed, my legs crossed over the mattress as I rubbed my hands together before digging into my plate. "You talk. I eat." I pointed a fork at Daddy.

He poured more maple syrup over my pancakes from a tiny dispenser before he spoke. Sweetening me up before the chat. Not good. "Did you look at your dress?"

"Choose another topic." I talked around the pancake in my mouth.

He sighed heavily, but chuckled. "Your mother has invited all of our friends to this party..."

"Next," I interrupted, cutting small pieces of the pancakes for easier consumption.

I waited three, four seconds for Daddy to talk again, but he didn't. He just watched me eat. His blue eyes were glazed over. Was it a side effect from his medications? How much pain was he in? Why was I giving him a hard time? I had to remind myself why I came back. Daddy.

I set the fork and knife aside, ready to surrender, but the words that came out of my mouth surprised me. "Why do you put up with her? With mom? She's pushy. She nags. She's really annoying. And she doesn't seem like she cares about anyone's feelings other than her own. I didn't ask for this party. I didn't ask her to get me a dress. I didn't ask her for anything. I would never ask her. And she does the same thing with you. So why, Daddy? Why do you let her do it?"

Daddy lifted the tray and placed it on my bedside table.

"Hannah..." he paused, possibly to think things through before he answered me. "When you left, your mother was all I had," he began. "When your sister disappeared, I had you, and you had me. Who do you think your mother turned to?" He didn't want an answer, continuing his explanation, "She had herself. And did you ever hear her complain that we kept to ourselves?"

"No." It was true. My mother only shed tears behind closed doors, when she'd thought no one was listening on the other side. "But I thought she had the Gee-gees?"

"Sure, it may seem like it. But you know her, she kept a lot to herself. When you left, I turned to her, and she didn't complain. She put up with me. Then, Danny returned home and he and I became close. Still, your mother had only herself. Not one complaint, Nugget, not one." Daddy raised a pointer finger in front of me. "And guess who picked up the pieces when I was diagnosed with cancer?"

Mom. I didn't say it out loud, but Daddy nodded.

"You see, Nugget, without your mother I would have fallen apart in an instant. She may seem difficult to you, but without her, I would be... I don't even want to think about it." Daddy squeezed my shoulders, then lifted my chin. "I am not putting up with her. I am grateful for each and every moment she has stayed with me through the good and bad. Anytime I can repay that, even if it means sitting through two hours of opera, I wouldn't hesitate."

Shit. When he put it that way, who could argue?

"Now, tell me, what's going on with you and Danny? Because you know your mother. If you don't clear it up with her, she'll have you sized up for another wedding dress."

That was cringe-worthy. "Danny and I are friends." I played with the hem of my dress.

He waited for me to explain further, but I couldn't, not if I didn't even know what the real answer was.

"Well, he did say he'll be your date at the party."

"Oh, shit." I did agree to that, didn't I? "It can't be that bad, can it?"

With a closed fist, Daddy nudged my chin. "I'm sure you can handle it." Daddy carefully got up, holding to the bed for support. "Rest up. Your mother hired the armada for tonight. I doubt you'll be needed for anything." And with a kiss to my forehead, he left.

꙰

"It's going to be horrible," I griped over the phone. "If my entire bedroom's pink, it could for sure cross my Mom's mind to choose a pink dress for me too, Nica." I had called her to get some kind of support. "There was no hiding from the party, but at least I could choose my own dress, right?"

"Just check it out first, Chase," she said.

"I knew you'd say that." I blew a harsh breath out between my clenched teeth, as I pulled open the closet doors. With the phone held between my ear and shoulder, I zipped open the garment bag. "Here we go. Moment of truth…" Then I released a dramatic gasp as I got a first peek of the dress. "Not pink." I continued to unzip it and gaped at the royal blue silk chiffon dress. It was simple, with thick straps and a sweetheart neckline. It was a layered sheath, and the fabric was a luscious silk. And there weren't any adornments on it. Not a single rhinestone. With swept up hair, a pair of diamond earrings, a silver cuff, and a pair of nude shoes, I would look glamorous in it.

"Chase? Chase, what does it look like?"

I nearly forgot about Nica. "Not pink."

"Black?"

"Nope. It's a rich, royal blue. Here I'll send you a photo." I held my phone up to take a quick picture and sent it to my best friend.

"Wow. That's wow. Try it on!" she screamed into the phone.

"Hey, no need to yell. Gimme a sec. You want me to call you back or..."

"Yeah, put it on, pair it with those gorgeous shoes you wore at last year's Christmas gala at the Benjamin's..."

See, this was why we were besties, we had like minds.

I did just that. My body shape had changed since my mother stopped buying clothes for me, and changed more after I'd been on my own. But the dress fit like a glove, displaying my tatas in an elegant way. I was a bit delighted that even with the lack of regular exercise, my arms stayed toned, and the swim from yesterday had given my skin a sun-kissed hue. I did my own hair, sweeping it up into a messy chignon, and applied my patented smoky eyes and blood-red lips.

Nica responded to my photo text immediately and captioned it with, **Rawr! Go get 'em, tiger!**

I wasn't entirely sure what she meant, but I sent a **Thanks!** just in case she meant it as a compliment.

I also sent Danny a text, asking what time he'd show up and if we should walk into the party together or separate. His response was instantaneous:

I've been here for half an hour.

Well, gee, thanks for telling me, date. But I replied with:

I'll be down in a minute.

Danny stood at the bottom of the grand staircase. His smile illuminated the room as he spotted me at the top. He wore a tux, as promised, and James Bond had nothing on him. He gave me a chaste peck on the cheek, whispering, "You look gorgeous."

"So do you." I hooked my arm into the crook of his elbow and walked with him toward the back of the house.

Danny leaned into me. "I have a few people I'd like you to meet."

"Oh, really? I thought this was my party," I joked, even though I would feel like an alien in it. A stranger, who guests would gawk at and chat about.

"It is. But these are very important people."

As soon as we were out in the yard, the sensation of a hundred eyes on me took effect in an instant. I wasn't shy by any means, but I often avoided being the center of attention, despite what folks in California had believed, unless it was absolutely necessary. Tonight was going to be the Chase/Hannah show. My own version of the parable, "The Prodigal Daughter". My own version of a nightmare.

In my bedroom, I'd convinced myself Danny would help me out and make things easier for me, make this whole night more palatable. But as we walked through the crowd, he shone. He loved the attention. This wasn't the Danny I'd known. This was someone else. I watched him curiously.

He introduced me to several politicians and influential members of the community.

When I reached for my third—only third—glass of champagne from a passing server, Danny muttered in my ear, "Slow down, Hannah." I gaped at him, and saw the rest of what he thought filling his eyes—*Don't embarrass me.*

I sucked in a breath and plastered the most polite smile I could muster on my face. "Excuse me, I need to use the..." Oh why bother? This party wasn't for me. This was for Danny.

As soon as I was far away enough from all of them, I

chugged the champagne and grabbed two more from a table. Those got chugged too. From across the way, I caught my mother's eyes and one raised eyebrow. I waved at her with the two champagne flutes in my hands, then proceeded to walk into the house.

"They do make a lovely couple," I overheard as I neared the sunroom.

"She is beautiful, and Daniel is very handsome," another said.

From the tone of their voices, I could assume that they were part of the Gee-gees, Mom's posse. What were they doing away from their leader?

"Well, they would photograph well together. It would help Daniel's image during the campaign."

Campaign? What campaign?

"That's if she doesn't run away again. The publicity would be horrible for Daniel. Who would want a governor who couldn't pin down his future wife?"

Governor? Future wife? What the hell?

I continued walking and stopped in front of the women. Their mouths popped open. They'd spilled everything, of course. I was Georgia-Anne Buford's daughter after all. By blood, I was part of them. But I had a bigger target, and I could see him past the windows of the sunroom.

Sehnsucht

y eyes were locked on Danny as I stomped my way out of the house and back onto the lawn. My fingernails bit the skin of my palms.

"Chastity, dear! Oh, Chastity!" my mother called out, waving her hand, smiling from one diamond solitaire earring to another. She reached me as I was halfway to Danny; my hackles raised.

"Not now, Mom," I shooed her away, but she grabbed a hold of my arm, and forced me to face her.

"Don't make a scene, Chastity," she said in a quiet, but firm tone. "You've done enough of that to last us a lifetime." There was a flash of anger in her eyes, so quickly gone that I thought I'd imagined it, but with the way her lips were set, I wasn't easily convinced of her rapid change in mood. She sent a fake smile across the way.

I stepped forward and she marched right with me. "Why don't we talk inside?" It wasn't a suggestion. It was an order.

Mom gripped my arm tighter. Past her shoulder, I got a glimpse of Daddy, a few feet away from us, with a worried look on his tired face, and I recalled what he had told me earlier. I turned away from my mother and walked back into the house, all the way to my father's office. The reprieve would only give me time to concoct a plan on how to get away with murder.

Even the office wasn't saved from my mother's ill

attempts at decorating. It was safari gone bad, mixed with tacky island knickknacks. I walked straight to the large leather wingback chair and stood behind it and under deer antlers nailed on the wall. I dug my fingers into the back of the chair.

"Now, pray tell what has gotten your panties in a twist?" Mom chose the lounger along the full bookshelves.

"It was your idea, wasn't it?" I lashed at my mother.

"Whatever are you talking about, Chastity?" She flung the back of her hand to touch her forehead. And the dramatics began.

I kept my hand on the chair. "Danny's political plans. Running for governor? It doesn't sound like Danny."

"I'm not sure what you're on about. Danny would make a fantastic governor. We all know he would be a great candidate."

"We? As in you and the Gee-gees? Will Danny have a say in this?"

Mom's lips puckered. Deep grooves lined her forehead and extended from her narrowed eyes. She straightened on the lounger and raised her chin. "You have no idea what we have gone through, child."

"What, Mom?" I cocked my head to the side. "Tell me what have you gone through that makes you think you have the right to put your nose into other people's business, into my life?" I jabbed my chest for emphasis. I didn't give her a chance to reply. "I know Daddy didn't ask to have cancer."

I rounded the chair to get nearer to where she sat. "And Danny didn't ask for his mother to die. And I know Charity didn't ask for her plane to nose dive into the ocean. I know she was your favorite daughter, but she was my only sister!"

Her eyes glazed. Her chin lifted a little higher even when the threat of tears welled up in her eyes. I stood above her, towering over her as she just sat there. "What do you have to say about that, Mother?"

My father's voice boomed in the room. "That's enough!"

Behind him, Danny appeared, his eyes full of confusion and worry. I should tell him to go, to leave us to deal with our own family problems, but the way he stood with Daddy, a hand clasped on my father's shoulder, I saw he was a part of this family as much as I was, if not more.

I stepped back when Daddy walked straight to my mother and held onto her, letting her cry on his tux lapel.

What was I doing? Why was I here? I didn't belong here. This hadn't been my home for years.

I pushed past Danny who called after me as I ran out the door into the suddenly frigid air. Right around the corner, I spotted one of the servers starting his Ducati. I waved at him, and he waited until I reached where his bike idled.

"Where are you headed?" I asked.

"Center town," he spoke through an open visor.

"Good. D'you mind giving me a ride there?"

"Sure, hop on."

⚜

With no clear direction to go, I wandered down Main Street.

I passed by the General store with the old-school wooden sign and green awning, and recognized a somewhat familiar face. Danny's secretary, the quasi-Nica. What was her name? Tessa? Trisha?

As she walked out of the store, with a little boy at her heel, she greeted me, "Hi, Hannah!" Cheery.

"Hey…"

"Tiana." She placed her hand over her chest, nodded and smiled.

"Yes, hi, Tiana." I looked down to the little guy hiding behind her maxi skirt. "Yours?"

She looked down and ruffled his dark, curly hair. "This is Sky. Sky, can you say hi to Miss Hannah?"

The little boy, with eyes as wide as saucers, hid further behind his mom.

"He's a little shy," Tiana explained. "That's quite a dress you have on. Isn't your party tonight? I remember Danny talking about it. He asked me to get his tux dry cleaned."

"Yeah, it got to be a little much." What else was I going to say? I couldn't exactly tell a near stranger my life had suddenly turned into one big soap opera.

Tiana just smiled and nodded again. "Well, we just bought ice cream and popcorn. It's our movie night if you want to chill with us."

Was this a ruse to get me talking so she could spread the word about my effed up life?

"Is that okay? You don't mind?" I asked.

She ruffled her son's hair again. "We don't mind at all. My car is down the block." I followed along, trying not to scare the sweet looking boy. "I hope you like *Despicable Me*. It's our favorite."

"Sorry. I've never seen it."

Sky gasped at my comment, and pulled on his mother's skirt. Tiana bent down to his level. He whispered something to her, which made her laugh. "Yes, Sky, we will have to watch it from the beginning again. Maybe you can hold her hand if she gets scared?"

"Scared?" I mouthed the word to Tiana. She shook her head. "Oh yeah, that would be great, Sky. I don't like scary things." It must have worked as Sky held my hand with his little fingers and we continued to walk down the street.

I gotta say, I was pretty proud of myself. Normally, kids gave me a wide berth when they see me coming. I couldn't wait to give Nica a call and tell her I might possibly seem friendly to her soon-to-be born child.

¨

Tiana and Sky lived in a small cottage fifteen minutes from downtown Stowe. The flower garden was in full bloom under purple and orange sky, and the air was fragrant with their scent. I noted the absence of another car or any movements in the house, much like the lack of a wedding ring on Tiana's finger.

If I had to guess, she was around Nica's age, and Sky looked about four or five, which would have made her twenty-one when she had him. A young single mom in a small town? That was almost as scandalous as me leaving Danny at the altar.

"Sorry about the mess." Tiana ducked her head as she unlocked the door.

"Don't worry about it." When I entered her quaint little home, it was evident she had nothing to worry about at all. Her place, although a bit sparse of furniture, was impeccably clean.

It was a real home, with walls and shelves adorned with photos of her and Sky, and kid's paintings and drawings. There weren't signs of a man living in it. It had a welcoming feeling, a warmth, somewhere love was shared. The house where my parents lived now used to have this feeling, even with the difference in size to Tiana's cottage.

I ached for that home, where, once upon a time, I felt loved.

"Sky, can you set up the movie? Hannah, if you want to change out of that dress, I might have something that will fit you." Tiana placed the grocery bag on the table.

I assumed I had to follow her, so I did, and found her rummaging through her closet. She pulled out a gray shirt and yoga pants. I lifted the T-shirt, possibly a guy's, but I didn't ask. Then I inspected the pants. It had 'maternity' on the tag.

"They were mine when I was pregnant."

"No shit!" I slapped my hand on my mouth as soon as I said it, looking back at the door in hopes that my voice hadn't carried into the living room.

Tiana laughed. "Don't worry about it. When he's concentrating on something, he doesn't pay attention to anything else."

"Just like anyone with a *Y*-chromosome." This time, both Tiana and I laughed.

She left me alone to change. The shirt was well worn and comfortable, and to my surprise, so were the yoga pants. I made a mental note to ask Nica if she owned a pair. Since my shoes looked ridiculous with my new outfit, I slipped them off and took them with me to the living room.

When I got there, Sky and Tiana were seated on the small couch, their feet propped on the large ottoman. Sky had a small bowl of popcorn on his lap, while she had a bowl of Ben and Jerry's in her hand. She patted the empty space beside her.

As I sat down, she handed me a spoon. "I hope you like Chubby Hubby."

"What's not to love?" We laughed.

In that instant, I knew Tiana and I could be good

friends, if—and it was a big if—I stayed in Vermont. At that moment, I yearned for San Francisco, for my friends, for my apartment, for my different assistants whose name I could never remember. I yearned for my own life.

I yearned for Chase.

Commuovere

"**S**he's asleep... What was I supposed to do? No...of course not..."

From where I was curled up on the couch, tucked under a thick blanket, I could hear Tiana's voice coming from behind me. She was on the phone, and if I were to assume, with Danny. Her voice grew faint as she walked further into the house, and I heard a door shut.

I opened my eyes. I must have been exhausted. I couldn't remember how the movie ended. I stretched on the sofa. I barely fit in it but I had one of the best sleeps since coming back to Stowe. There was a clink of a utensil hitting a stoneware, and I looked over to see Sky seated on the dining table having his breakfast—a big box of chocolate-flavored cereal beside his bowl. I gave him a wave.

Sky slipped off his seat and ran into the kitchen. Maybe I should check to see how I looked since I slept with a pile of makeup on. My feet hit the area rug and I stretched up again as I stood. Sky came back with a bowl and spoon, placed it next to his, and poured sugar-filled cereal and milk in it. Then he walked over to me and led me to the table.

Aw, what a sweetheart.

"You are going to be a heartbreaker when you're older."

Tiana came back soon after, clutching her phone in her hand. "Oh you're up. We have other food with more sustenance. If you want I can make you an omelet."

I shook my head. "This is great."

"I was just on the phone with Danny," she said as she sat across from me. At least she's an honest person. "He asked me to call him back as soon as you're awake."

I waited to see what she would do. Danny was her boss after all. Tiana smiled at her son and me, scooping soggy cereal with our spoons.

"That does look good. I'm going to get a bowl. Coffee?"

My shoulders sagged. "Please." Ten years on my own and not bothering to learn how to cook, a pot of coffee was my usual breakfast.

"Good choice, Sky. I think I'll pick up a box of this for myself," I said, pouring more cereal and milk into the bowl.

Sky was a boy of few words. I had only heard him laugh the night before. He did keep saying "banana" while we watched the little yellow minions in the movie. Either I'd missed a part or he thought they looked like bananas. There was intelligence in his light brown eyes, and often, a thoughtful gaze, or a curious stare.

When Tiana returned with her bowl and two cups of hot coffee, she offered more news. "Danny sent a text. He said he's coming in ten minutes. Apparently, your friends are at your parents?"

"My friends?" I dropped the spoon into the bowl. "Oh crap. Nica!" She must have called me last night or this morning, but my phone was back in my bedroom. "Did he say how many people were there?" I couldn't exactly ask if Alex had also come with his girlfriend. Would he dare?

"No. Just a text saying your friends came." She placed a cup in front of me.

Raising the cup, a gloomy reflection on the dark liquid stared back at me. I looked a fright! My hair was a nest and my makeup had smudged all over my eyes. I was surprised Sky didn't scream when he saw me earlier.

When I finished my second bowl of cereal, I darted off to the bathroom with Tiana, where she handed me her makeup remover and a small washcloth. I was able to mangle my hair into some semblance of neatness when I heard Danny's voice. He wasn't exactly the person I wanted to see today but I didn't want to drag Tiana and Sky into our little drama.

When I made my way back to the living room, he was seated on the couch where I'd slept, with Sky on his lap. He seemed comfortable with Sky, and Sky with him. It was a surprise, since Danny didn't want kids, and he had never been around enough of them while we were growing up to be comfortable with them. But things could change in a decade.

"Hey," he greeted without a smile, his eyes full of concern and something else I refused to think of.

"Hey." I turned to Tiana and gave her a big hug for being my savior the night before. "Thanks for letting me crash your movie night and letting me drool on your couch."

"You're welcome anytime." She rubbed my back like Nica used to do, which was weirdly soothing. Maybe it had something to do with being a mom, although my mother had never done it to me.

I grabbed my dress and shoes, not bothering to put them back on, and walked barefoot out of the house, waving goodbye to Sky and his mom standing by their door.

"Bye, Sky!" I even blew him a kiss.

"Bye, Miss Hannah! Bye Uncle Danny!" He waved back.

I didn't wait for Danny to open the car door for me as I expected he would. I was pissed off at him, and I wanted to wring his neck, but not until he drove me back to my parents, and after I saw Nica.

We'd been in his Camaro for two quiet minutes, but the tension was thick enough to choke us. The radio was off and the loud engine was a welcome distraction.

"I'm sorry."

What was that? I glanced over at Danny with my lips set into a thin line. "What?"

For a second or two, he took his eyes off the road to look at me, gripping the wheel as his car crawled on the empty country road. He was taking his time and doing it on purpose. "I said I'm sorry...about last night. Your Dad told me you found out."

I scoffed and spat, "Yeah." I could claw his eyes out. During all those talks we'd had, not once had he ever mentioned running for governor.

"It wasn't my idea and truth be told, I don't think I'm going to do it. They've been pushing me for the last year to run in the next election."

He didn't have to specify who "they" were.

Danny continued, "You know how it can be around here. People speculate. They hear one tiny bit of information and paint a larger scenario in their heads with it." Out of the corner of my eye, I could see his hangdog expression. He could pout as much as he wanted; I was still going to remain unengaged, both in this conversation and in marriage.

"Please, Hannah, please know I had nothing to do with all of that. I didn't tell you about it because I didn't want you to think I was using your family's influence in the matter." Danny slowed the car even more and stopped along the side of the road. He angled his body toward me, and reached for my hand.

I sent him a seething look, which was hopefully enough to convey I wanted to bite his head off if he made another move. Danny was smart. He got the point. He lifted his palms up in surrender.

"I like you. You know that. One day, I hope we can continue what we started years ago, but right now, and until you're ready, I'd like us to be friends."

What could I respond with? Danny was a nice guy. He was one of the good ones, and he would make a great husband, but I wasn't sure if I was still marriage material. Apart from him, and for the last decade, I'd had no other serious relationship. I'd stayed away from that because of my past with Danny. Even with Alex, I hadn't been ready to explore that scenario. I couldn't say if I would ever be ready. Being in a serious relationship meant falling for someone, loving that person, and it would only result in heartache.

I had enough of that in this lifetime.

❦

I ran into the house and straight into the sunroom where I could hear Nica talking to my mother.

"Nica!" She sucked in a gasp when I wrapped her in the tightest hug. "Oh my god, I missed you!"

Her eyes widened into saucers when I held her an arm's length away. Her eyebrows were drawn together and her smile was toothy. She regarded me up and down and mouthed "what the heck" as she took in the zero makeup, plain gray shirt, yoga pants, which stopped above my ankles, and my bare feet. "Did you forget we were coming?" The curiosity and concern in her eyes spoke more. Was I allowed to tell her Vermont broke me?

"No. I...give me fifteen minutes to change and I'll be back down." Back to my usual self, I hoped.

"Okay," she squeaked out.

I gave her another hug before straightening, and only then did I note who else was in the sunroom with us. My mother, Daddy, and Levi. No Alex. No Alex's girlfriend. I didn't know if I should be happy or sad.

{🍂}

After showing them around my parents' estate, we drove to Maple Farm. Danny prepared everything for us, and volunteered to drive us in my Daddy's truck. I didn't argue. It would only make Nica more curious. I needed alone time with my bestie before I could spill the beans.

I spread out a large blanket under the maple trees and started handing out the food Chef Paul had made. Levi was very attentive to his wife, helping her sit on the ground. She'd grown so much bigger since the last time I saw her. Danny and Levi got along splendidly as they had back in San Francisco. If this wasn't bizarro world, the two of them would have made great friends.

The chatter was mostly about Nica and the baby, the business we owned, and changes in the weather in San Francisco.

When Danny offered to show Levi and Nica how the maple syrup was harvested and processed, Nica declined politely, telling him her feet were starting to swell and ache. Levi bent down to give his wife a kiss, and ordered me to take good care of her while he was away. I stuck my tongue out at him.

"Okay, spill." Nica clapped her hands. "What the hell happened to you? You're not yourself at all. You're so...docile."

Glancing away, tears prickled behind my eyes. Without another word, because I couldn't stop the world from spinning in the wrong direction, I cried.

"Geez Louise, Chase, what the heck did they do to you?" She rubbed my back and let me lean my head on her shoulder while my tears continued to fall.

Words wouldn't come out, and if they did, they were garbled nonsense. We weren't sure how long Danny and Levi would take, and soon after they rested, Nica and Levi would immediately head back to San Francisco. My head ached from all the crying and my chest filled with hurt and sorrow. I missed Nica. I missed my best friend. There were things we couldn't talk about over the phone. I took advantage of the short time we had.

I told her everything. I told her about my secret rendezvous with Alex. About Charity and why I had to leave Vermont and Danny, to search for my lost sister. I opened up about why I wanted to marry Danny back then, and why I couldn't see myself with him now.

Nica was speechless through all of it and right after. She didn't have to say anything. Her presence and listening were all I needed. She never judged me. She produced tissues from her purse and lent me her compact mirror, face powder, and her sunglasses to cover the horror of makeup I'd made with my tears.

I was a right mess. Moreover, I wasn't me.

We could hear the rumble of the truck drawing near.

"Chase," Nica started, her hands squeezing mine. "You know who you really are. Are you Chastity Hannah from Vermont, Princess of Maple? Or are you the feisty, takes no nonsense beast of a woman Chase who rode a Harley and lived a full life? Forget Alex and Danny for now, because I truly believe you can't love another person without loving yourself first. And if you don't know yourself, you can't love yourself. You said so yourself."

Fuck me, I did tell her that.

"I will love you no matter who you choose to be. You

know that, right?" God, this woman was good through and through. Why wasn't the world filled with people like her?

We hugged each other, with her belly squished between us.

Before they left for the airport, Nica reminded me that I would have to return to Napa for her baby shower. Gerard and Jewel were planning the damn thing. We both shuddered at what a colossal collision it could be. She also said she couldn't wait for me to meet Cara, Levi's half-sister, and the *special someone* Alex had talked about in New York.

With that short stay, Nica had given me something I knew no other person in my life right now could.

Hope, acceptance, belonging and unconditional love.

Pareidolia

ALEX

I'd gone off the deep end.

Cray-cray, as Cara put it. Half of the words she said weren't real words. I feared for her generation.

But she wasn't the reason I was going mental. It was that damn woman. Why couldn't I get *her* out of my mind?

Every morning, before the break of dawn, I would go for a run to try and rid my mind of her. The high from running was much more exhilarating than a cigarette. And it was much healthier too, no argument there.

During the visit with Levi, he'd asked me point blank over a pint, "What the devil are you on?" He'd somehow made me admit I was aching for a woman who'd cast me aside as though I were rubbish.

He'd called me a 'git'. And said I should either get her back or get over it.

I chose to run.

The trip back to France had a purpose. I'd planned it a while ago, and would have asked her to join me if she hadn't kicked me to the curb. If she'd asked, I would have given her the world, handed it to her on a fuckin' silver platter.

Duty to her family, or me. Those were her choices. I'd been in her position before, and I had chosen to live my own life. But the second time 'round, I'd chosen to do my due diligence and claim my rightful place on the Laurent throne. I would have understood the reasons, her reasons —it wasn't easy to deal with a family member threatened by illness—but not the fiancé that came with it.

I'd offered her all of me and she had given me nothing in return. I was in too deep. I was fuckin' hurt. Crushed and defeated.

Though I'd never said the words, I'd wanted to show her. Experience love with her.

Chase.

That was the joke, wasn't it? I was chasing a tail that belonged to someone else, like a mutt too stupid to realize and not change course. How many times had she tried to dissuade me? All along, I'd thought she was playing hard to get, but no, she was just playing me.

"Are you sulking again?" Cara looked up from her phone once and kicked my shin. She'd made herself home in Martina's house in Bordeaux. She took to the open air, and the sun shining over the vineyards. Martina, as expected, adored her.

"I don't sulk," I gritted out, sinking deeper into the well-worn chair.

"Mm-hmm. I know what sulking looks like, big bro."

Out of nowhere I had the urge to stick out my tongue at her, and so I did. She guffawed, slapping her leg with her free hand. I needed more time with adults, especially after a hard day in the fields. Once we arrived at Chateau Laurent, Martina had immediately set me to work, crouching down and plucking grapes off the vines. Muscles I didn't know existed creaked and caused me discomfort, but I couldn't complain about it. Not when Martina herself was out under the sun with us too. I bet people thought because I was the CEO of the business, I had it easy. Martina would never let me sit on my ass all day.

Whenever I was in the fields, shadows on the ground

would remind me of the curves of her body. My mind was playing havoc on my flailing sanity.

I scrubbed a callused hand over my face and groaned. Enough of this wallowing in self-pity. She was one woman. I'd had many women before her. I could have plenty more after her.

I planted my feet on the floor and tested my balance. My knees didn't give out, but my back ached if I stood erect. I could use a drink and better company. As I made my way to the door, Cara jumped off the sofa and rushed to reach me.

"Where are you going?" She didn't bother looking up from her phone as she spoke. I suspected she was about to post another entry on her blog. She'd admitted lately most of them were about me. I didn't bother arguing.

"Out," was my curt reply.

"No, duh. But where?"

"Pub."

Cara stopped short, twisted the sleeve of my shirt to halt me, and finally, lifted her chin to stare directly into my eyes. One of her brows rose. "You know there's a huge wine cave thingie in the back, right?"

I rolled my eyes, and continued to drag my ass to the door. "I'm not in the mood for wine. And I'm in need of more mature company." I stared pointedly at her.

"Right." She dragged the word out like it had more than one syllable. "Okay." She raked her lip between her teeth, and cheered. "That sounds fun. Do I need ID?"

I vehemently shook my head when I entered my bedroom, slipped out of my shirt and threw in a fresh one. She, of course, followed me around. "You're not coming with me, Cara."

"Yeah I am," she argued, adding a nod. "Martina said

she won't be back 'til later tonight. I don't want to be here by myself."

Jogging out to my Triumph and trying to dissuade Cara from following, I swung a leg over it, straddled the seat and started the engine. "Martina has people in the house at all times. You'll be fine."

Cara, naturally, did not listen and settled behind me. "I'll drive this back when you get drunk. So yeah, I'm going with you."

Swearing under my breath, I relented. "Fine." I donned my helmet and ordered her to use the extra one. There was no point in arguing with her, ever.

*

I chose the closest English pub to the property, which had changed hands several times. The bartender, an Irish bloke about my age, recognized me from previous nights I'd banged out a pint or two. He nodded by way of greeting when Cara and I sat at the bar, and I threw my keys on the bench.

"*Bon soir, Alexandre, comment ça va?*" Kieran wiped the weathered wood in front of us.

"*Bon soir!*" Cara beat me to a reply. She'd been learning French with Martina; it was passable at best. "*Je m'apelle Cara,*" she carefully enunciated, pressing a hand on her chest.

Kieran, with a massive grin plastered on his face, crossed his arms over the bar and leaned over. I'd seen this sort of behavior around Cara before.

Clearing my throat, I made introductions, "Kieran, this is my sister, Cara. She's nineteen." I emphasized the words 'my sister' and 'nineteen', but to ensure the warning was clear, I added, "Don't even think about it."

Cara slapped my arm at the same time Kieran's smile dropped. He polished the bar again, and laughed. "What can I get you both?"

"I'll have a diet coke please." Cara raised a dainty finger.

"The usual for me."

While Kieran fetched us our drinks, Cara jabbed me in the ribs. I glared at her, but she was turned in the opposite direction.

"What is it?" Why did I agree to bring her here again?

"Someone's checking you out." The always-friendly Cara waved at someone across the bar.

The woman, sitting alone at the far end waved back, stood, and sashayed toward us in a black and red dress, which hugged curves that appealed to me. Her hips swung from side to side in a sultry Tango.

"Ehmergerd, she's coming." Cara practically shook in her seat. When the woman approached us, Cara's smile brightened, and she held out a hand. "Hi!" Her tone was giddy from excitement.

"*Bon Soir*, I am Marielle." Marielle gathered her dark hair and let it tumble over one shoulder, leaving one side of her smooth, regal neck exposed.

Kieran brought our drinks. "Another one, Marie?"

"*Oui, s'il vous plâit*." She returned her attention back to me and Cara. "Would you mind if I joined your party?"

"Not at all!" Cara answered and scooted over the next stool, leaving Marielle to sit between us. The hem of Marielle's dress pulled higher up her thighs.

"I'm Cara, and he's my brother, Alex."

"It's very nice to meet you, Cara, but I know your brother very well." Marielle spoke in accented English. Not a French accent, but Italian distinction.

"You do?"

Marielle flitted a hand over her chest, and I couldn't help but appreciate the sight in the vee of her dress. "I used to work for your grandmother. As a matter of fact, my entire family did."

I dragged my eyes from her cleavage to gaze at her verdant eyes, rimmed with thick curly lashes. A few lines crept from the corners of her eyes and lips as she smiled and winked. I knotted my brows together, trying to conjure any memories. The only Italian family who worked for Martina were the Cerillos, and if I could recall correctly, they had two daughters and a son. Marielle was several years older than me but she'd worked hard alongside her parents in the vineyard during harvest.

The only evidence of her age were those little crinkles in her eyes. I could have spent hours exploring her flawless olive skin. Her thick, black curls framed a beautiful face. She licked her lips every time she glanced my way.

"You know what I just remembered?" Cara piped up.

Marielle and I turned to Cara who sipped her soda before standing and grabbing the Triumph keys off the bar.

"I have some blogging to do. I'll take the bike, Alex. You gonna walk or do you want me to pick you up?" It didn't take a genius to figure out what Cara was doing, but I wasn't going to fight her. Marielle might be the distraction I needed.

"I can give him a lift," Marielle offered, smiling back at me. My eyes darted to her red lips, the tip of her tongue sticking out between them.

"Great! Nice to meet you." Cara hugged Marielle and kissed my cheek and whispered in my ear, "Have fun, brother."

Then there was just Marielle and me. I hunched over my drink, three fingers of Scotch, neat—*her* usual drink of choice—as I felt Marielle's hand snake over my leg. Through the smoky mirror behind the bar, I caught her sultry gaze. I didn't look away. I didn't flinch or move. I didn't think of the chase. I just let it be.

Alexithymia

CHASE

*T*he last thing on my list to worry about was what I should wear, but stressing over it in front of the mirror helped contain my raw emotions.

Daddy's dying.

I swiped the runaway tears from my eyes, cursing at each drop. My face had turned splotchy and no amount of cover-up would help. Screw wearing makeup too. Any sort of mascara, even the so-called waterproof ones, would only cause black streaks down my puffy face. I showered but I hadn't bothered with shampoo, so why should I care about brushing my hair? The ends soaked my back, turning the loose white shirt transparent against my back.

The shirt didn't belong to me. It was Alex's. It was the only thing I had of his, and for some reason, today, I'd wanted to wear it. The shirt vaguely smelled of him. I should be disgusted with myself for a lot of reasons, but today, I didn't care.

I let the thoughts run through my head. If I didn't, I would lose my mind.

Today, my father had his first chemo treatment since finding me in San Francisco. I met my parents out at the front courtyard, and kept quiet when I got into the car. Nica's glasses covered my reddened eyes, and I hid the rest of my face behind my curtain of wet black hair.

The hospital wasn't far, but the trip seemed to take

hours. My mother had hired a local man to take the wheel. I would have volunteered to drive if I weren't a total basket case.

The silence was excruciating. I stole glances in the rearview mirror to check on my father. Every now and then, I caught him kissing her hair or her temple. I pretended to scratch my cheek with my left hand, and I spotted their hands tangled on my father's leg.

My father loved her. That much was obvious. But what did she really feel about him?

In the mirror, I saw my mother's expression hadn't changed. She was quiet, but not contemplative. She wasn't in a panic, but neither was she calm. Her eyes were hidden behind dark lenses, but her mouth was set into a flat line. Not a smile. Not a frown. Not a hiccup or sob. Not hate. Not love.

Yet, my father held onto her like she was his rock.

I never thought my mother was someone who'd stick around through thick and thin, but like my father had said, she had been there when I left. Was that how she showed love? And was it enough to ignore all her imperfections?

My mother was manipulative. She'd always been the kind of mom who pushed her kids to get better grades, kick the ball harder, jump through higher hoops. Be faster. Be smarter. Be better. Was I ever a disappointment to her! Charity was the brainy one. She was the natural athlete. She was creative. Her toes were pointier in ballet. She scored more goals in peewee soccer. Her horse had never bucked and thrown her off its back. All because of my mother. Had all of her pushing caused Charity to flee? I'd always thought so.

When Char left to explore southeast Asia, my mother had set her sights on me. But I had Daddy on my side. He'd been my shield. Still, Mom had been a force I couldn't mess with or ignore. She'd found ways to get into my head. I'd competed on all fronts—sports, arts, academics, but never dance. That had been Charity's forte, but I couldn't even do the hokey-pokey. I'd shredded my tutu after my first recital. I was five, climbed up a ladder and dropped the pink, frilly skirt into the tree chopper.

Then at fourteen, Danny became my boyfriend. Was Mom ever ecstatic! From then on, she'd tuned into my life through Danny. She'd known how intelligent Danny was. She'd known that despite his father running off, Danny had turned into a man's man, responsible, polite, and respectful. He was adored by many, emulated by some. He was a star set to shine over all of us.

Now, he had become my mother's pet project.

I wondered...if Alex were here, how would he handle my mother? He had been so at ease with my father the only time they'd met outside my apartment. Would he recognize my mother's uncanny ability to poke her nose into other people's business? Would he let her?

The car slowed to a halt in front of a low brick building, and all thoughts of Danny and Alex filtered out of my head like gray smoke. My heart leapt into my throat, gagging me. I grabbed the door handle and squeezed it, and waited for my entire body calm down.

"Let's go, Chastity. We haven't got all day." My mother climbed out of the car, rushed to the other side and helped my father into a wheelchair.

With my jaw clenched, I held off the bark I was ready to release at my mother. I wasn't here for her. I was here for Daddy. Quietly, I followed them into the oncology wing.

❧

How could a life depend on clear liquid trickling from a bag into a catheter?

For my benefit, Daddy's oncologist explained the procedure. The doctor fiddled with his glasses and averted his eyes when I asked if it would cure my father.

"We'll hope for the best," he replied, clicking his pen on my father's chart.

"What the fuck does that mean?" I shouted, garnering a warning look from my mother.

If my mind had been functioning properly, I would have done my research. I would have read more about the drugs my father was to receive. I would have familiarized myself with the benefits, the rates of survival under such treatment, and the possible side effects. Instead, I'd wasted my time reminiscing with Danny, going on a picnic with him, and flirting with him, even though he was someone I barely knew, and wasn't sure if I wanted to know at all.

Mom profusely apologized on my behalf as she walked the good doctor out of Daddy's room.

I watched everything, and I held his hand when they flushed out the port in his chest. I told him I loved him as they administered the first dosage through the tube.

"Does it hurt?" I asked Daddy when the nurses left.

"No, Nugget." The seconds ticked on before he answered. "Not now that you're here." And he had just enough energy to lift our intertwined hands and press a kiss on my knuckles.

Afterward, we did nothing but sit and listen to the monitors and the movements outside his room. I didn't bother checking on my mother.

❦

I didn't remember falling asleep. It might have been after

Daddy closed his eyes. But when I woke, he was gone. Standing, I rolled my shoulders and called out to him. The room was dark except for the light seeping out from underneath the bathroom door. When I neared it, I heard shuffling.

When I opened the door, I found my mother on the floor rubbing my father's back as he bent over the porcelain, throwing up his guts. The only sound I could make was a shaky gasp, but it was enough to capture my mother's attention. My knees weakened, and I held onto the doorjamb for support.

"Go back out, Chastity. You don't need to be here," she ordered in a quiet, firm tone, without looking directly at me.

Daddy hurled again and again until he was too weak to continue, and he collapsed into my mother's arms. Mom held him and cooed sweet nothings into his ear. I didn't know I was crying until I brushed my cheek and felt wetness.

Nurses came into the room, pushed me aside, and left me leaning, useless and helpless, against the wall, as people helped my mother lift Daddy off the floor and back onto the bed. My knees buckled when he puked again all over his hospital gown. Everyone who came into the room had something to do, while I sobbed like a lost child on the sidelines.

Mom came to me, and squeezed my right arm. "We need to step out of the room so the nurses can clean up your father and change his clothes." I shook my head. She had to drag me out. Mom sat me on a chair in one of the visitors' rooms and left. When she came back, she held a cup against my lips.

"Drink this."

I did. Ice-cold water flowed down my throat and hit my aching chest.

"This is all my fault. I should have listened to your father." Mom tilted the cup back to my lips. My gaze flitted up to her face. For once, Mom wasn't all put together. Her hair was combed back but it wasn't done neatly. There was a dark smudge of makeup under her left eye, and she hadn't bothered re-applying her lipstick. "He didn't want you to see him this way."

"What happened?" My voice sounded strange even to my own ears.

"It's a side effect of the chemo. He didn't have it too bad the first time. They've given him anti-nausea pills. Hopefully, it will take effect soon and he can get some rest." Mom sighed, and swept my hair off my face.

She forced me to drink more. I squeezed my hands together to stop my fingers from shaking, and crossed my ankles to keep my legs from bouncing. "How are you so calm?"

Mom produced a tissue from her pocket and wiped my face. A memory of how she'd done the same thing when I was little popped into my mind. Her forehead smoothed. Her lips pursed and parted a smidgen. "I've been through this with your father before, and I won't lie...it never gets easier." She had a faraway look in her eyes.

A nurse came to let us know they had finished helping my father, and that he was asking for us. When I moved to get up, Mom reached for my hand.

"Go see him, but I don't think you should stay the night. The nausea pills might not work, and what you saw...it might become worse. I've booked us a hotel for the next few days. Randy can take you there so you can get some sleep. I've also bought you some clothes."

"I'm not leaving Daddy."

Mom nodded. "I understand—" and for once, I believed her "—but your father will want you to leave. He would rather you remember him healthy and happy, and not like..." She pressed her lips together and covered her mouth with the back of her hand. Her shoulders rose and fell as she took cleansing breaths.

"Okay, Mom. I'll go if he asks."

He did ask. His voice was hoarse and tired when he suggested I got some rest for the night. Daddy said exactly what Mom had told me. Mom handed me a key card for the suite she'd booked us and rang Randy to have the car ready to meet me downstairs. I kissed my parents goodnight, and like a good daughter, I obeyed.

When I got to the hotel suite, I crashed onto the bed. I rummaged through my purse for my phone, and dialed a number I thought I'd long forgotten.

After a few rings, a voicemail message played.

Tears overflowed and sobs filled the dark room. I couldn't breathe. "I need you," was all I could say over the phone.

*S*audade

*M*uch of my days were filled with waiting. Waiting for the sun to push through the space between the closed curtains. Waiting for Nica to call me first thing in the morning and ask how I was feeling, if I was ready to face the day. Waiting for my father's treatment to take effect so he could be better, be stronger, be himself once again.

The morning after Daddy's first treatment, I woke up with a throbbing headache from lack of sleep and the stubborn, salty tears which had poured out of me. My phone had startled me awake. I'd picked it up and grumbled a response to Nica, and then I'd lost my shit.

Then a knock had come at the door, so I'd ended the call with her. The man on outside announced that my breakfast orders were ready. Mom had thought of everything, even a breakfast I couldn't stomach. She'd picked up clothes for me, all my size, all white or black, nothing pink. An olive branch in the form of denim and cotton shirts. She'd also bought me bathroom crap, which I'd need if I ever decided to shower.

I couldn't get myself to think of myself, until the third day, when Nica threatened she would unleash her crazy pregnant hormones on me if I didn't take care of myself.

Pain and sorrow were natural reactions to what I was going through. Nica understood. She'd gone through it too, but at a much younger age. Nica's father had passed away when she was five. All she remembered were his big brown eyes when he smiled and his fondness for life.

After poking at the various pastries on the cart, I sneered at them and went for the coffee. Coffee was my lifeline. It would help to have a bottle of Irish liquor, too, but I couldn't remember the last time I'd had anything alcoholic and feared it would just upset my stomach. There was no need for me to make myself voluntarily sick when Daddy was suffering in his hospital bed.

I would arrive at the hospital over-caffeinated, jumpy and snarling. Mom would hand me a glass of iced water before I relieved her for the morning. She never came to sleep in the hotel with me. I never argued that she should. It made Daddy happy to see her first thing in the morning, and that joy extended when I traipsed in with a newspaper or a book in hand. Daddy and I chatted about everything except our lives. Sometimes, I would read him hilarious posts I'd find on Twitter. This was our routine.

On the third night, Danny called to say he would be over for a visit the next day, and asked if I wanted him to bring me anything from my bedroom. I declined, profusely and politely. I didn't want him touching my stuff or going through my things.

He also asked me out to dinner. I replied with a yes, but only because I had said no to him picking up my things, and it would be a much better time than dawdling in the hotel, waiting for the sleeping pills one of the doctors had prescribed me to kick in.

When Danny came, he brought my Mom and me lunch. He sat with Daddy and they talked college football. As Daddy was reminiscing about his college varsity games, I was able to observe the little changes in him since the chemo had started. His eyes were sunk deeper.. There were sores around his mouth. He had trouble getting food down and had lost more weight. He looked frail.

But he smiled and laughed. He kissed my Mom before she left and again when she returned, even if she'd only gone for a quick bite to eat or a cup of coffee.

After Danny's visit, he excused himself and said he would pick me up later from the hotel. Both my parents were obviously pleased, though neither one commented on it.

"I'm going to grab some coffee." I stretched, grabbing the edge of the seat and pushing myself up.

"You just had coffee. You should eat." Mom waved in the direction of some packaged food on a side table.

"I'm not really hungry," I told her. "I just need a little boost. The sleep meds make me lethargic." It was the truth, but I didn't want more coffee. I needed to find a bathroom I could use. If I told them that, Daddy would just get me to use his private bathroom. Hell no, I was not going to sit and pee on the toilet he'd have his head in later on.

I walked around the hospital to look for a clean, unoccupied bathroom, and somehow ended up in the gift shop, where I found a blue teddy bear on a shelf. It resembled something I'd had when I was little. With a thought of giving it to Daddy, hoping he would remember, I purchased it. Not rushing, I walked around some more before heading back to his room, and ended up in one of the family waiting rooms.

Danny saw me before I could turn around. "Hannah," he called before he slowly unwrapped his arms from Tiana.

I was stuck, staring at Tiana's tear-soaked eyes. There was only one explanation why she was here—Sky.

I ignored Danny as he walked toward me, but he halted

midstride while I made my way to Tiana. She hid her sobs behind her hand and shook her head.

"Is Sky okay?" I asked as I closed the gap between us. My arms flew around her when she hiccupped and sobbed. I looked to Danny for answers, but he'd sat down, his hands buried in his hair. He was as distraught as she was. There was no denying the closeness between these two. It was written thickly in the air between them.

I waited until her sobs quieted and led her to a chair beside Danny. It was like instinct for him, or maybe a habit, to reach for her, hold her tight and kiss the top of her head. Tiana still couldn't talk, and so Danny did,

"We came to have Sky tested."

"For what?"

"Huntington's." The word sounded ominous coming out of Danny.

I tried to squeak out a word, but what was there to say? There were more questions to ask, even though I posited what the answers were. How did I not see the connection before? Sky's eyes might be the same color as his mom's, but the shape was distinctly Danny. Sky had a darker skin tone, but apart from that, he was Danny as a kid. I'd seen the photos numerous times when Abigail was still alive. She had been fond of telling me stories about little Danny. It was a shame Abigail never met her grandson.

"We asked for genetic testing, because he'd been showing signs and symptoms."

"What was the result?"

"Negative." The answer came from Tiana, her voice flat and small.

"But that's good, isn't it?" It was. Sky could live a normal life, free of the disease, but why was Tiana in tears? They couldn't be tears of joy. I recognized them as similar to what I'd been doing these past few nights.

"It is." Danny freed Tiana from his embrace, and kissed her hand, like a man who loved a woman and sought her support.

This was what I had missed before. These two were together, or they had been once, long enough to have a child together. And long enough to have stayed good friends.

Danny hung his head. "Sky's tests were negative, but mine were not."

He tilted his head and stared me squarely in the eye. I couldn't even begin to list the myriad of emotions in them. Danny had Huntington's disease, a condition which caused his mother's eventual death. How long would Danny have? Ten? Fifteen? Thirty years?

I averted my gaze. I didn't know what his eyes were telling me, but the rest of his actions spoke volumes. He might try and deny it, but whatever he had felt for Tiana before was still there. And she was there for him. His disease would be a battle they would have to face together. I was only a witness to what would eventually happen. I had no doubt in my mind she would be by his side the entire time. I only wished he knew.

"Where's Sky?"

"He's not here. We only came to get the results. He's with a sitter," Tiana explained.

The three of us sat there, staring at the light blue wall under the flickering fluorescent light. At some point, Mom called my cell phone and I made my exit. What could I offer Danny at this point?

"Call me later," I said. "Call me anytime."

I hugged them both, one at a time, then together. They'd figure it out. They didn't need me there.

I took the bear out of the white plastic bag, handed it to

Tiana and asked her to give it to Sky, her little boy, their son.

꿏

Since my dinner with Danny was cancelled, and I didn't have the heart to tell my Mom without spilling my guts about his condition and his relationship with Tiana, I went to a bar by myself near the hotel.

It wasn't much of a place, and I counted about twenty people in attendance—people with nothing better to do on a beautiful, summer night. The bartender eyed me as I chose a stool and ordered a lager and chicken wings. I picked at the wings and sipped the lager. Much like the twenty or so bar patrons, I had nowhere else to go, nothing to do and no one to see.

My cellphone rang in my jacket the moment I finished my drink and I let it go straight to voicemail. It might be Danny calling, as I'd asked him to, but I couldn't get myself to answer. In any case, he needed to sort things out with Tiana. He should talk to her, not me.

My phone bleeped, announcing a voicemail had been left. Good. I'd check it later.

When I paid for my drinks and barely-touched food, my phone rang again, and I slipped it out of my pocket and wondered about the unregistered number. I hadn't asked where Danny was staying, if he was sticking around tonight. Otherwise, the hotel name would show up on my phone. I hit answer, but I was too late, and whoever the caller was would get my voicemail again.

And again, my phone bleeped. Another voicemail.

When I returned to my hotel room, my first stop was the bathroom. It had a large jet tub, and after the shocking news today, I could use a bath. I turned on the faucets and poured bath salts and oils into the tub. By the time I was out of the water, I'd smell like the entire Bath and Bodyworks store. With my clothes off, replaced by a robe, I set the pajamas my Mom had bought for me on the bed. Nica would be proud of my preparedness.

I checked the two voicemails while I waited for the bath to get full enough for me to get into, and received a shock that rocked my entire body. My mind numbed. My extremities tingled. The world around me ceased to exist.

Hi... It's me... It's Alex...

He sounded distant. He *was* distant. Nica had informed me that he'd returned to France with his half-sister, Cara. But my god, hearing his gravelly voice—the smooth, sexy mixture of accents that were unique to Alex—was enough for my stomach to flip and my heart to lurch, simultaneously.

I didn't mean to take this long to ring you back...

The pulsating of my blood in my head minimized the clarity of his message. I held onto the phone before it slipped off my hand and landed into the water.

I haven't been using my mobile and the reception out in the field is staticky at best. I would have rung you right away, after you called and left the message...

I called him? I left him a message? What did I say?

You can call me again. A pause. A hesitation. *If you want to. I'd like to hear from you, know how you're doing.* Another long pause, followed by a deep, heavy sigh. *I want to say that I—*

He what? What? I stared at my phone when the robotic female voice told me I'd gotten to the end of his message.

"No!" I shook it like it would continue Alex's message, force the rest of his words to come. Then the robotic voice let me know another voicemail was waiting for me.

Alex had called me twice that night. Five minutes apart,

and left two voicemails. I held my breath as I listened to the next one.

It's me again. He chuckled without mirth. *I got cut off. Just call me, Chase. Whenever. Don't worry about the time difference. I will answer. I will be here...whenever you need me. Just call me.*

There was a bit of a shuffle, a sigh then static before I heard *End of messages.*

It had taken him five minutes to call again. What did he do in those five minutes? Did he pace, wherever he was, like I was doing now in my hotel room? Did he feel like his heart was ripped out of his chest when he heard my outgoing message? Or did it speed up when he began talking, knowing I would be listening to it?

I miss him.

If I closed my eyes, I could imagine him whispering to me, drawing out passion from deep within. I missed Alex, and I hoped he missed me too. He hadn't said it, but if I paid close attention, I could almost hear it in his messages. Or was I making it up?

I listened to his messages again, memorized them, tried to hear between the fucking lines as I dipped my feet into the tub. The water had gone tepid.

The last time I'd taken a bath was with him. Alex was fond of baths. He'd prepared one before I'd even replied to his text message asking for yet another secret meeting. The hotel we'd ended up that night had a claw-foot tub, and we'd barely fit in it together, but still managed to have incredible sex in it. It was the kind of lovemaking that lingered in one's mind. My first and only bathtub sex, probably the last.

Before I played the messages for the umpteenth time, I accessed my outgoing calls. Alex had said I called him. When?

There wasn't much on my list. On Monday night, the

first night my Dad spent at the hospital, I saw I'd broken down and dialed his number. With everything going on, I'd somehow blocked it out. I'd deleted his number a while ago, but somehow it had imbedded itself in my brain, and I'd punched in each number from memory.

Once, I'd only called him once and it hadn't lasted a minute. Alex had received a message from me, but what could I have said? Whatever it was had been enough to make him call me back.

The question now was what should I do?

Halcyon

*B*reathy. "Hi, Alex, yes it's me, Chase. Sorry I missed your call..."

Nope. Not good enough. I wanted breathy not out of breath.

I was a fool, looking at myself in the mirror, twirling the ends of my hair, as I practiced what I would say if—big if—I gathered enough courage to call Alex.

I puffed out my chest and held in the air, raising the phone to my ear as I said, "Hey...yeah...I'm chill." Ugh! He would never believe I was chill. Was chill even an acceptable word these days? I'd lost my touch. I used to be on the in. No matter, Alex probably wasn't too impressed with my huge vocabulary. It was difficult to think of any big words when my entire head was full of him.

Try again, Chase. I flipped my hair, almost giving myself whiplash. Think sexy. Alex thought I was sexy. He thought I was beautiful.

He also thought I'd betrayed him.

The smile fell off my face. I stared at my phone. Who was I fooling? This wasn't going to work! He had family and business obligations in France. He jetted off to various parts of the world and I could barely sit through the few hours it took to fly from California to Vermont. My passport had zero stamps on it, while his was riddled with them. I'd seen it one time and was awed at all the places he'd been to. That had been the night he had asked to go to the Serengeti with him on a NatGeo assignment. I'd refused.

I'd refused Alex. I'd shooed him away. He'd been nothing but sweet and gentle and caring and achingly tender with me. And I'd slapped him with my baggage from my past.

I pressed a number on my phone and sighed as I heard Nica's voice on the other end of the line. It was a Friday night and the noise in the background told me she was at a huge event.

"Chase? You okay? What's up?" she asked, almost shouting over the brouhaha.

"He called me," I began, also yelling into the phone even though it was as quiet as the desert night in my room (not that I had ever been in a desert). "Alex called me!"

"Hold on." Nica spouted off directives to the people surrounding her, ending with a 'please and thank you'. She might be the big boss lady, but to Nica, politeness was a key to success. "I'll look for a quieter area and you can tell me what he said."

I waited for her, listening to her breathing and movement. I imagined her waddling while rubbing her protruding belly. After a groan and a grunt, she spoke again, "Okay. You said Alex called?"

"Which party?"

"Burgess-Maclean. Five hundred guests."

Nica was my best friend for many reasons. Her tenacity was incomparable. Her dedication was limitless. And even as she managed a large event, she paused to take a panicked call from me.

"Chase, don't dawdle. What did Alex say?" she asked again.

I sat on the edge of the bed and fiddled with the hem of

my robe, lowering my voice as I spoke. "I didn't talk to him. He left me a message. He asked me to call back."

"He called you out of the blue?"

"No. I called him a few days ago."

"You did?"

"I left him a message. I told him that I needed him."

"Oh."

As I'd continued to listen to his messages, I'd remembered what I'd said when I called. I'd told Alex that I needed him. Like my life would end if I didn't breathe in the breath from his lips. Like my heart would cease to beat if I didn't experience the heat of his touch, the urgency in his kisses, or the quiet whispers he muttered in my ears. Like food would lose its flavor. Scents would lose their smell. Like the world would become a hazy shade of gray if he didn't exist in my life.

"He asked me to call him back, but I haven't. I don't know what to say. We left things a little... well, not pretty, Nica."

My best friend sighed into the phone. It was so heavy I could almost feel it in my ear. "He's still in France. It would be around five in the morning there. And it's harvest season, so he's probably in the fields. I don't think he'll have his phone with him." She paused and it gave me enough time to picture Alex, shirtless, hard at work under the hot sun. I squeezed my eyes shut to ignore my overactive imagination.

"Levi spoke to him earlier today. I didn't get a chance to ask him how Alex was doing. I assumed they talked about the business, and maybe Cara, since last time I heard, she was getting on Alex's nerves. If you just want to leave him a message, now would be a good time." Before I replied, she spoke again, "If that's what you want. Unless you really want to talk to him, then wait a while to make sure he has his phone."

"I just don't know what to tell him." I pulled at my hair in frustration.

"Whatever feels right, Chase. Only you know what's in your heart. For once, maybe you should listen to what it's saying."

Neither of us said anything for a couple of minutes, then Nica had to end the call since the party hosts were looking for her. I mumbled a hesitant goodbye.

I had established how much of a coward I'd been before. I couldn't say that I'd changed now. Or at least, not at that moment. Nica had said Alex would be too busy to answer the phone. I could spill my heart out in a message, then maybe chuck my phone into a lake right after.

Before my mind switched gears, I pressed redial on his number. My heart thundered in my chest. My teeth chattered even though I wasn't cold. Breathe in. I listened to the phone ring. Breathe out. It rang once more.

Then I heard a voice on the other line, "Hello." And I promptly hung up.

I threw my phone at the far wall so hard I had doubts it would work again.

A woman. A woman had answered Alex's phone.

❧

Two weeks later, I found myself sitting across from Tiana in her cozy home. Over a cup of coffee, and with both our nerves jangled, we talked about Danny and his condition.

"Do you still love him?" I asked. Wrapping my hands around the warm cup kept them from trembling. Putting my nose in other people's business wasn't anything I was used to, or enjoyed. But this was about Danny and Tiana, and their sweet boy, Sky.

Before she answered, she traced scuff marks on the tabletop, avoiding eye contact. "Yes. I've never stopped loving him."

"Why aren't you guys together? Are you married or something?"

There wasn't anything I could do about Alex and myself. But I could help Danny and Tiana figure out what they were missing—a chance on a true family.

"We had one night. I had just moved here when his Mom passed away. At that time I was trying to forget my past. We met at the bar, and nine months later, Sky was born." She offered me a small smile. "He was very supportive, but he was afraid of something. It took him a few months before he even picked up his son." Tiana turned away as she continued, "I had to find out on my own how Abigail died, and right after, I heard about you." What could I say to that? She regarded me shyly. "Do *you* still love Danny?"

I suddenly didn't know what to do with my hands. I brought them down to my lap, then I scratched my ear, and raised my coffee up to my lips. "I care about him. We had a great time when we were younger. He was a lot more fun then." I cringed as soon I said that.

"It's okay Chase," her tone turned motherly. "I like the serious Danny, but I do wish he would smile more. He's really good with Sky though."

"About Sky... does he know Danny's his father?"

Tiana shook her head.

I reached across and patted her crossed hands. "Don't worry, I'll have a chat with Danny. Someone has to knock some sense into him."

And that was exactly what I did the next night. Danny didn't fight it. I knew he wouldn't, but he still seemed surprised when I told him how Tiana felt about him. I also told him he was stupid if he didn't marry the girl.

Daddy had begged to come home. He wanted familiar surroundings. He wanted comfort. Since they could afford it, the oncologist agreed and gave me directions on how I could prepare for his homecoming. Danny and Tiana were there to help me the entire time.

The first night Daddy was back, I sat by his bedside. Without saying a thing, he knew what I had come in for.

"You're leaving," he stated.

I could have held off for a few more minutes, but why bother? "Yeah."

Daddy nodded and as I leaned toward him, he kissed my forehead. "It's about time you go back home, Nugget."

An hour before that, I had spoken to Nica. All we had talked about was how busy our company was getting. Her due date was coming fast, and I'd be left to run Bliss while she got used to being a parent. She didn't ask me to go back, but she did say how much everyone missed me. I, of course, snorted at that. I very much doubt that anyone else missed me.

Daddy was getting stronger every day, although the length of his time with us was still unknown. Now that Daddy was back in Stowe and Mom could care for him better, with aid from a couple different hospice nurses, I could travel back and forth between Stowe and San Francisco.

Always the smart one, Daddy was right. It was time I went back to San Francisco. It was time I went home. What was waiting for me there was another story.

Quaintrelle

During the weeks leading to the day I would return to San Francisco, the two Pauls became determined to fatten me up. The irregular meals at the hotel where I'd stayed while Daddy was in the hospital had caused me to lose weight.

When Daddy became comfortable getting treatments in his own house, I started my training. I did laps in the swimming pool, and he turned into my personal cheerleader. I also helped more at the farm. Throwing bales of hay was a good workout. Then I added long distance runs to the mix, every day from my parents' house to the maple grounds. It wasn't exactly Delicious Diego's boot camp, but he would have been proud of my determination.

The night I returned to San Francisco, I reinstated my gym membership. It was the best way to battle loneliness.

By the time I hit the sheets—my own high thread count charcoal sheets—I thought I'd be so zonked out I'd instantly fall asleep. Wrong. Alex invaded my mind.

Since hanging up on the woman who'd answered his phone, I'd never called again.

To keep myself from going crazy, I kept to a strict schedule before going to Nica's baby shower. I scrubbed my whole house clean, shopped for food (thanks to a determined Chef Paul, who had taught me how to cook some basic meals), bought new clothes that weren't all black, religiously went to the gym, and finally had my hair done.

When I was five, I had strawberry blonde hair. I discussed returning to that color with my hairstylist, who was appalled at the state of the mop I'd piled atop my head. Zero care had gone into my hair while I was in Stowe. My roots showed. With the healthy tan I'd received from running and helping at the farm, he thought I might be able to pull off. But was I ready for the change back to my natural color?

It turned out, I wasn't. My hairstylist had exceptional expertise. He did a fabulous job at getting rid of the dark hair. But the strawberry blonde...wasn't me. It was Hannah, and not Chase.

What was supposed to be a quick phone call to my hairstylist about dyeing my hair black again the morning I headed to Napa, turned into an hour-long chat. At the end, he convinced me I looked fantastic with the change, and I should embrace it. But it also made me late for the party.

I loaded up my beautiful and sorely-missed Harley with bags for a week of pure fun with my best friend.

The party was to take place behind the main house. I went through the gardens and stopped short. Gerard and Jewel had planned the baby shower. Nica was having a girl. This apparently meant bright pink tabletops, pink-frosted cake, pink cookies, pink punch, pink flowers and pink ribbons on pink chairs. It was like my bedroom in Vermont had thrown up in Nica's backyard.

There was enough chatter to pull me further in. Jewel and Mateo were by the punch. Sandrine was huddled with Natalie and another woman I didn't recognize around a table, all speaking in French. Sandrine and Natalie's toddlers were running around. There were several girls from work, whose names I hoped would come to me sooner rather than later. Lily, Nica's mom, sat at another table with Nica's sister, Maggie, one other girl about

Maggie's age, and Gerard. Nica was nowhere in sight. Neither was Alex. I breathed a sigh of relief. I wasn't sure I wanted witnesses when I faced him again.

Gerard saw me first. He waved me over but instead of waiting, he came to me. "Va-va-voom, Chase, love the hair and the new outfit."

I wore one of my recently purchased finds, a gray crop top, printed leggings and a red leather jacket. Not what I'd intended to wear, but since I was late, I didn't have time to change into my purple shift dress. I'd applied very little makeup as I wasn't sure if it would have been able to withstand the heat of the day.

"Thanks, G." I raised my hand to ruffle my hair a bit, thinking that it may have gotten flat under the bike helmet, and removed my jacket. "I see you and Jewel went for..."

"Pretty in pink!" Gerard exclaimed, throwing his hands in the air.

'Pretty' wasn't my choice of word, but I bit my tongue. This was for Nica. Nica liked pink. "Well, there's also the Parisian theme."

He pointed out the features added into the decor: miniature pink Eiffel Tower cookies, and pink and sparkly Eiffel Tower sculptures on the tables.

"You know there's more to Paris than the Eiffel Tower," I told him.

Gerard rolled his eyes. "Well, the French love it!" He pointed at Sandrine, Natalie and their friend.

"Yeah, who's the new Frenchie? The Monica Bellucci wannabe?" I nodded my head at their table, eyeing the raven-haired beauty.

"Oh my gahd!" Gerard gripped one of my shoulders, and placed a hand over his heart. "That my dear is the fabulous Marielle. You've got to meet her. She almost forty but you wouldn't know it."

"Marielle?" The woman might have antennae. She looked over at us and waved at Gerard.

Gerard stretched his arm over my shoulders and whispered into my ear, "That, my dear Chase, is Alex's new squeeze."

"His new what?" My loud voice halted the chatter around us. All eyes drew to where we stood.

"You heard me." Gerard lowered his voice again, ignoring the curious stares. "Alex brought her here from France. Seems serious."

My head spun.

Alex had a girlfriend?

And not just any girl. I watched her throw her head back as she laughed. She had an undeniable amount of sex appeal, paired with the self-confidence I knew Alex liked in a woman. I could hear my inner self bawl. I could hear my heart scream as it was crushed into tiny little pieces.

"G, I need a drink." I patted Gerard's pockets. He always had a flask hidden somewhere for emergencies. This was an emergency. It was red alert.

"Girl, get off." He gently pushed away my hands and shook a finger at me. "Why would I carry my holster when I'm at a vineyard? Take a few steps down that way. You'll hit the cellar, and you can siphon wine off the barrels."

My throat closed up as Marielle's voice carried over, and I couldn't help but gawk at her. The wind whistled past and caused her thick black hair to dance with it. The way she moved her hands as she spoke was graceful.

"Where's Nica?" I gripped Gerard's shirt. I needed my best friend before I imploded.

"She's in the house."

I ran in the direction Gerard had pointed. I called out for Nica. As I neared the front of the house, I heard her answer me.

"In the library!"

We sat on a sofa beside the desk. Her stomach had grown more, and it made it difficult to hug her, but I still clung to her.

"Alex has a girlfriend?"

Nica's mouth opened, then closed again. After a heavy sigh, she spoke, "I didn't know until they came last night. I would have called you but I wasn't sure how to tell you about her."

"Are they staying here?" My voice quavered. Nica nodded. "I can't stay here. I have to leave."

"Chase, no. Stay. I'll be with you the whole time. I don't want you going home alone."

"Nica, he has a woman with him!"

"I know. I know." We heard Levi calling her from outside the library. "Please stay. We'll figure this out together. You'll be fine. I'll be here for you the entire time. Plus I missed you." Nica pleaded with her eyes.

How could I say no to her? She'd been with me through thick and thin. She'd been the one person I'd depended on for years. Despite the stabbing ache in my chest, I agreed, but I didn't say how long I would stay. The vineyard and the house were big enough to get lost in and hide from people, from two new lovers.

"I better get out there to see what Levi wants and get the party started now that you're here." She squeezed my hand before she pushed up to standing, cradling her swollen belly with one hand. "You look great, by the way. I love the hair. Take your time to gather yourself and when you're ready, come and join us out there."

"Yeah," I breathed out through clenched teeth.

I listened for the tapping of her shoes, and when I was sure that she was out the door, I aimed for the liquor cabinet. Levi wouldn't mind if I broke into it. After two shots of eighteen-year old malt, I headed out the door, determined to at least see the party through.

I stepped out of the library and slammed right into someone.

"Chase!"

My knees weakened and I stumbled back, but Alex held me tight against him. My ribs constricted. Suddenly, I found it difficult to breathe, think or speak. I just held on.

Had his eyes always been that blue? Were his shoulders always so wide and toned? Did his lips use to appear as tempting as they did at that moment?

"Chase, are you okay?" he asked, looking at me in wonderment.

I spread my hands and lifted them off his shirt, stepping back as I gathered my thoughts. My palms tingled but my fingers were numb. I kept my breathing shallow, trying not to gulp in the air that he breathed.

I flattened my shirt with my palm and pushed my hair off my shoulders and face. When I glanced his way, the smile on his face stretched even bigger.

"You're blonde now?"

"Yup. Back to blonde." *Unlike your girlfriend.*

"It's nice," he said.

"I better head out to the..."

My words were interrupted when a husky-toned voice called him. I might not have met her officially yet, but I knew Marielle was the one looking for him.

"Alexandre," she said his name like it was caramel oozing off her lips.

Alex turned away from me and we both watched Marielle sashay to us. When she reached him, her hands slithered up his arms and chest—a lot more toned than last I'd seen them—and cooed words in French.

"*Oui*, Marie," he replied. Not darling or sweetheart or *hayati*. But it didn't lack sweetness or warmth.

They turned to me, her hand pressed against his chest where I could almost see his heart beating furiously. He was nervous.

"Hello," Marielle greeted me.

"Marie, this is Chase." Just Chase. Nothing else.

Marielle stretched her hand to me, but before I could shake it, she wrapped me in a hug and kissed my cheeks, saying, "*Ah, oui*! You are Chase, Veronica's best friend, *non*? I saw you talking to Gerard earlier." She held me at an arm's length and smiled. "Ah! You are as beautiful as they say!"

"Who say? Ahm, said?" I cocked my head to one side, avoiding eye contact with Alex, who was standing behind Marielle and running his fingers through his hair.

Marielle flicked her hands up. "Everyone."

Had her boyfriend said it too? I bit my tongue, and reminded myself that I was there for Nica. She wouldn't want me to claw this woman's eyes out. No, she was a guest. And Alex's woman.

"Are you joining us?" she asked.

I thought at first that she had meant joining her and Alex to do god knows what, but it dawned on me that she'd meant the baby shower.

"Yeah. I just have to grab something from my bike." Or jump on it and leave before my heart leapt out of my rib cage.

When the heat of the sun hit my face, I felt the prickle of tears in the corners of my eyes. I fanned my cheeks and forced myself to breathe as I jogged to my bike. Before I reached it, I heard someone behind me.

I surreptitiously wiped the tears from my eyes and sucked in a breath before I looked over my shoulder. The girl who had been seated with Maggie earlier leaned against a post. She waved at me with a hand holding a cellphone.

"You're Chase, right?" she asked, making her way to me.

Her hair was cropped short and dyed a pink that matched the baby shower palette. She had on a summery dress and sandals. There was bounce in her step which told me that she was indeed as young as Maggie. I suddenly ached for the younger, care-free me.

"Do I know you?"

"No." I faced her, waiting for her next move or word. "I'm Cara."

"You're Al—Levi's sister! Hi!" I offered her a hand.

She switched her phone to her left hand before she shook mine. "Yup, that's me. I didn't recognize you at first with the new hair color."

"How do you know about that?" I patted the top of my head. "We've never met before."

"I've seen your pictures," she answered.

"What pictures?"

Cara hesitated for a bit before she said, "Nica's wedding pics. We looked at them last night. I feel like I know you already. I've heard so much about you."

"You have? Well whatever they said... it's all true."

Cara laughed. I didn't know what it was about her that I felt this sudden relief, an ease in my chest and a peace in my mind. For the first time in a while, I laughed as well. It almost sounded alien to my ears.

"You're not running away, are you?" Cara asked and I immediately clammed up.

I glanced over to my Harley. "I was just going to get a change of clothes. It's too hot to be wearing this." As I answered her, I believed it.

Cara shrugged. "You look fine to me. Let's go ahead in. We have some catching up to do."

I wondered why she would say that when I hadn't met her before, but I let her drag me inside. Nica was happy to see me with Cara, and quietly informed me that Levi and Alex were gone for the rest of the night. For the entirety of the party that afternoon, Cara never left my side as though she was guarding me from something...

Or someone.

Nyctophilia

ALEX

The heat of the night clung to my skin, even as I pushed the sheets off me. It seemed that yet again sleep evaded me. I groaned into my hands, careful not to shake the bed as my feet hit the floor. Straight off to the balcony I went, hoping to take in some of the fresh California air.

When was the last time I'd had a full night's sleep? Weeks, possibly even months. With her. That night I had come from a run and found Chase in the shower, drowning her sorrow under the rush of hot water. It hadn't been clear then why she had resorted to tears. The reasons came later on, and I didn't understand right away. Things had been going great between us, despite her not accepting a more serious relationship. As long as it was just us, she and I, nothing else had mattered.

I leaned over the iron railing, looking up at the night sky.

I could use some clarity at the moment.

Out of the corner of my eye, a figure flitted into the night, toeing the edge of the pool. She was like an apparition in a white dressing gown as the moonlight hit her blonde hair and illuminated it. I'd thought I was prepared to see her.

Why wasn't she in bed? What thoughts ran through her mind that kept her awake and wandering at night?

I pushed away from the railing, and turned back into the bedroom. I padded toward the door, not even caring that I only had on pajama bottoms. My hand wrapped around the handle of the door when I heard Marielle stir on the bed behind me.

"Alexandre? What are you doing up? Come back to bed, darling."

I glanced over my shoulder quickly and saw Marie slowly sit up in bed, her hand outstretched to me. Then I looked down and stared at my hand. One turn and I would be out into the night with Chase. But I had come here with Marie, who had been nothing but good to me.

She had eagerly volunteered when Martina couldn't make it.

"Alex?" Marie called again in her tired voice.

Sighing, I released my grip on the handle.

CHASE

*W*hose idea was it to ply me with drinks?

Oh, right, mine.

With my arms crossed over my head, I groaned as an explosion threatened my brain. The bright sun in Vermont had followed me to California. I wished I'd listened to Nica when she told me to stay away from the cellar.

I couldn't help it. Not when every single time I saw Marielle, I remembered how she had felt up Alex. Felt him up! Right in front of me!

I suspected that Alex hadn't said a thing to her about us. Why would he? There was never really an us.

Oh, give it up!

There was a clear us, and if I had been completely honest with Alex, there would still be an us now. He could be spooning me this moment, massaging my pounding head, and telling me he wished I didn't drink so much. I wished I could tell him that it had been a while since I'd drank. That last night's binge had been caused by heartache.

I whined as I accepted once again that it was indeed heartbreak that I was feeling at that moment. And what I'd been feeling for a while. I pulled the sheets over my head. They would have to drag me out of bed if they wanted to see me today. I had zero energy or courage to face everyone, anyone, Alex and his perfect woman with the perfect tatas and perfect red lips.

Those lips kissed his, and probably more. Ugh! Why couldn't I stop torturing myself?

I should get up and get out of here. Nica would understand.

"Oh, Alex." My chest hurt. My throat was parched and the throbbing discomfort in my head wasn't anything compared to the pain of a heartbreak. "Why him? Why now?" I asked myself.

Maybe my answers would never come.

I had to have a chat with Nica to convince her to let me go back to San Francisco today.

After a struggle with clean clothes, giving my face a wash, and brushing my teeth, I walked out of the bedroom. When I reached the steps, I noticed how quiet the house was. Something wasn't right. This place was full of energetic morning people. Why the stillness? I tiptoed down the steps, silently thankful once again that Alex and Marielle were staying in the opposite side of the house. I would have stayed in the guesthouse with Gerard and Mateo if it didn't bring too many memories. Maggie and Cara were there too. I wouldn't have gotten any sort of rest at all.

Cara. What a sweet girl. She'd kept me entertained yesterday, and my surliness had made her laugh. She hadn't asked too many questions, thankfully, and she had mostly talked about her blog and the secret boyfriend she had in New York City. Why she'd opened up to me was beyond my comprehension (it was difficult to think clearly when I was getting drunk). But I was glad she did. I doubted very much that after this we would remain friends, because Alex and Marie's relationship seemed awfully serious. Why else would he bring her here to the

States? I had overheard, too, that Martina was fond of her, although I believed this information had come from the cow, er...Marielle herself.

I should have asked Cara. I could have, but I didn't. She didn't seem to suspect anything, and I wasn't ready for explanations.

By the time I reached the kitchen, my curiosity had grown. I expected everyone to be around the massive island, but again, no one. Nothing but the quiet drip of the coffee. So I continued my search, and finally heard mutterings as I neared the front rooms.

There in the living room were all of my friends, staring silently out the large window that looked out to the courtyard.

"What the hell is going—"

"Shhhh... come." Gerard waved me over without even taking his eyes off the window.

I hesitated, but moved forward, and then I saw what had them stumped. I covered my mouth when a gasp came out. Nica threw me a sympathetic look.

Out in the pebbled yard, Alex was talking to Marielle. One of the vineyard's trucks idled beside them. My pulse rate increased as I became witness to what seemed like a lover's quarrel. Marielle would put one of her suitcases into the truck and a moment later, Alex would take it out.

"What are they saying?" Gerard spoke. "Is that French?"

"No. I think that's Italian," Maggie answered.

"Someone translate it!" Gerard ordered, but everyone ignored him.

"I can't believe this is happening. Somebody do something." I wasn't sure who'd said it but I felt all eyes on me.

I faltered and stepped back. "Why are you looking at me?"

"Pshhh...not you. Levi, can't you do something?"

I turned to Levi, who shrugged, shoved a hand through his hair, and headed out the door.

Marielle successfully moved all of her bags into the truck, and Alex stopped fighting her for them. He hung his head, gripping Marielle's hands. His lips moved but we couldn't hear what he said. His shoulders sagged. His eyes were focused on the ground. Marielle's stance was the same. Then she lifted Alex's hands and kissed the back of each one before cupping his face, and tilting his head to her.

They exchanged words, and Alex nodded. When they kissed, I gripped the nearest hand to me, grateful it was Nica's.

"Shit. They're coming in!" somebody said, "Everyone, spread out!"

My friends' movements were swift, but I was stuck to the floor. I could barely breathe much less run. When the door opened, and Alex came back in, his gaze found mine.

Two loud heartbeats. That was how long our moment had lasted before he turned away and disappeared further into the house.

I could've easily fainted from the lack of oxygen, but I felt the squeeze on my hand and remembered Nica was there to support me.

"What just happened?" I muttered under my breath.

*A*fter two full days of constant noise, laughter, muttering, and bickering, the house went quiet. The rest of the family and friends who had gathered for Nica's baby shower had returned to San Francisco. The silence unnerved me. I remained as Nica suggested.

What could only be called as a lover's quarrel—even possibly a breakup—we'd all witnessed, confused me. Ever since Alex had left with Cara, right after Marielle's departure, I'd asked around for what had started the misunderstanding. No one could verify what had caused Cara and Marielle's arguments. They'd insisted all they had heard were yelling from the two, which eventually drove Marielle packing and Alex running after her.

"Cara called Marielle a gold-digger," Gerard assumed, but no one else could confirm if it had happened.

Lily argued, "No, Marielle discovered something Cara's hiding and threatened to exploit it." I would have looked to Nica to confirm this, but she'd been so distraught over the incident that Levi insisted she'd needed to rest. Everyone knew and understood this. With another month to go before she popped, Nica couldn't be under any amount of unnecessary stress.

After breakfast on the fourth day, Levi had a meeting to attend which left Nica and me alone at the vineyard. He had given his staff the day off. The sun was strong by mid-morning and the two of us had decided that time by the pool was the best plan. An easy, relaxing time after all the craziness, just as the doctor had prescribed.

Nica had gone into the kitchen to scrounge up some snacks for us... or rather, for her and her baby. I stretched out on the lounger, soaking up the heat of the sun. Then my phone beeped beside me.

Hi, it's Cara. I got your number from Nica.

My response was short:

Hi, Cara! Are you back in NYC? I typed 'with Alex' at first, but at the last second, I erased it.

Yeah. My mom's already on my case. I need to talk to you about stuff.

What stuff?

Things that concern you and my brother.

The lump in my throat grew and remained stuck in my throat. **Which brother?** I feigned ignorance and rolled my eyes at myself.

The controlling one over there. Alex.

I thought Alex went with you.

Her response was instantaneous: **He did, but he went back there. He said he needed to think things through.**

Why didn't he go to France to see Marielle?

I hoped my desperation didn't show.

Go after that bitch? No way! Not after all the BS she said.

This was when Nica came back from the kitchen, carrying a bag of chips and a carafe with her. "Can you grab these, Chase?" Nica handed the snacks and drink to me. Her lips pursed. "I have to go pee again." She looked down at her belly and rubbed a hand over it. "She's so active too. It's okay, little munchkin. Mom will make room for you."

"Nica, before you leave..." I cocked my head to the right, toward the direction of the guesthouse. "Is somebody in there? I think I saw someone pass the window?" I adjusted the sunglasses on my face, grateful that the dark lenses shaded my eyes from my best friend.

She bit her bottom lip and averted her eyes. "Well... okay, don't freak out." She offered her hands for me to hold and I took them, titling my head up to her. "Alex came back after dropping off Cara."

"Why didn't you tell me?"

"He asked us not to tell anyone. He said he needs time to think some things through. Levi and I thought it would be best if you and Alex didn't see each other for a bit until he got everything sorted out." Nica pulled her lip between her teeth once again. Her apology and regret hung in the air. "I hated not telling you Chase, please trust me. It's really for the best. You both have been going through a lot."

She shut her eyes and her forehead creased. Nica moaned as her lips twisted, and she squeezed my hands harder.

"Nica, did you just pee your pants?"

Nica grimaced and groaned again, and my laughter died. I rose to my feet to get to hold her up.

Both her hands went to protect her belly. She pinned me with a worried look. "I think my water just broke."

"Oh gah! It's... no! It's too soon!" I stepped back to study the liquid that gushed down her legs and pooled around her feet. "What do I do? What do I do?"

Before Nica could answer, she buckled. The strength of her grip on my hand was enough to make me wince. Sweat beaded on her forehead as she twisted from another contraction.

"Nica, Nica, what... What do I do?" She didn't answer. She couldn't. My phone laid on the ground, on the other side of the lounger where it had fallen when I stood. "You have to let go of my hand, Nica, so I can call for help."

She let out a scream and some choice words.

Alex sprinted toward us, hurdling past the flower gardens and stone wall which separated the guest house from the main house. He knelt on one knee in front of me and Nica, not even concerned about the icky wetness underneath him. In two seconds, he had the situation assessed, and he smoothed his face into calmness. Alex turned to me and nodded, a silent way of telling me that he was here to help. Everything would be fine.

"We have to get you inside and out of the heat," he spoke in a steady tone, lifting Nica's chin to get her to focus her attention on him. "I'm going to carry you into the house, alright, Nica?" Nica nodded. "Let go of Chase's hands so she can call Levi."

"Levi," Nica managed to squeak out. Alex picked her up as though she was light as a feather and hurried to the house.

I swooped down to grab my phone and tapped Levi's number. I bypassed the greetings as soon as he picked up. "Nica's in labor. Come home!"

"What? It's too soon." Despite the uncertainty in his voice, I could tell he started to run, as I heard him panting through the phone. "Where is she?"

"Alex just brought her in. I'll keep you posted." I hung up. He would understand. Then, unsure of what to do, I called the emergency line while I jogged to where Alex brought Nica. An early, unexpected labor constituted a call to 911, didn't it?

"Nine-one-one, what's your emergency?" a woman asked.

Nica screamed before I could reply. I scrambled to her side on the floor. Alex had her laid on a thick blanket and her head propped on pillows. She had her legs bent and her feet spread apart. Somehow he seemed to know what to do, as he sat with her.

"Hee-hee-hoo," they breathed in unison. Alex's focus was on her.

"Ma'am? Ma'am, what's your emergency?" The voice on the other line pulled me back to the call.

"My friend. She's pregnant and I think the baby's coming." There was no way I could stay as calm as Alex. I informed the woman that Nica wasn't due for a month. I rattled off the vineyard's name and address.

"Is she crowning?" the woman asked.

"What? Crowning? I don't know." I looked to Alex for an answer. "Is she crowning?"

Alex's eyes widened. "I can't look..." He wiped the sweat off Nica's forehead. "She's my sister-in-law, Chase. You'll have to do it."

"What?" My brows shot up to the edge of my forehead. "I'm not... She might be my best friend but that's not... No way!"

"Ma'am, is she crowning?"

"Chase, you have to check," Alex told me.

I muttered a curse as I maneuvered between Nica's legs, pushing her dress up to expose her bikini bottoms. I held the phone between my ear and shoulder. Then I undid the strings of her bikini. "Holy hell!" I squeezed my thighs together, reminding myself to refill my birth control pills, and trained my eyes back at Nica's face. "Yeah, she is. I see the baby's fu—fudging head," I informed Alex, Nica and the 911 operator.

Nica continued to writhe.

"The ambulance is on their way, ma'am. Is there someone who can meet them at the door?"

"Shit. No... Alex, can you go to the gates to let the ambulance in?"

"Yeah. Stay with her." He leaned down to press a kiss on Nica's sweaty forehead. "Keep breathing, luv, you're doing great."

Nica nodded and continued to breathe as Alex had instructed her. Once he left, she turned that breathing into red-faced grunting. I didn't know if she should be pushing, but I had a role as her best friend and the only other person in the house with her. Make sure she and the baby were safe. It was my duty. Our friendship had just reached insanity level.

There was a loud screech of tires outside the house, followed by running, and Levi calling out his wife's name. Nica's answer was another scream and a curse as she bore down.

"Sweetheart, I'm here." Levi skidded to a halt and dropped beside me. "Is the baby really coming?"

"What the hell do you think?"

People always called birth a form of miracle. It was a miracle Nica wasn't tearing Levi's skin off while she went through birthing pains. I took Alex's job of getting Nica to keep her breathing steady and let Levi witness his daughter's birth. Several minutes later, a tiny wail echoed, and Levi held a mini-person covered in grossness up to show Nica. I grabbed another blanket off a chaise lounge and handed it to him so he could wrap his baby in it.

Then I witnessed the real miracle.

"She's here. She's beautiful," Levi choked up, staring in awe at his wife and daughter. His eyes welled up and so did Nica's.

It was beautiful to see so much love. I swiped at a tear that rolled down my cheek.

The ambulance came soon after. I stood aside, frozen, while I watched them take and check on the tiniest being in the world, cleaning her up in the process. They brought

Nica out on a stretcher and Levi stayed beside her the entire time. I shuffled behind them, my heart hammering in my chest. My hands felt sticky. They loaded Nica and the baby into the ambulance and Levi rode with them. When the vehicle pulled away and the sirens died down, I felt a strong presence behind me. It could only be caused by one person. And I was alone in the house with him.

Kyoka suigetsu

I was a mess in more ways than one. I didn't know what to do with my hands, my sticky, icky hands. So I stood there like I was about to do jazz hands.

"That was quite an adventure." Alex followed this statement with a nervous chuckle behind me.

That low timbre of his voice hit me right in the solar plexus, right in my core, and produced a delightful warmth. I rolled my eyes and squeezed them shut. His voice made me all tingly (and girly—which I wasn't too keen on).

Breath held, I turned to him, with my hands splayed at my sides. Had he been half-naked all this time? No, I would have noticed earlier. There was a thin film of sweat covering his top half. I bet if I took a step forward, I'd get that manly, sexy, rugged scent. I dragged my gaze away from the low-hung waistline of his running shorts and focused instead on the skin between his eyebrows. Yeah, that was a safe place. Nothing sexy about that.

But he moved, wiping his forehead with the back of a forearm—the one with the tattoo. I followed his toned arm muscles to his bulging biceps. Yes, bulging. It was safe to focus on that rather than the other bulge below the waistline. Those biceps met strong pecs. The pecs introduced me to ripped abs.

"I suppose I should clean up the mess in there," Alex said hitching his left thumb over his right shoulder, his arm stretched over his chest. Then he pinned me with those blue eyes a second too long, before strutting away.

I snapped out of it, out of staring at his firm butt.

Shower. I required a shower. Besides washing off the birthing grime, it would help cleanse the lust swimming in my unfiltered mind. Using the breathing technique Nica had used earlier, I hoo-hoo-heed my way to the bedroom en suite, jumping into the cold gush from the shower head. I let out a few curse words at the bite of nearly freezing water on my skin.

Then I remembered Nica hadn't brought a bag for the hospital. I'd been in the room with her when she'd packed it. I bet it would still be in the walk-in closet where she had set it aside for when the day came. Well, that day was today. There was a good chance that she'd be staying in the hospital longer, since little bundle of joy wasn't supposed to have come for another few weeks. I paused by the door, sending a quiet prayer that Nica and the baby were okay. I wasn't a religious type, that was my father's forte; he had always believed miracles could happen.

Sure enough, the luggage was in her closet, where she had left it. Thank Nica and her OCD preparedness. I'd take it to her, and at the same time, pay them a visit. As I walked back to my bedroom, lugging Nica's bag with me, I was shocked to see Alex pacing in front of the closed door. He looked like he was having a conversation with himself or trying to make a decision. His hand massaged the back of his neck. His hair was wet. Had he taken a quick shower too? Had it also been an arctic shower?

"Alex?" I called to him, and he raised his head. "What's going on?" I stopped a good few paces away.

He smiled, that panty-twisting brilliance of a smile, and I sucked in a deep breath. Only to inhale his fresh shower scent. Was that a combination of lemon and verbena? Gad, he was killing me! Couldn't he see my stomach quivering under my white shirt?

His smile disappeared when he saw the luggage in my hand. It didn't take long for me to assume what he probably thought. I rolled my eyes.

"This is Nica's. I was going to bring it to the hospital," I explained.

"Oh, perfect," he said, with his smile back on again with a lower wattage this time. "I came to ask if you'd like a ride... to the hospital."

"Yeah, that would be great. It would have been tricky to strap this on my bike." I waited for him to walk ahead of me so I could get my bearings.

We sat comfortably, yet uncomfortably, in Levi's car. He had left the keys in the ignition. Alex and I took advantage of that. I entered the address of the hospital on the GPS, and buckled myself in. The inside of the Audi felt constricting and I'd almost plastered myself to the car door, because I didn't want to get too close to Alex. It was too dangerous.

Halfway to our destination, a beeping sounded in the car's interior. A phone number and Martina's name popped up on the dashboard screen. Alex pressed the answer button and greeted his grandmother in soft-toned French.

"Olivier?"

"No, Onna. It's Alex." He glanced in my direction with a quirk in one corner of his lips. He continued in English, and I knew it was for my sake, "Levi is with Veronica. She had the baby today, and we're on our way to see them." *We.* I liked 'we'.

"The baby? It is too early?" his grandmother asked.

"Yes, Onna. About a month too soon. Shall I call you once I have more news?"

"*Oui, Alexandre...* and who are you with?"

Alex peered at me sideways. "Chase is with me." Damn right I was! "You remember Chase, don't you? Veronica's best friend?" He paused, tapping his fingers on the steering wheel, as if he was going to add more, but nothing else came.

There was also a bit of hesitation on the other line with Martina. For a second, I thought the call was dropped, but she spoke again, and this time in French. From the corner of my eyes, I watched Alex grip the wheel tighter. To say I wasn't eavesdropping would be a lie, as I listened carefully, picking up any familiar words from the rest of the conversation. A name was thrown in—Marielle—more than once.

Alex ended the call, and the rest of the ride was spent in uncomfortable silence.

❧

The maternity wing of the hospital was on the third floor. The neonatal intensive care unit was further down the hallway. In a private room, we found Nica resting on the bed and Levi, shoulders slumped forward, hovering over an incubator. I looked to Alex for guidance. Would it be right for us to be in the room with them? I didn't say anything out loud, but Alex nodded and we entered the room quietly.

Dropping the bag, I walked gingerly to the bed. I hugged Nica gently. She was hooked up to all sorts of tubes and monitors. A stray tear escaped my eye as she sobbed in my arms, and I patted her hair until she was able to talk.

"Did you see her? She's so tiny, Chase. They did so many tests on her," she said to me, staring past my shoulder to where her baby rested, encased in a temperature-controlled incubator. I eyed Levi and Alex and bit the inside of my cheek to keep myself from crying when I took note of other equipment in the room.

"The doctors said she has jaundice. And they're monitoring her heart and lungs," Nica continued.

I sat beside her, and held her close to me. She had to be one of the bravest people I knew. She couldn't have been doing one hundred percent as well, judging by the heart monitor and IV attached to her.

"How much does she weigh?"

"Four pounds and twelve ounces," Nica whispered. "We'll have the test results later."

We all remained quiet when a nurse came in the room and checked on the little nugget in the incubator. Nica held onto me. Neither of us could breathe.

Levi caught my attention. His eyes were red-rimmed. How long had it been since I'd seen him in the house running to his wife's side? A couple of hours? Had he been in tears this whole time? I couldn't forget the enamored look on his face the first time he saw his baby girl. I offered him a tiny smile, a form of quiet support, and he acknowledged it by nodding my way.

Alex was right beside him, his hands stuffed in his pockets, paying close attention to everything. I could see how he would be as an uncle. He'd be the cool kind. The one who'd spoil his niece. The sweet yet overly protective one. I wondered idly how he would be as a father.

On the way to the vineyard, the two of us were back in the cramped car. We were in our own worlds, sitting side by side, but it wasn't hard to guess what was on his mind. He would release a sigh every so often. The tension was palpable.

As we entered the vineyard's gates, Alex asked, "Ever thought of having kids?"

It almost knocked me off my seat. "What'd you say?"

He blew air through pursed lips. "Nothing. I'm sorry. My mind..." He sent me an apologetic look, his lips quirking on one side, but not a sign of a smile.

And because I was tired, and the question threw me off balance, I told the truth, "Not after witnessing Nica's childbirth. I think I'll have my thighs stapled together."

Alex's reply was a chest-rumbling chuckle.

⁊

People came trickling in and out of the vineyard the next few days. Lily, Nica's mom, came back with Maggie in tow, followed by Gerard, Mateo and Jewel—who visited Nica for a few hours before heading back to San Francisco as a promise to our friend. Every day I went to the hospital with Alex, but never alone.

However, we had formed some sort of routine. We'd have coffee first thing in the morning—and it hadn't escaped me that he'd developed some dark circles under his eyes, much like I had—and he would cook a quick breakfast for the two of us. He never asked what I wanted, but I ate everything he offered. In the kitchen, we'd be alone for a couple of minutes, standing side by side in front of the island, and sipping coffee. Then someone would come in and break the peaceful moment. I was grateful for the disturbance, but missed the proximity of him at the same time.

When we came back to the house after our visit, he'd say goodnight and wander off toward the guesthouse. Levi's housekeeper would have dinner prepared for anyone who returned for the night. Alex never joined us for meals at the dining table. And I couldn't help but worry about him.

On the fourth morning, after another restless night, the smell of coffee filtered into the house. Coffee-making was my only way of being useful in the kitchen. Someone else had beat me to it. When I walked in, Martina was seated on one of the stools beside Maggie.

"Good morning," I greeted everyone.

"Good morning, Chase. We made coffee," Maggie said.

"Thanks." I smiled at her and Martina. When our eyes met, I felt exposed, like she was privy to a secret about me. "When did you come in?" I asked her.

"Late last night, dear," she replied in dulcet tone. She reminded me of Cara, and only then did I realize that Cara hadn't sent me a text since Nica had her baby. I made a mental note to give her a ring later.

To avoid looking like a fool, standing there gaping at her like she was some kind of sideshow, I proceeded to make myself a cup of coffee. Out of habit, I brought two cups down from the cupboard, but I only poured coffee into one.

"I'd like some of that," Levi said as he came into the kitchen. He had a bit more spring in his steps. The baby was doing better every day. The tests showed there weren't any major health concerns. Nica was healing well too. She didn't have any worrisome complications during pregnancy and the doctors had said the premature birth had been due to a weak cervix. When she'd found out and shared this with me, she was well enough to joke that she would need a boot camp for her cervix for baby number two.

I handed Levi my cup and poured coffee in the second one. "Who's with Nica?"

Before answering, Levi took a sip from his cup. "Lily stayed with her last night. She forced me to get some sleep, because I had to drive to the airport to pick up Martina and drop Alex off."

My hands trembled and I hid it by gripping the edge of the coutnertop. Alex left? And he didn't tell me? I controlled my breathing, careful not to arouse suspicion. But when I tilted my head up and caught Levi's gaze, there was no escaping the truth. He knew. I averted further eye contact and focused on my coffee.

Chairlegs scraped on the floor as Maggie and Martina stood and shuffled out, telling Levi they'd be ready to leave for the hospital in a few minutes.

"I better get ready too." I stepped aside to excuse myself, but Levi stopped me by placing a hand on my arm.

"Chase, a second?" Levi and I had had rough times together. Or rather, I'd given him a tough time while he was dating Nica, and even a more difficult time when he was about to propose to her.

I leaned my back against the opposite counter, and crossed my arms over my chest. "Yeah?"

Levi narrowed his eyes at me, studying me, scrutinizing my features. "Are you in love with my brother?"

"It's none of your business, Levi..." was my quick reply. I pouted when I thought once again who I was talking to. This was my best friend's husband. He was my best friend-in-law. Was that a thing? It should be. As long as he was there and he continued to love her, I'd have to tolerate him. "Yes, yes I am...but it's still none of your business."

Levi chuckled, and I gave him a gentle push.

"Hey, have you guys decided on a name?"

"Yes, we did," Levi replied, "Her name is Aimee."

ALEX

*I*t didn't matter what part of the world I was in, when true love presented itself, I knew what it looked like. All I had to do was open my eyes and see.

My camera was an extension of myself and because of it, I'd witnessed true wonders of the world. Nothing took my breath away more than when I saw true love. I raised it, I breathed in, and took the shot. Trying to capture the meaning of love in one photograph wasn't a hard feat when I understood what it was like. It was beyond two people kissing, holding hands, while embraced by the warmth of the sun. It was present in what wasn't easy to see. The simplest caress, the whispered care, knowing that nothing else mattered without each other.

Walt Buford sat beside his wife in the sunroom, an extension of their home, which faced their grand estate, and what I'd gathered was his sanctuary. When he heard the second shutter noise my camera made, he raised a hand, slightly trembling from the obvious weakness he felt but continued to hide.

"Alex, good morning," he greeted, his voice hoarse. "Why don't you come and join us?"

I didn't hesitate, stepping forward until I was soaked by the brightness of the sun. "Good morning." I bent down to greet Georgia-Anne, who'd offered one side of her cheek for me to peck.

"Did you get enough sleep?" she asked, waving a hand to an empty seat.

"Better than expected." I reached for the carafe of freshly squeezed orange juice and poured myself a glass.

I'd been their guest for the past two days. I'd come for one purpose, and hadn't expected the need to stay for another. Despite my own protestations that I would overstay my welcome if I didn't leave sooner, it felt right to be here. To be near the people who'd raised the woman I'd fallen madly in love with.

I wanted to understand her. Who she was before I met her, before she became the woman who'd driven me mental, who'd made having another woman by my side felt wrong. When I left my brother's vineyard, I'd made a rush trip to New York City and reclaimed the motorcycle I'd left behind. As soon as I rode it, my direction had been clear. It hadn't taken long to arrive in Stowe and when I got here, I'd been welcomed with open arms depsite only meeting Walt once, and never having met Georgia-Anne at all.

"I'll head over the kitchen and fix you up some breakfast." Georgia-Anne patted my hand before she stood. There was no point in arguing with her that I was quite capable of doing the task, she was as stubborn as her daughter. I'd learned how to choose my battles.

"Thank you."

I placed the camera on the table and sipped the juice in comfortable silence, which didn't last long when Walt spoke. "When will you see my daughter again?"

Rubbing the growth on my jaw, I contemplated on my answer before saying, "Right after I return from Istanbul."

He nodded and craned his neck over a shoulder. When he returned his attention back to me, my heart ached for Chase. Her father was getting weaker. Every movement exhausted him; every word out of his mouth was a challenge. But he continued to fight because of his love for his wife and daughter.

"Take care of her."

His words gripped my heart. "I intend to."

He nodded again. Not long after, Georgia-Anne returned with a tray of food and Walt continued to smile for his loving wife.

This was the kind of care Walt wanted his daughter to have, an all-consuming love. Before I dug into my meal, I caught his eyes again and nodded my head. It was a silent promise, and he accepted it as the truth.

I loved his daughter. I'd been wrong to think I could ignore how strong my feelings were for her, that by seeing Marielle, I could easily erase the memories Chase and I had had together. Marielle had known the truth from the start, and the night I'd seen Chase out in the vineyard alone, Marielle had admitted what was so clear to her. Still, I tried to deny it. My heart didn't wander. I couldn't possibly love a woman when another warmed my bed. I wasn't like my father. I continued to deny it even after Marielle had packed her bags and left. Cara might have ignited the argument that morning, but at the end, Marielle and I had understood our time came to an end.

But it would be days before I finally admitted it—before I could surrender to the fact Marielle and I had been over before we'd begun. It took seeing Levi and Nica and the unfathomable happiness they shared when they held their daughter for me to believe I had love in my heart. Except Chase needed time on her own. I couldn't have her thinking I'd jump right into a relationship with her days after I'd ended one. I wanted to know everything about her, and since she wasn't forward about any of it, I'd come to do research on my own.

A visit to her family had been an eye-opener. I found

out about the sudden disapperance of her sister, and a friendly chat with her ex-fiancé, Daniel, had given me insight on what had driven Chase out of her hometown. Chase had spent years on her own before she met Veronica. I ached for the young woman who'd walked through life searching for something only she could say.

"Are you sure you need to leave today?" Georgia-Anne asked, pulling me out of my reverie.

I nodded and reached for the coffee she'd brought me. "I should have left yesterday. I'm promised Daniel I'd meet with him before my flight tonight."

She hummed and stared far off into the distance. "It's nice to see you guys get along." She lifted her teacup to her lips and sipped quietly before continuing. "My daughter said she'll come next weekend. Would you be back then?"

"I think I might be." I smiled, more to myself than to my companions. It would be a surprise for Chase to see me here, comfortable in her parents' home, sleeping in the room across from hers, eating breakfast in the sunroom with her parents, having a pint with Daniel.

I could see it all clearly in my mind.

I could breathe when I was around her, even better when I was with her. When I had her in my arms, nothing else had mattered. If it would take longer for her to realize we belonged together, I was ready to challenge each minute head on. She was worth fighting for, even if it was her own stubborn behavior I had to battle against.

Her love was worth it all.

CHASE

I never truly believed in happily-ever-afters. That was Nica's territory, and every day she became a testament that such a thing existed. There was zero doubt in my mind that Levi loved her through and through, and now, they had baby Aimee to shower affection to, as well.

Could a non-believer get their happily-ever-after? I supposed it would help if I had a Prince Charming around. He was in Arnavutköy, Istanbul, last I heard—mostly from eavesdropping on Levi and Martina's conversations. A quick Google search of the location hadn't produced much information. The photos looked welcoming, but we were in California. If Alex wanted deep blue sea, all he had to do was take a short drive to the coast...and use the perfect camera filter. What could Alex be doing there? More importantly, why wasn't he here? He was missing out on quality bonding time with his one and only niece.

Levi hadn't mentioned or hinted at the short conversation we had in the kitchen. I was both grateful and disappointed about that. I didn't expect a thorough study on the topic, just a few clues, perhaps an insight on how Alex felt about me. Though, to be honest, I'd rather hear it straight from the ass' mouth. Besides, Levi had more pressing matters to focus on.

When Monday came rolling along, I prepared my bags to head back to San Francisco. Now that Nica was out of commission for work—and since I owned part of Bliss—it was up to me to take the brunt of the responsibility, something she and I had agreed on. For me, it was a driving force behind my move back to California, instead of staying in Vermont. My parents' home was in Vermont. Like the song, I left my heart in San Francisco, and if I didn't come back, I would wither and die.

Martina walked out of the house while I rearranged the Harley's side bags. She and I hadn't been alone since her arrival, something else I'd been grateful for. I didn't know why, but she made me nervous. There was something in the way she looked me, like she was studying and scrutinizing me.

"Levi mentioned you're leaving today, Chase," she said, spreading her lips into a polite smile.

I peered at her through my sunglasses. "Yes, I have to get back to work." Short and sweet. Then I busied my hands, stuffing them into the bag so she wouldn't see how they trembled.

She stood in front of me for a few minutes, taking all of my Harley in. Would she think it was inappropriate for a woman who was in love with her grandson ride a beast like my baby? But when she opened her mouth to speak, what came out surprised me.

"My husband and I used to ride. After the war, he and I spent our early wedding years travelling the States." Martina stepped forward and ghosted a hand over the leather seat. "I can still remember the thrill of it."

I smiled at her, and climbed onto my Harley. "I'm visiting Nica at the hospital before I head home." Sliding my butt forward, I patted the back of the seat. "I can give you a lift?" Was it the right thing to do? Oh, Alex would have a heart attack if he knew. Served him right for not being here.

"Oh, what a lovely idea." She glanced toward the house. "But, I'd promised my grandsons I'd behave."

"I won't tell if you won't." Martina shifted her weight from one foot to the other. What was I doing? Alex would have my head! "Maybe next time. I'm in Levi's good graces right now. Wouldn't wanna ruin that, would I?" I pushed my sunglasses up and winked at her.

Martina let out a demure laugh, hiding her mouth behind a hand. "I thought it was Alex you were concerned with?"

My mouth dropped to the ground. Martina's eyes lit up and she lifted one hand to cup my cheek, speaking in smooth-flowing French. What she said I had no idea, but it somehow caused goose bumps all over my body.

❧

I arrived at the offices of Bliss Event Designers with my head in the clouds. As soon as I got off the elevator, my phone buzzed. A text message from an unknown number: **You left?! I just got here! It's Cara BTW. New phone, new number.**

I'd sent her a couple of messages the past few days, and hadn't received anything back. I'd been worried but I couldn't ask Levi or Martina. They might not have known that she was in contact with me.

I sent a quick message back: **Where have you been? I've sent you messages. I guess you didn't get them.**

Her reply was even quicker: **I broke my phone. Long story. It took me a while to get my contacts back. So where are you?**

I'm back in SF. Back to work.

Cara sent: **Are you coming back? We have so much to talk about, and I can't say it over text.**

We did? I paused in front of the office entrance, reading and re-reading the text again. I was just about to type a text when a knock startled me. I looked up to see Gerard and Jewel waving frantically on the other side of the window to my right. They rushed out of the office to get to me, squeezing me in a group hug—without my permission!

"You're here!" they both said.

Gerard propped a hand over one hip and quirked an eyebrow. "And you're late for the meeting. Come on."

"Hold up, guys, I just need to send a quick message." I waved my phone at them. Bad idea. Gerard snatched it out of my hand and ran into the office before I could take it back.

"Who is more important than your welcome back to work meeting? Is it lover boy Danny?" he said, giggling as I chased him.

"Danny?" Jewel asked.

"It's not Danny! And he's not my lover. Get your facts straight!" I yelled at Gerard, tackling him in the hallway the moment I got close enough. My Daddy had taught me some moves when I was little and the boys at school had started picking on me. Gerard and I both dropped.

"Get the phone, Jewel!" he screamed, as he grappled with me on the floor.

"Jewel, if you touch that I will fire you!"

"You can't fire her. She's part owner now." Gerard wrapped his large legs around mine, effectively keeping me from squirming out of his grip.

"Yes, you are!" I squeaked out from Gerard's hold. "That's why you have to do the responsible thing!"

My argument worked. Jewel picked up the phone and ordered Gerard to let me go. "We should really start the meeting."

Gerard huffed and released me. I punched him a couple

of times on the upper arm. Not hard enough to make him grapple with me again. Gerard was like a brother to me. A brother I had never wanted, but was glad I had.

I straightened out my clothes and took the phone from Jewel. Then I sent a rapid text to Cara that I would have to talk to her later.

❦

Unfortunately, later didn't come. Right after the meeting, Gerard was on me again, asking about Danny.

"So you're single? 'Cause we thought you..." He didn't finish, looking to Mateo and Jewel for some kind of affirmation that the rumors were true.

As I'd said, these people were my family now. Opening up to Levi about my feelings for Alex had given me some sort of ease. I'd left San Francisco weeks ago without telling my friends, apart from Nica, the complete story. I guess today was the right day to straighten out speculations.

With the conference door closed, I told Gerard, Mateo and Jewel my story. I spread out all my cards and came clean, everything from my father's condition to my previous engagement to Danny to our current non-relationship relationship. Well, not everything per se. I did leave out what I had with Alex. Some things were meant to be kept as sacred secrets.

"So you are single!" Gerard repeated, clapping his hands together in absolute glee. "Do you know what this means?"

I narrowed my eyes at him. "The answer is no." I stood to walk out of the conference room. Confession time was over.

"Yes!" Gerard clasped his hands together and knelt in

front of me, blocking the door with his large frame. "Please, Chase, can we please have an un-engagement party?"

"Oooh!" Jewel quipped from behind me.

I looked over my shoulder and squinted at her, shaking my head as a show of disappointment. Then I turned my sights to Mateo, pleading him for some sort of help.

He shrugged. "You know he's never going to stop," he said to me.

"Ugh!" He was no help! "Fine! One party. Tonight. Just us." I figured we would all be too busy for the rest of the day for anyone to make a grand plan for this cockamamie idea.

How wrong was I? I had underestimated the powers of a group of event planners.

❧

When I awoke the next day to a thrumming on my bedside table, my mouth felt like the Gobi desert, and it took me a few more moments to notice the phone vibrating beside me. Not my phone. And someone named Honey Boo was calling. She was pretty in a piled-on makeup kind of way. I sat up to find the owner of the phone to, one, ask him or her what his or her phone was doing on my bedside table and, two, why had he or she been in my bedroom in the first place. Then the taste of bile crawled up my throat, sending me off to the bathroom.

After a quick discharge of projectile vomit, followed by a couple more heaves, I washed the smeared make up off my face. I was fully clothed, in the same clothes I'd worn all day at work. As I changed, the phone vibrated once again. Out of my bedroom I went, and into a war zone. From the state of the rest of my apartment I could have easily called the army and reported some kind of national emergency. Anybody living in this country who partied like my friends did should be thrown onto an island where they couldn't hurt those around them, particularly me.

I looked around the living room and to the pathetic state of my so-called friends scattered all over the sofas and the floor. I deliberately stomped my five-inch heels onto the parquet floor to rouse them. Mateo was the first to groan, followed by Gerard's protestations.

"Why am I vomiting glitter?" I asked. "What happened?"

Gerard chuckled. "You're vomiting glitter? Must be because you wouldn't stop licking Rocco's abs last night." Everyone else, still half asleep, snickered.

"Who the hell is Rocco?"

"That would be me."

I followed the voice and found it belonged to a half-naked man walking out of my kitchen, sipping what I assumed was coffee from one of my cups. My eyes fell on his ripped abs. Some kind of word gurgled out of my mouth.

"Ah, and you have found my phone!" He stretched out his hand for the phone I had clasped in mine.

"It was on my bedside table." My own words slapped me into reality. "In my bedroom... oh my god... what was your phone doing in my bedroom? Where you there too?"

Mateo spoke for him when all Rocco did was chuckle. "Relax, Chase, you're not really Rocco's type."

I was slightly appalled by that comment. "Why? What's wrong with me?" My own ego tried to inflate itself back to its regular humungous size.

"For one, you're not a man," Gerard answered.

"Oh." Right. For a moment, I forgot where I was. "Well,

get your asses up. It's Tuesday and we have work to do. And did anybody see my phone?"

"Check the freezer," Nica's assistant, Becca suggested. My assistant, whose name I'd finally remembered was Stephanie, stretched out her arms and legs beside Becca. Glad to see that they'd had a great time too.

"The freezer?"

"No, it's okay." Rocco placed a warm hand on my arm. "I saved it. It's in the kitchen, been ringing all morning."

"Oh shit." I walked around sexy Rocco toward my kitchen, then turned around before I could get to my phone, yelling out, "And Honey Boo's been calling you, Rocco!"

He strutted into the kitchen and calmly prepared a cup of coffee for me. "She needs to learn about boundaries." When I raised a brow at him, he shook his head. "Thank you for throwing a great party." Then he handed me my coffee.

Once my head was clearer, I'd have to speak to Nica about hiring Rocco. He'd been more useful this morning than the rest of the crew. Whatever he did with his time off was his own business.

I scrolled through my missed calls. Ten calls from my parents and fifteen from Danny. I also had numerous voicemails waiting. I skipped checking any of them and rang my parents' home with no success. So I called Danny.

"Danny, what's up?" I asked as soon as he picked up.

His voice sounded tired and heavy. I didn't like it one bit. "Hannah, it's your Dad..." He sighed, and I felt the weight of it on my shoulders and on my chest. "It's time for you to come back to Stowe."

My entire body numbed.

Lacuna

ALEX

At thirty thousand feet, while I watched the right wing of the plane get swallowed by white clouds, I received a message. I feared that my heart would stop beating if I didn't get to her sooner. I couldn't even imagine the pain she was going through.

Right at that moment, a vision appeared clearly in my mind—a photograph burned into my memory—of Chase somber, looking out the hotel window one rainy night. The light from a lamp post outside illuminated her figure, a silhouette in the shadows.

I'd said, "Tell me. What's on your mind?" as I'd walked up to her, sliding my arms over the smooth skin of her naked stomach, and pulling her flush against me. My body's reaction was instantaneous, firing up the craving I'd had for her.

She hadn't shied away, instead, she'd pressed her buttocks harder against me, no inch spared between us. I'd produced a hiss, not of pain, but of satisfaction. Her scent had infiltrated my senses, and I'd been addicted to it, to her, to all of her. Chase had breathed, pushing her chest forward, urging me to cup her breasts, and she'd welcomed my touch. I couldn't get enough of her. I would never get enough of her.

"Alex," she'd begun, then paused and turned to face me, hooking her hands over the back of my neck. Her fingers played with the ends of my hair. I'd splayed my hands over her buttocks, and squeezed. "Have you ever been in love?"

"Once," I'd answered, "Once I thought I was." It was the truth. I remembered what I'd thought I'd felt for Simone, thinking that my world revolved around her. I'd been careless. I'd been blind. And I'd paid dearly for it. Chase knew about Simone.

But her next question had terrified me more.

"Is there anything you regret in life?" Her fingers massaged the muscles of my neck, easing the tension this line of questioning had created.

I'd breathed her in again, leaned my head forward and released a warm breath over her shoulder. "I'd like to think that I shouldn't have any, but...the separation between Levi and me was hard on me, on the both of us." Where was this going? "Do you have any regrets?"

"Plenty." There had been no hesitation on her part, and no pause before her next question. "If there's one person you could talk to right now, who would it be?"

I'd chuckled drily. "I am talking to her now."

"No." She'd grazed her lips over mine before kissing me. "I mean someone who's not in your life anymore."

I'd nipped at her soft, sweet red lips. It wouldn't do me any good to keep the answer to myself. She'd never let it go. She was a naturally curious person. "My father."

"What would you say?" Her voice had become almost a whisper against my skin.

"That I forgive him."

Chase had pressed her lips over mine. Desire had burnt through me. There had been no other questions asked that night.

But now, I wish that I had asked. I wished that I'd asked her the same question—What would she tell her father if he were in front of her? I imagined she would tell him that she loved him. I imagined those were the same words she could be saying to him now, as my plane flew over the Atlantic.

I'd received a different message several hours ago. A message which had sent me packing in a haste and abandoning my assignment. The preparation to leave Turkey had been quick, but the departure had been pain-stakingly slow.

His condition worsened due to a complication. Chase had made it to Stowe and by her father's side the entire time. Daniel had been sending me daily accounts. At first, they all thought he'd be on the mend, but his condition had turned overnight.

My phone lit up and vibrated as it received another message. It had only been a few minutes since I'd been told Walt Buford was sent to ICU. But it was too late. He couldn't be saved.

I pressed a number in my contacts and immediately connected.

"How is she?" I bypassed the greeting. There was no need for it. My call was expected.

"Holding everything in, like usual. When will you get here?"

"About five hours. The skies are clear," I said.

"Get some rest while you can. You'll need the energy. See you when you get here."

I gripped the armrest of my seat, cursing myself for leaving the US in the first place. "I should have been there right from the start. I should have been there for Chase."

My heart felt the pain of loss. What she'd be feeling now was insurmountable compared to mine.

"Just get here." The line went dead as Daniel ended the call.

❧

When I arrived at the Buford Estates, the house was packed. I stayed hidden in the shadows. My presence would pique people's curiosity. Who was I, a stranger amongst them?

"Alex." There was a soft tap on my arm. I'd been staring into nothing, focused on the memories in my head.

"Georgia-Anne, I'm sorry for your loss." I hugged her. She was fond of hugs, unlike her daughter.

"Thank you for coming. I'm sure Walt would have been thrilled knowing you're here. I know he's watching us right now." She leaned forward and lowered her voice. "Have you seen my daughter? Does she know you're here?"

"No, I haven't." I made a gesture of looking around although I knew Chase wasn't near us at all.

"She's probably in her bedroom. Go and find her. She needs you right now." Georgia-Anne patted my arm before hugging me again. "You know the way. Go on."

I turned to the stairs, which led to the second floor of the large home. She was right. I knew the way to Chase's room. How many times had I'd gone there before, searching for a clue to how I could reach out to her, and prove my love? Her bedroom walls were covered in pink chintz. I knew that she must have hated it. It was an exact contrast to her bedroom in San Francisco.

My heart thudded inside my chest as I drew near it. I rapped at her door and waited for an answer. Nothing. I knocked again. With courage, or insanity, or a mixture of both, I turned the handle as I quietly called out her name. And it opened to an empty room. The black dress she'd worn during the funeral service laid across the undisturbed bed.

CHASE

There's no rewind button in life.

How I hoped it wasn't true. All I had were memories and mementos. The letter from my sister. The last few words from my father. The sound of my heart breaking.

It was always so easy to just run away, turn my back on the past and start anew. But I'd done that before and eventually it caught up to me. A big part of me wished it had stayed in the past, but a larger piece of my heart was grateful that it hadn't. I didn't know what I would have done had Daddy passed away without me knowing. Yes, his death had taken a bite out of my life but he had given me peace at the very end. Only he could've done that.

When I'd told him that I regretted leaving Stowe years ago, Daddy had said, "You must learn to forgive yourself. What you did was something you felt was right." He'd paused to cough, taking his breath away momentarily, but then he'd trudged on. "You're a survivor. You're a proud Buford, and as stubborn as your old man here. But you're also a lover and a fighter. It's okay to follow your heart."

He'd said the words to me when we'd been alone. Daddy had continued, despite my urging to save his breath, "And don't worry about your mother. She will be fine. She's been running the farm with me since before you were born. I know she'll manage on her own. You...you need to go everywhere and see everything. And be with that person who can take care of your heart. Be with the person you ought to be with, my Nugget."

My father had given me sound advice throughout the years, particularly on matters of the heart. Even while I'd been away I'd kept his wisdom in my thoughts. But at the end of it, I'd chosen to be alone.

Or fate had chosen it for me.

My chest heaved as I controlled my breathing, gazing out into the reflection of the orange sky over the silent, still water. Just yesterday my father had been alive, offering pieces of his soul to me. Then he was gone. And in Walter Buford fashion, the funeral service had been simple and quick. "Like pulling off a Band-Aid," he would have described it. He hadn't wanted anyone mourning him for days, especially not me. Yet, it didn't stop the hollowness in my heart. My heart was overfilled with sorrow. With loss and heartache.

My plan had been to chuck several bales of hay to exert some energy. I hadn't slept. I hadn't eaten. I hadn't stopped crying when I was alone. And I'd thought that by making my muscles hurt, I could try and release the other kinds of hurt I was feeling.

When I'd reached the farm, though, I couldn't get myself to do anything but sit on the dock and stare at everything around me, wiping away tear after tear rolling down my cheeks. As I sat with my arms around my legs, I contemplated on the words he'd offered to me. Daddy had wanted me to live, to love, and to experience the world. Charity had had the same sentiments.

I wondered what the rest of the world looked like. In Alex's photos, I'd seen the beauty it offered. But to feel the searing earth in Africa, to smell the aroma of spices in India, to hear the chatter of birds and all sorts of animals in the Amazon, to taste the sweetness of freshest fruits in Thailand, what would those experiences be like? How would I react to them?

As I dipped my feet into the lake, I patted the paper beside me, weighed down by a large river rock. Charity's letter. She'd encouraged me to see and experience the world all those years ago. And my father had done the same before he'd taken his last breath. I had the urge to run and hop on the next flight out of the country, but some time during the last decade, I'd grown up. I would have to start making plans. I'd travel to respect my father and sister's wishes. I'd do it for the little girl who'd learned to climb the tree all on her own just to experience what it was like to be that high up, reaching tiny hands toward the clear blue sky. She'd want me to climb a mountain too.

I'd do this for them. I'd do this for me. It was time to live.

I heard the crunch of gravel behind me. I knew Danny would come looking for me once they discovered I'd left the estate. I glanced quickly over my shoulder at his truck stopping by the docks. The lake water was cold, like the air around me. While I sucked in another calming breath, and swiped at the last tears from my eyes, I swirled my toes and watched the ripples on the still surface. There was something beautiful about the circles forming over the lake. It was almost soothing. I could talk to him, but I didn't want him to see me cry.

Behind me, a car door shut, followed by footsteps on the wooden dock. Hesitant footsteps. I made another ripple with my feet. I sniffed the air and touched my cool hands to my reddened cheeks.

"I'm fine, Danny. You didn't have to come and get me. I just needed some time to myself," I said without looking over.

The footsteps halted. "Would you like me to come back in a minute or so?"

The speaker wasn't Danny. I turned and saw Alex with his hands in his pockets, looking every bit as handsome as I last saw him. When I stood to face him, I lost my balance. My hands flailed to keep myself on the dock, and Alex reached forward to help me.

I fell into the cold water, pulling him in with me.

I shouted a few curse words as I resurfaced and pushed myself back up to the dock, not ignoring Alex's splayed hands on my butt as he helped me up. Once seated back on the wood, I stretched out my hand to pull Alex up beside me.

"Is that water always this cold?" he asked, pushing his soaked hair off his forehead. His black shirt and trousers clung to him like second skin.

I gathered my hair to one side and squeezed the water out of it. My teeth chattered. "Nope. What are you doing here?"

Alex peeled his shirt off and as he stood, he started unbuttoning his pants. "I came to look for you. You weren't at the house."

"What are you doing? Why are you getting naked?" I forced my eyes away from his toned, tanned, wet body and up to the concerned look on his face. "Hold up. You were looking for me at my parents' house?"

"Yes. You're going to get a chill if you don't take your wet clothes off." He undressed to his boxers and left the pile of clothes by his feet.

"I'm fine." I swatted at the air around me, but the thoughtfulness in his voice caused a tightening in my chest. A pressure built in my head, and I felt the prickle of unshed tears in the back of my eyes.

"No, Chase. Come to the truck. I think I spotted a

blanket in the back. I don't want you to get sick." Alex spread his hands in front of me. "Take my hands or I'll pick you up and carry you." One corner of his lips quirked.

Encouraged by that hint of a smile, I nodded. As I got on my feet, Alex held me, wrapping me in a tight embrace. It was too much for me, and I sobbed. My shoulders shook. The outpouring was relentless, but Alex did not let go. He murmured foreign words into my ear. And as my legs gave out from under me, Alex held me closer. He kissed the sensitive skin on corners of my lips, then he pressed his lips on my forehead. When my sobs died down, he guided me toward the truck.

"Wait. My letter." I pointed at the soaked paper beside his wet clothes.

Carefully, he picked it up and handed it to me. Then we proceeded to the truck. Before I stepped in, he helped me take off my shirt and jeans, and wrapped me in the blanket, which he grabbed from the back. Alex lifted me into Danny's pickup. I reached over and started it, letting the heat warm the cab. I placed Charity's letter over the console to dry. As Alex scooted beside me, he wrapped his arms around me, and I in turn, shared the thick blanket with him. We stayed in silence for a while.

"What are you doing here, Alex?" I asked in a soft voice, hoarse from my crying.

Alex's shoulders rose then fell. I couldn't ignore the quick tattoo of his heart as I pressed my head on his chest. He inhaled deeply and exhaled into my hair.

"I received the message about your father when I was in Turkey. I'm sorry I couldn't be here sooner."

If he expected me to accept that answer as it was, then he was mistaken. "I don't understand. How did you know?"

Alex held my chin and raised my head so that I could

see the tenderness in his eyes. "Yes, Levi and Nica told me about your father. Daniel called me to say that his condition had gotten worse, and later on, he called me when Walt died."

"But..."

"Chase, you should know that I'm here for you, and only you. When I left Napa after Aimee was born, I decided to pay your father a visit."

"Why?"

Alex offered a half shrug. "I wanted to get to know the man who raised you. Who meant so much to you, while I still could. I met Daniel then too. I came before I worked the NatGeo project in Istanbul." He looked out of the window. The sky had turned into a rich mix of purple, red and grey. "I promised him that I'd show him the photos I'd taken when I came back. I didn't think..."

He let the words hang in the air. Nobody had foreseen Daddy's death. The probable months we had been given as he'd undergone chemo had turned into days, then hours. No matter how much I'd tried to prepare myself for it, my heart had broken. Alex said he was here for me. Would he help me heal?

"He was a great man, Chase, and he spoke of nothing and no one else but you." He brushed the hair off my face, and ran his thumb over my lips. "I promised him I would take care of you. Will you let me do that? Will you allow me to keep my promise to him?"

I'd be stupid to say no. I loved this man in front of me, and it seemed he felt the same way. I raised my arms and tangled my fingers behind his neck. "Just moments ago, I was thinking of you. Daddy asked me to find the person who had my heart. I guess I don't have to go looking too far, now that he's in front of me." With my heart sighing Alex's name, I pressed my lips onto his.

Sweetness and sorrow co-mingled in that kiss.

We drove back to the house as the night took over the sky, and the brightest stars came out to greet us. The people who had gathered earlier had all gone back to their homes. My mother had retired for the night, and the house stood in comfortable silence. I didn't have to lead Alex to my bedroom.

With the moonlight filtering through the bedroom windows, Alex skated a thumb over my cheeks and followed the shape of my lips. *"Hayati,"* he whispered, while our foreheads touched and our eyes closed. "My life." A single tear left a moist path down to my lips before Alex covered them with his.

We slept in the same bed, in my pink bedroom. We kissed. We cuddled, but not much more. We had the rest of our lives for more. Alex was there with me. Neither one of us ran away from love, instead, we embraced it. We held onto it.

Logolepsy

acing the full-length mirror, I ran my hands over the white silk dress, with the cathedral-length train bundled up behind me. I tugged at the ends of the sleeves at my wrist and fixed the high-neck lace collar.

Who was this woman in front of me? I raised my chin, looking down at the reflection.

"Wow."

My shoulders shook when his voice startled me. My eyes darted to the corner of the mirror. My hands were poised to unzip the bridal gown. I panicked and it got it stuck in my hair.

"Ouch!" My lips twisted into agony.

Alex came to my rescue. "Hold on, Chase, let me help. Push your hair aside. Wait, I'll zip this and... take the piece off... Voila!" Through the mirror, he teased me with his playful eyes.

Warmth spread up my neck and to my cheeks. "Don't say a word," I warned him.

He sniggered. "You look beautiful. It may need a few minor adjustments. Maybe take out the sleeves..."

"I said not a word!" I huffed and as soon as the dress was fully unzipped, I stepped out of it and dumped it on the floor. "It's my mother's not-so-subtle way of telling me she wants me hitched." She had sent me her old wedding gown this morning, with a note saying that she'd had luck with it, and maybe it would work on me too.

Alex circled his arms around my waist and turned me to

face him. "You looked beautiful in it," he repeated, with a smile tickling his lips. "You look beautiful in anything." Then he ran his eyes over my nearly naked body. "You look beautiful in nothing."

I sucked my bottom lip between my teeth, while he nipped the tops of my boobs. My fingers worked through his long hair. He'd been away on another assignment, which I hadn't been able to go on since Bliss had received more contracts for events within the coming months. We'd had to hire more people (including Rocco, whom Alex wasn't too keen on) to work the weddings, bashes, and galas.

"Do you want to talk about it?" Alex stopped nipping. He stared at me through thick lashes. His stubbled chin rested on my cleavage. His arms tightly wound around my body. His looks and his touch electrified me. But his words jabbed at my gut.

"Talk about what? You need a haircut." I wasn't stupid. I knew what he wanted to discuss. To distract him more, I tugged at his hair. He moaned, but the distraction was short-lived.

"Chase." Alex trapped my face between his hands and made me look at him.

"What?" I pleaded with my eyes so he'd drop the subject.

Alex and I had never talked about marriage. We'd spoken about kids once. Once. Months ago. And my thoughts on the matter hadn't changed. I wasn't the maternal type. I was a good friend, a fairly good daughter, a fantastic lover (just ask Alex), a smart business owner, but I was not a mother.

Alex stroked my left cheek with the back of his hand. "What are your thoughts on marriage?"

Fear gutted me. I loved Alex. He was my one. The one.

I'd been engaged before and left Danny at the altar. And Alex also had been engaged once, to Simone. I'd seen photos of her. She'd been a beauty. She'd also broken Alex's heart in a most unforgivable way. Two wrongs didn't always make a right. Two broken engagements didn't mean we should try for marriage.

Sucking in a breath, and then letting it out before I answered, hadn't helped quell the tight rope in my gut. "I don't want to get married," I blurted out.

I locked eyes with him. Intense blue on blue. My heart thudded madly inside my chest while I waited for him to reply.

His answer was a deep, maddening kiss, followed by, "Then we won't get married."

We stumbled onto the bed. Alex pinned me under him, his legs trapping mine in between. And his hard-on pressed on my soaked panties. This usually meant it was game on, but his answer had me curious.

"Are you sure you're okay not marrying me?"

Alex propped himself up with elbows tucked closely to either side of my arms. He licked my bottom lip and caused shudders down my spine.

"I love you, Chase."

"I love you too." I searched his icy blues for some sign of hurt and found none.

"I'm committed to you in every way," he told me and his eyes told me that it was true. His pupils dilated. "If I could survive without my heart beating inside my chest, I would rip my ribs open and offer it to you."

I drew my brows together and twisted one corner of my lips. "That's...sweet?"

"I'm with you, even without a contract. We'll do it our own way, whatever that may be. Just as long as you're with me, loving me." His lips this time made my heart stutter.

"But I would like to keep doing the things that people do on their honeymoon." He dipped his head on my shoulder and sucked the skin along my collarbone. His hips undulated and the action produced a guttural moan from me.

"We have to get ready," I said the words without conviction. "Nica will kill us if we're late."

Alex wouldn't listen. His lips searched for all the buttons that made me melt. "We'll be fast."

"No you won't." I raised my hands to try and push him off but the traitorous things grabbed his butt instead. "We'll be fashionably late."

Alex offered me his wicked grin. "I love every bit of you, but especially your naughty side." He followed that by unclasping my bra and pulling down my panties. Then he stood before me and stripped.

Yeah...we were going to be so late.

&

In the car, on the way over to the party, I typed a reply to Nica's fifteen text messages, all of which I'd missed because...well, I had been busy doing something else. I glanced at Alex. God, he looked so yummy in a tuxedo. I idly thought of skipping the party altogether. But Nica would have my head.

Our party was the first one she'd planned by herself since little Aimee was born. She'd been hush-hush on the details, telling all of us that she'd like it to be a surprise for all the work we'd done while she was on leave. She'd given us the date, time, and theme, and sent cars to pick us up and take us to an undisclosed location. Decked in our black-and-whites, per Nica's instructions, we stopped in front of a postmodern building.

Alex held his hand out for me when I stepped out and stood for a second in front of the new art gallery. I didn't even know one had opened. We walked in and were greeted by a server who offered two bubblies with blackberries in them.

"I didn't even know this place existed. It was a deli two months ago," I told Alex while I shrugged off my faux-mink shawl and bundled it on an arm.

"A garage actually," Alex said. I regarded him with curiosity. "It was a garage...er...an auto shop before."

I crossed one arm over my chest. "And you know this because?" But I didn't need his explanation. Behind him, on a stark white wall, the word HAYATI was projected, and under it was one of Alex's black-and-white photos of me facing away from him in front of the windows of his Paris apartment, wearing his white button down and black lace underwear. The photo was life-sized. I turned to Alex for an explanation.

"Levi had been thinking of opening a gallery and he asked me to..."

"Post my naked pictures?" I thumped my purse on his chest.

"They're not all naked..." I hit him again. So much for honesty. "They're not all of us."

"Us? Us!"

"There you are!" Nica popped around the front wall. She'd kept this from me too. I growled at her. "What?" She pressed a hand on her chest.

I nudged my head toward my photos.

"Oh... yeah..." Nica glanced at Alex then propped a hand on her hip. "Well if you'd been on time, you would have seen them before everyone else did."

"I—uh—it was his fault!" I thumped my purse on Alex

again then gulped down the champagne, avoiding Nica's you're-in-so-much-trouble gaze.

Alex took my hand and pulled me to him. "It was entirely my fault, Veronica. I'll make sure Chase punishes me for it later." He chuckled, and I felt the reverberation of his chest on my back.

Nica rolled her eyes at us. "Will you keep your hands off each for a few minutes to mingle with everyone else. They've been admiring your work, Alex. Truly amazing." Then she left us to join the rest of the party.

I wiggled out of Alex's grasp. "You're in deep shit, mister."

"I know. I'm sorry. You know I hate keeping anything from you, but Levi and Nica made me promise not to give any details. We all wanted this to be a surprise for you." Alex reached out for my hand. I let him hold and kiss it. "Forgive me?"

How could I not? "Fine. On one condition." He cocked his head on one side. "I want this framed picture in my bedroom," I said, hitching a thumb over my shoulder.

Alex was right, of course, the gallery wasn't filled with only photos of me, although I counted five of mine, and only one showed my face. And there was a shot of us—standing in front of a mirror while I held the camera up to my face, and Alex guiding me, while he looked straight on. The rest were of different people from all over the world, and of Levi and Nica, of her and Aimee, of Levi and his daughter and of all three of them. There was one of Mateo and Gerard. One of Cara, looking out into the New York skyline. Even one of Tiana, Danny and Sky. And one of my parents.

Wonderment directed me straight to it. Around me, my colleagues laughed and chided each other, while I studied the scene before me. When had Alex taken it? Mom and

Daddy were in the sunroom, their foreheads touching. Daddy's hands cupped Mom's cheeks. Their eyes were closed. I'd never seen this kind of display of affection from my parents.

I felt Alex before he even touched me. He stood strong and steady behind me, his hands snaking around my belly. I reached out to touch the photo, letting a tear drop down my cheek.

"I took this when I'd gone for a visit." His breath warmed the sensitive skin behind my ear. "There was so much love between them. I sent a copy to your Mom last week."

"I never... I didn't think they could be like this," I told Alex, my voice low to avoid revealing my wrenching emotions. "He loved her so much."

"She loved him just as much, Chase. I witnessed it. They had no idea I captured this until they heard the click of the camera. I can show you the rest later."

I nodded, and swiped at the stray tear. "This is supposed to be a party." I spread my lips into a smile, turned and pressed my hands on his lapel. "Can I have that photo too?"

"You can have whatever you want. Anything and everything I can offer." Alex took my hands in his and leaned in for a kiss.

Our surroundings blurred. Voices turned into white noise. I got lost in that kiss. We both did. Alex had offered the world to me and everything else I'd only dared to imagine. What more could I ask from him?

❦

Two weeks later, I woke with the filtered sun shining through slits of the *nipa* hut roof along a beach in a southern island of the Philippines. Something long and hard pressed on my buttocks. I wiggled my hips, claiming every inch between Alex and me.

"Good morning to you too. Is that what I think it is?" I kissed his arm that wrapped around my body.

Alex adjusted himself behind me and pulled out a flashlight. "Sorry, darling, that was the torch."

I laughed. We'd sat outside the previous night for a bit until we couldn't stand the mosquito buzzes any longer. We'd star-gazed, something that made the world both smaller and bigger somehow. No matter how many miles we'd travelled, how high the mountains we'd climbed or deep the oceans we swam in, the stars stayed the same.

Alex dropped the flashlight on the wooden floor. The sounds of the waves drew me outside. But Alex had other ideas. He showed me something else long and hard. I was powerless to resist.

Our fingers intertwined over my thighs while I straddled him. I rode him for my morning exercise. And he feasted on my lips for breakfast. We listened to each other's galloping hearts after I'd collapsed, spent, on him. Our skin slicked with sex sweat. The air co-mingled with our sensual scents and the salty ocean air.

This was our commitment to each other. More than a piece of paper could offer us. We'd see the world together. Mine, completely new. For him, a different vantage point through my eyes.

THE END

ACKNOWLEDGMENTS

I'm always grateful to the people who continue to help me throughout this journey:

To my amazing editors, Dayna Hart and Elizabeth Roderick, you ladies rock!

To Lucy Rhodes of Render Compose who makes my books so pretty, and Alyson Hale for giving it a new look.

To my family, my parents and siblings, whose support knows no bounds.

To my children, thanks for keeping mom in check.

To my husband, for always believing in me.

I am constantly surrounded by strong women who inspire me in my daily and writing life—Amie, Emily, Charity, Liz, Jade, Amanda, Michelle H, Aline, Krista, and Cathy! Thank you all for the encouragement and words of wisdom.

To my readers, you make this possible!

To Samantha Marie, girl, thanks for reading all of my books. You make me feel legit.

To ARC reviewers and bloggers, a warm thank you for giving authors like me a chance.

ABOUT THE AUTHOR

USA Today Bestselling Author, Michelle, is addicted to romance. She believes in happily ever afters and loves writing about couples who get there.

When not writing, she props her feet up on her favorite lounger and binges on Netflix shows, or reads one or two books at the same time. She enjoys red wine, dark chocolate, cake, and can talk your ears off about delicious food. Travelling is high on her list, whether alone, with friends or family.

Michelle lives in Ontario, Canada with her husband, two amazing children and a cuddly maltese-yorkie dog named Scarlet.

DON'T MISS UPDATES ON UPCOMING WORKS, SALES OR GIVEAWAYS, SIGN UP FOR MICHELLE'S BI-WEEKLY NEWSLETTER:
BIT.LY/MJQUINNNEWSLETTER

www.michellejoquinn.com
michelle@michellejoquinn.com

ALSO BY MICHELLE JO QUINN

www.michellejoquinn.com

THE BLISS SERIES

Planning Bliss

Proposing Bliss

Chasing Bliss

Santa Bébé (A Christmas Bliss Novelette)

Finding Bliss (Winter 2017)

WHEN HE FALLS (A New Adult Novel)

WHEN SHE SMILES (Coming 2018)

LOVE IN BLOOM (A Collection of Short Stories)

STANDALONE

THE MISTER CLAUSE (A Holiday Romance)

HARLEY (A Rockstar Romance)

WINTER'S KISS (part of IMAGINES ANTHOLOGY)

SUMMER OF BUTTERFLIES (Coming Soon)

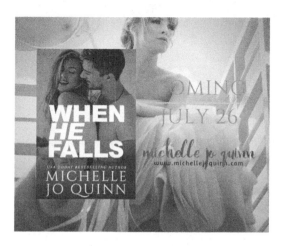

I thought I had found the man I was going to spend the rest of my life with – until he ran off with my best friend on our wedding day. I had to get away from it all - my meddling mother, the cheating couple of the year, and the embarrassment of being stood up at the altar.

My sister's house in San Francisco is the perfect escape. I can get lost in a big city where nobody knows who I am, where I can mend my broken heart in silence.

But someone crashes my pity party.

Zach Faustino was the quiet boy who lived next door ten years ago. He was my first kiss and - if a young heart can be trusted - my first love. That was before he and his mother left without saying goodbye.

Ten years have shaped him into an irresistible, charming young man. But the same ten years have also sharpened his edges, his dark past paving the way to a career that could end in a heartbeat.

And despite it all, Zach hopes to change my mind about giving love another chance.

But is a broken heart a willing heart?

And if we're both broken, is a second chance at love enough to fix us?

Made in United States
North Haven, CT
29 December 2022

30309194R00171